A TERRIBLE GUILT

BOB ROTHMAN

Black Rose Writing | Texas

ISBN: 978-1-68513-475-4
PUBLISHED BY BLACK ROSE WRITING
www.blackrosewriting.com

Printed in the United States of America
Suggested Retail Price (SRP) $22.95

A Terrible Guilt is printed in Minion Pro

*As a planet-friendly publisher, Black Rose Writing does its best to eliminate unnecessary waste to reduce paper usage and energy costs, while never compromising the reading experience. As a result, the final word count vs. page count may not meet common expectations.

PRAISE FOR
A TERRIBLE GUILT

"A riveting tale of a double-murder suspect caught up in the struggle between a zealous district attorney who demands the death penalty and two lawyers who believe in his innocence."
–Gail Ward Olmsted, best-selling author of the *Miranda Quinn Legal Twist* trilogy

"A fast-paced blast through the legal maze of a capital murder case. Bob Rothman's powerful realism, and ear for courtroom conversation, made the courtroom scenes so genuine they transported me back onto the trial bench, against my will."
–Morris Hoffman, retired Colorado state trial judge, author of *Pinch Hitting*

"A poignant and masterful story about a capital murder case, and the devastating impact it has on everyone involved. Rothman's knowledge of the courtroom, and his empathy for the people whose lives intersect with the justice system, shines through."
–Bob Carlson, Butte, Montana, trial lawyer for more than 40 years

"Rothman expertly guides the reader through the intricacies of a capital murder case while detailing the emotional toll the case takes on all those involved. Fans of legal thrillers will not want to put this book down."
–Gary Gerlacher, MD, MBA, author of *Last Patient of the Night: An AJ Docker Thriller*

"A brisk-paced legal thriller packed with twists, turns, and tension!"
–Cam Torrens, award-winning author of *Stable* and *False Summit*

"A riveting legal thriller. Rothman ratchets up the suspense of a murder trial through skillful use of dialogue that pushes the action forward."
–Karen Brees, author of *The Esposito Caper*

"The believability of this novel sets it head and shoulders above other legal whodunits. Rothman's deftly developed characters face real-world problems in a fast-paced plot filled with crime, corruption, and law firm politics."
–Nancy Scott Degan, New Orleans, Louisiana trial lawyer

"Bob Rothman's new legal thriller starts with a sensational murder and ends with a desperate fight to save a man's life. Rothman tells a story that will grip you from the opening pages and have you cheering for the two lawyers who take on a seemingly impossible fight for justice. An entirely realistic and immensely satisfying read!"
–Robin M. Maher, Executive Director, Death Penalty Information Center

To Dee,
for her love, support, and patience from the first word to last,
which made this book possible.

A
TERRIBLE
GUILT

PART ONE

CHAPTER ONE

On a brisk morning in late September, Steve Tillotson and his chef, Eduardo Gonzales, prepared for the morning rush. "Coffee's ready and the biscuits are out of the oven," Gonzales called out as he began stuffing the golden-brown biscuits with eggs, ham, and cheese in varying combinations. He wrapped each one in foil, then stacked them in a basket under a warming lamp at the drive-thru window.

The window opened at 6:00 a.m. for truckers and commuters in a hurry. But those with time to sit and enjoy their breakfasts at the Harrington Diner enjoyed a magnificent view of the heavily wooded mountains to the north, bathed in the first rays of golden morning sun. The leaves in the foothills of the Blue Ridge mountains were showing a hint of fall colors that would soon attract carloads of visitors to north Georgia.

"We're good to go, Steve," Gonzales told Tillotson. "Turn on the light whenever you're ready."

Tillotson took a quick look around to make sure the early-shift employees were at their stations. "Where's Owens?" he called out to nobody in particular.

"Haven't seen him," Gonzalez said. "Guess he'll be late . . . if he even bothers to show up. Which really wouldn't matter much since he doesn't do diddly-squat, anyway."

"Well, we can't wait for him," Tillotson barked as looked at the clock above the drive-thru window. It was 6:01 when he flipped the switch to illuminate the bright-red neon sign atop a thirty-foot pole just outside the restaurant. It was visible to truckers, commuters, and tourists driving north or south along Interstate 75 in plenty of time to swing off the highway. Within minutes, there was a long line of vehicles waiting to grab breakfast on the run.

"Thanks, and drive safely," Tillotson said with a smile as he handed a large bag to two regular customers in a white Chevy Silverado. Then, glancing toward the back of the restaurant, he saw Joseph Owens walk through the rear door and meander into the kitchen.

"You're forty minutes late," Gonzales yelled before Owens had time to remove his jacket. "Get over here and take the trash to the dumpster before it spills all over the floor."

Owens pulled the black plastic bag out of the trash can in the kitchen, tied it closed, and replaced it with a fresh bag. Then, he walked to the drive-thru window to get the trash bag there.

"After the breakfast rush," Tillotson said, "you and me are gonna have a talk. Understand?" Owens nodded. Then he carried both trash bags through the kitchen and out the back door. When he didn't come right back inside, Gonzales called out, "Where the hell did Owens get to now?"

"Probably stuck in traffic between here and the dumpster," quipped Elaine Jessup, a waitress getting the dining room ready to open at 6:30. But Gonzales wasn't laughing.

"Take it easy, Eddie. I'll check on him," Tillotson said. He asked Elaine to take over at the drive-thru window and was barely out the door when he yelled, "Break it up, both of you. Eddie, give me a hand here. Quick!"

Gonzales, who was stronger than Tillotson, pulled Owens off the assistant cook, Alberto Guerrero. "My God," Tillotson said as he bent down to help Guerrero get up, "your face is a bloody mess. I'm gonna take you to the hospital."

"No, no," Guerrero said, "I'm okay. I'm fine. Just give me a little time to clean up in the bathroom."

Tillotson grabbed Owens by the arm and shoved him inside the back door, toward the storage room, which doubled as his office. "Sit down in there and don't move!"

Sitting in the chair with his head down, his hands clasped behind his neck and his elbows resting on his knees, Owens stared at the floor. When he looked up a few minutes later, Tillotson was staring at him. "You not gonna believe nothing I got to say, so I might as well just go."

"Let me decide for myself who I believe and don't believe."

"Man, that sucker jumped me from behind while I was tossing the trash bags into the bin. He's got an arm around my neck, punching me in the face, and trying to get me down to the ground. I was like, man, I ain't having none of that shit. Hell, I didn't even know who the sucker was. So I just swung around and slammed him against the dumpster with my back. He lost his grip on me and hit the ground."

"Why didn't you just come inside and call for help instead of jumping on him and beating his face to a bloody mess?"

"You gonna stop and think if somebody jumps you from behind and is trying to twist your head off your shoulders, other than how the fuck to get him off you and even the score? C'mon, man!"

"Watch your language around here!" Tillotson admonished. "I'm going to hear what Alberto has to say, and I'll be back." As Tillotson approached the door, he turned around and pointed his finger at Owens. "Do not move from that chair. Understand?" Owens's head shot up and he glared at Tillotson but said nothing.

"He's full of shit!" Guerrero told Tillotson and Gonzales. "I'd just parked and was walking toward the back door, minding my own business, when he grabbed me from behind and started pounding on my face with his fists."

"Why would he do that?" Tillotson asked. "You guys been having some trouble?"

"I've got no idea. Why'd he swing at Malcolm the week before last? He's a lunatic, that's why. Everyone 'round here knows it. Just ask some of them." Tillotson didn't need to ask the others.

As they walked back to the kitchen, Tillotson looked at his friend. "Eddie, whaddaya think I should do?" he asked.

"No question in my mind," Gonzales said. "We've never had trouble around here until we hired Owens. And we've had nothing *but* trouble ever since."

"But how do you know he's not being provoked? Y'know, he's a little different. A little moody, perhaps. But he's also our only Black employee. Maybe some others are goading him and trying to get him fired."

"Perhaps. But it's not just the arguments and fights. Every day it's something else with him. Either he doesn't show up or shows up late or he's disappearing in the middle of breakfast or lunch hour. His attitude sucks. Personally, I think he's nothing but trouble. If you don't get rid of him and then he really hurts someone—or worse — you could take the blame."

"I don't know," Tillotson muttered as he shook his head slowly and walked back to the storage room. When he got there, it shocked him to see Owens standing just inside the door.

"I told you to stay in the chair," Tillotson yelled.

"Don't make no difference. You 'bout to fire my ass, right?"

Tillotson's eyes widened and his face reddened before he regained control. "Joseph, I've bent over backward trying to help you. But this isn't working out," he said. "You show up late almost every day. You're constantly getting into fights with a bunch of the other guys and it's really hurting my business. I'm sorry, but I'm gonna need you to leave and not come back."

As he pushed the back door open a few inches, Owens turned and glared at Tillotson. "Man, I thought you was different," he said. "Joke's on me." Then he shoved the door open so hard it swung completely around, hitting the outer wall as he stormed out.

"Did you see that look on his face?" Gonzales asked. "I'm worried about that guy. No telling what he might do."

"Relax," Tillotson said. "We've seen the last of him."

CHAPTER TWO

Three days later, the restaurant remained closed well past opening time. Instead of the red neon sign, flashing blue lights from five police cars pierced the early morning darkness in the restaurant parking lot. Two ambulances, their engines idling and red lights flashing, were standing by. Yellow crime-scene tape running across the driveway from a light pole to an orange-and-white-striped traffic cone kept the morbidly curious, as well as news reporters, outside.

"All right, what do we have so far?" Captain Gerald Smith asked as soon as he arrived.

"Two victims," replied Lieutenant Ted Randall, a fourteen-year veteran of the Harrington Police Department and a former Marine. "We've recovered two shell casings and bullets at the scene. They're from a .45 ACP cartridge. We'll send them to the Georgia Bureau of Investigation lab for analysis.

"Look over here now," Randall continued as he led Smith a few feet away from the body to where there was a yellow marker on the floor. "This is where we found a piece of the victim's skull."

"How'd that happen?" asked Smith, his head swiveling back and forth between the spots where the body lay and where the stray skull fragment landed.

"See, this is where we found the owner," Randall said, gesturing toward a toppled chair in the dining room where Tillotson's hands remained tied behind him to one of the chair's horizontal wooden slats. "The perp must've been holding the gun right close to his forehead, because the force of the blast shatters the poor guy's skull and exits out the back, sending this fragment flying over here while the chair, with the victim attached, falls back the other way."

"How'd you know he's the owner?" Smith asked.

"Me and the guys stop by now and then for biscuits and coffee," Randall said. "Name's Steve Tillotson. He was the kind that always welcomed his customers, walked around, stopping at each table, chatting them up. He did a nice business. Real nice, from what I could see."

"You could do with a few less biscuits, Ted," Smith said to his friend.

"No worse than those donuts you wolf down every morning with your coffee," Randall shot back. "Now, better c'mon over this way and I'll show you where we found the other victim."

A moment later, they were standing in front of another body with a large pool of blood beneath it, just a few feet inside the restaurant's rear door. The victim was about five feet, six inches tall, with black, wavy hair. Blood had poured from a gunshot wound to his chest, drenching the front of his shirt.

"This victim—Eduardo Gonzales, the cook—must've arrived just after the assailant shot Tillotson and came face-to-face with the perp as he was fleeing the scene. Bad, bad luck. If he'd showed up just two minutes later, well ...," Randall said, his voice trailing off.

"Anything else I need to know?" Smith asked. "Chastain will be here any minute demanding answers so he can put on one of his classic performances for the media."

"We've found a few fingerprints, some partials, on the rear doorknob," Randall said, "and some at various locations around the restaurant. Chairs, tabletops, and such. We're sending them to the GBI for processing, which we'll also do with the prints of all the restaurant employees as soon as we collect them."

"Have you verified the whereabouts of all the employees?"

"Not yet," Randall said, "but we're working on it. Several showed up for work not long after we arrived, and I've gotta tell you, it devastated every one of them. Many had worked here for years. Seems like a close-knit group. We're interviewing the ones who are here and tracking down the others."

"Any witnesses?" Smith asked.

"No, which isn't too surprising since the restaurant doesn't open its drive-thru until six and the dining room until six thirty, so there weren't yet any customers there yet."

"Who's that?" Smith asked, gesturing toward a middle-aged redhead sitting in a booth, her arms folded on the table with her head resting on them.

"Name's Elaine Jessup. A waitress. She's the one who reported it. Got here around five forty. Says she arrives about that time each day to have breakfast and chat up Tillotson and Gonzalez before getting the dining room ready," Randall said. "When she got out of her car, she noticed the back door was ajar. Says she called out for Tillotson and Gonzales, whose cars were in the parking lot. She thought she heard a moaning sound, so she pulled the door just enough to peek inside. When she spotted Gonzales on the floor just a couple of steps inside, she kneeled next to him, heard him gasp and try to say something, but couldn't make it out. Says she was holding his hand when he died moments later.

"When she stood up and looked into the place, she saw Tillotson laying on the dining room floor with a hole in his head. She remembers nothing after that, including placing the call to 911. Once the operator calmed her down enough to understand what she was saying, we had officers on the scene within minutes. Unfortunately, she didn't see anyone else at the scene when she arrived."

"Good thing she didn't show up before the perp fled or we'd have another body on our hands," Smith said. "Ted, are there any video cameras?"

"The restaurant doesn't have any, but the convenience store across the street has one facing the restaurant. We're working on getting access to that one."

"Wait. Is that the same convenience store where the fatal overnight shooting of the attendant took place a few weeks back?" Smith asked.

"Yes, sir, it is," Randall said. "Hard to believe this is a coincidence, eh?"

"Let's get our hands on the store's video ASAP. Anything else from the forensic team?"

"Not yet."

"Okay, keep me updated. Would've taken some balls for the convenience store shooter to come back here and strike again."

"That's for damn sure," Randall said.

"We may have a serial killer on our hands," Smith said. "Remind your team nobody talks to the damn media. Anything that's released to those vultures comes from me. If there are any leaks, somebody's gonna lose their job. Got it?"

"Got it, Captain. But what are you gonna do about him?" Randall asked, looking over Smith's shoulder as District Attorney Paul Chastain got out of his black Chevy SUV.

Smith turned around and saw Chastain walking straight toward him. "Pray," he said.

CHAPTER THREE

"It's Owens," Chastain told Smith three days after the murders. "No question about it. Neither of the victims had any other enemies."

"Paul, don't start jumping to conclusions," Smith replied. "Owens would've been the stupidest criminal on earth to go back there and shoot those guys just three days after being fired. We've got a lot more work to do, and I'm nowhere near ready to pin this on Owens."

"What are you talking about?" Chastain exclaimed. "We've got the guy dead to rights."

"You don't have diddly-squat!" Smith yelled. "You don't have the murder weapon. You don't have any witnesses placing Owens at the scene. And you haven't given us nearly enough time to make a connection between these murders and the convenience store murder just across the street three weeks earlier. We've got to have time to investigate."

"There are no witnesses because, as only someone who'd worked the early morning shift, such as Owens, would know, Tillotson and Gonzales were the only two people at the restaurant at that hour," Chastain countered. "Besides, Owens had motive and, knowing nobody else would be there that early, he had opportunity."

"Paul, for God's sake, what's the rush? We need to get this right the first time."

"In case you've forgotten," Chastain replied, "we've got a community that's gripped by fear and looking for someone to blame. It's getting worse by the day. Or have you just not bothered to read the papers lately?"

A light went off in Smith's head, but he quickly put it out of his mind.

"Look, Paul, give us some more time. If I'm right and you arrest Owens now, you'll end up looking bad. In the meantime, we'll keep a close eye on him, and if he gives us the slightest reason to think he's going to flee the jurisdiction, we'll have him behind bars before he knows what hit him."

"You keep him under twenty-four-hour surveillance," Chastain demanded. "If he gets away, I'll have your badge. Do you understand?"

Smith nodded.

"You've got ten days," Chastain said. "If you haven't come to your senses or arrested someone else by then, I'm gonna take the case to a grand jury, and I *promise* you they'll return an indictment of Owens for two counts of murder."

On his way back to the police station, Smith called Randall and told him to gather the group working on the convenience store murder in the conference room at 10:00 a.m.

"What's up?" Randall asked.

"Aww, Chastain's hell-bent on indicting Owens for the restaurant murders unless we can find a connection with the convenience store murder," Smith said, "and he's given us ten days to do it."

"Ten days? Why not ten hours? We'd be just as likely to solve it in that time as we would be in ten days."

"Well, this has nothing to do with what we can or can't do. Personally, I think it's driven by some rumblings about a likely challenger in the upcoming election."

"Okay, I'll get the group together. But I don't know that we've got a lot to go on yet."

"We need to go over that video again," Smith said. "There's got to be something there that we're missing."

"Ten-four," Randall said. "I'll have it ready. But I think I've looked at it a hundred times if I've looked at it once."

"We need to get a fresh set of eyes on the video and case file," Smith said. "Find out if any of the detectives are around who haven't worked on the case."

When Smith walked into the conference room, Randall and Lieutenant Alisha McKee were waiting for him, along with Detective Steve Shorter, who'd been on vacation when the convenience store murder occurred.

Smith reached into a bag he was carrying and pulled out a box of donuts. "Help yourselves," he said after grabbing a chocolate glazed out of the box and pouring a cup of coffee from the insulated pitcher in the middle of the table. "Ted, have you told everyone what this is about?"

"Yes, sir," Randall said. "I've also made a few inquiries, and I think your hunch about what's motivating the DA to move quickly was right on the money. In fact, I believe there'll be an announcement by a challenger within a few days."

"Who is it?" Smith asked.

"I hear it's gonna be Dick Shaw."

"Didn't he work for Chastain before starting his own criminal defense practice?" Smith asked.

"He did," Randall said. "In fact, Shaw was the chief deputy DA for a couple of years, if memory serves me right, until they had a falling out over what Shaw thought was an unreasonable position Chastain took on a sentencing recommendation in one of Shaw's cases. As I recall, Shaw was none too subtle about letting the court know he didn't exactly agree with the recommendation the DA ordered him to make."

"That must've frosted Chastain," Smith observed.

"Oh, for sure," Randall said. "Shaw resigned less than a month later to go into private practice."

"So Shaw knows where the secrets are buried," Smith mused. "The campaign should be interesting. But let's keep our eye on the ball here. Steve, I want you to watch this video from the camera outside of the convenience store across the road from the diner and just tell us whatever jumps out at you."

As the video started playing, everyone except Shorter grabbed a donut and poured themselves a cup of coffee. Shorter stayed focused on the video.

"Well, for starters, we got a pretty good look at the suspect, although his cap shields the top of his face," Shorter said. "White male, I'd say about five foot eight, and I'd guess around 140 to 150 pounds. Looks like he was driving a black Camaro and peeled out of there fast, heading toward I-75. Can't be a hundred percent certain of the year model of the Camaro. The 2012s and 2013s look damn near identical. Can we get a close-up of his face?"

Randall quickly accommodated the request.

"I'd say the guy's probably in his late twenties or early thirties with a fair complexion and a small mole on the right side of his chin," Shorter said.

Smith looked at Shorter. Nobody else had noticed the mole. "Get that added to the description of the suspect on the BOLO and wanted posters," he barked. "And circulate it to all law enforcement agencies in the state."

CHAPTER FOUR

Ten days later, Smith's phone rang at 7:30 a.m. "The grand jury meets at nine, and by noon, I'll be announcing the arrest of Joseph Owens for the murders of Tillotson and Gonzalez," Chastain said.

"I still think you're making a mistake," Smith opined.

"Yeah, well, have you seen the morning paper?"

"No. What's the daily rag saying today?"

"Go look for yourself," Chastain said and hung up the phone.

The article, on page one, reported exactly what Smith had expected, but left unsaid, in his conversation with Chastain ten days earlier.

Harrington criminal defense attorney Richard Shaw will announce on Tuesday that he will run against his former boss, District Attorney Paul Chastain, in the upcoming election. "Criminals are destroying our way of life in Harrington," Shaw told the Harrington Press-Tribune. "Since the incumbent doesn't seem able to do anything about it, I intend to put the law back in 'law and order.'"

At the press conference later that day, Chastain told reporters that Owens, who had lived in Harrington for just fourteen months, had been fired from the Harrington Diner three days before the killings. "Besides having a substantial motive based on revenge, Mr. Owens has a history of violent behavior. That's all I'm going to say about the case for now."

"Paul, any comment on Dick Shaw's forthcoming announcement?" a reporter called out.

"The great thing about America," said Chastain, "is that any fool can run for office, even if they're totally unfit for the job."

"Are you saying Shaw is unfit to serve as district attorney, a fool, or both?"

"I didn't say any of that," Chastain said as he flashed a Cheshire-cat grin and walked out of the conference room.

Chapter Five

Jasmine Owens was washing the lunch dishes when she heard screeching tires outside of the apartment. "What's that about?" she muttered to herself.

Seconds later, she screamed as the front door shattered from the force of a metal battering ram. Then she saw four police officers, guns drawn, come running into the apartment. "Where's Joseph Owens?" one of them demanded as the others, with shields in front of them, began searching the apartment.

"He went to the store," she gasped. "He'll be back any minute."

"Which store?"

"The grocery just one block over next to. . ." she started. At that moment, Owens came through the broken door carrying two plastic bags filled with milk, cereal, and canned goods.

"Drop the bags, show me your hands, and turn around. NOW!" the officer commanded.

Owens, shocked by the sight of armed police in his apartment, did as he was told.

"Slowly, get on the ground, face down, keeping your hands in view."

Owens complied. Then, two other officers pulled his arms behind him and handcuffed him, patted down his back, helped him up, and patted down the front of his body from neck to toes.

"What'd I do?" he asked. "What'd I do?"

"Joseph Owens," the lead officer said, "you're under arrest for the murders of Steve Tillotson and Eduardo Gonzales on the morning of September 27 at the Harrington Diner."

"I didn't kill them!" Owens yelled. "I didn't do it."

"Mr. Owens, you do not have to say anything," the officer continued, "but if you choose to do so, anything you say may be used against you in a court of law. You have the right to an attorney. If you cannot afford one, one will be appointed for you. Do you understand each of those rights?"

Owens didn't respond. He just looked at his wife, whose hands covered her face, but she couldn't stop the tears pouring from her eyes and down her cheeks before dripping onto the worn linoleum floor.

"Do you understand your rights as I've read them to you?" the officer demanded again.

"Jasmine, listen to me, baby. I didn't do this," he whispered, turning his face toward her as the officers led him out the door. "I swear to you, I didn't kill nobody. This is bullshit! Call Hector and tell him I need a lawyer. Fast!"

CHAPTER SIX

"Elena, it's Karen Cepeda." Channel 3's news editor greeted Fox Stern's newest partner.

"Hey, Karen, how's the news biz these days?" Elena Samuels asked.

"Busy," Karen said. "We've got the legislature in session while the governor's getting ready to launch his reelection bid, and murder and mayhem throughout the city. And then there's Harrington."

"The small town up I-75 in north Georgia?" Elena asked.

"You're familiar with it?" Karen asked.

"I've been through there once or twice on my way to the mountains. It's a peaceful, charming sort of place in the foothills of the Blue Ridge. What's happening there?"

"There's a restaurant right off the interstate that I'm told was popular with locals, truckers, and tourists, especially during leaf-peeping season, until it became the scene of a double murder a few months back. Actually, that was in September, so it's been more like six months. We gave the killings and the indictment of a suspect a few minutes of airtime, but you know the news cycle. It quickly became yesterday's news."

"Sounds pretty awful!" Elena said. "But I can't say I really remember it."

"So the victims were the restaurant owner and his chef. A waitress found them shot to death shortly before opening one morning. Both were well liked. The owner was a civic-minded type, and the chef was a respected member of the Latino community. Anyway, there's a preliminary hearing coming up on Thursday and the public defender who's representing the defendant has moved to keep the media out of the courtroom," Karen said. "And that's where you come in. We'd like you to be there to represent the station and argue against the motion."

Samuels, an Atlanta native, had graduated from the University of Georgia near the top of her class and, after teaching elementary school for several years, received a full scholarship to Yale Law School. After graduation, she returned home to be close to her widowed mother and accepted a job offer from Fox Stern, the largest and fastest-growing law firm in the city.

"I'd be glad to do that. Can you send me a copy of the papers the public defender filed?"

"Check your in-box. I sent you an email a moment before I called and attached the indictment along with the motion to close the courtroom. Look at the attachment and let me know if you've got questions."

"Will do. Do you want me to handle this, or should I get Greg involved?"

"It's all yours, Elena. You've done excellent work for us, and Greg's told me several times you're ready to handle most everything on your own. Speaking of which, congratulations on making partner."

"Thank you. I've enjoyed working with you and I'm grateful for your confidence. And Greg's. Hard to believe it's already been seven years since I joined the firm."

"Let me know if you have questions once you've reviewed the defense motion," Karen said. "We'll have a reporter there who'll want to speak to you after the hearing is over. I'd appreciate it if you'd give her a moment."

"No problem," Elena said. "Oh, I almost forgot to ask. Do you know the name of the judge assigned to the case?"

"It's Janice Hinton. I haven't been able to find out much about her. She was appointed to the bench by the governor around three years ago."

"I'll check her out and send you a copy of our brief in opposition to the motion as soon as it's ready to file."

"Okay, but I'm up to my eyeballs, so don't wait for me to sign off on it. Fire when ready and call me after the hearing."

CHAPTER SEVEN

A scruffy-looking, middle-aged Black man in handcuffs and leg shackles, wearing an orange prison jumpsuit, shuffled slowly into a courtroom on the second floor of the Noonan County Courthouse. There were deputies on either side, each gripping one of his arms. The prisoner made his way to the wooden table occupied by his lawyer, all the while staring at a man in a gray business suit sitting in the first row of spectator seating.

The look on the prisoner's face startled Greg Williams, who accompanied Elena to the hearing. He didn't know the man, but instantly seemed able to look inside his troubled soul. He'd seen that same haunted look of emptiness only once before. It was a look that was bereft of life, of a psychic void that cried out of nothing so much as utter, hopeless despair. As Williams stared at the prisoner, unable to look away, his mind raced back across decades. The face of another prisoner, one Williams had tried desperately to forget, was clawing its way back into his consciousness. The look on Greg's face jolted Elena.

"Greg, what's the matter?" she whispered, but he made no response.

"Greg, what's going on?" Her voice was a little louder and tinged with anxiety at what she was witnessing. "Do you know this guy?"

Again, Greg didn't respond, and it wasn't clear whether he'd even heard her. His gaze remained locked on the prisoner, mesmerized by whatever it was he was seeing, or thought he was seeing, in the guy's face.

Just then, the courtroom bailiff called out "All rise" as Judge Janice Hinton entered through a door behind the bench. Greg remained in his seat, so Elena placed a hand behind his right elbow and gently pulled him up, which seemed to break the trance—or whatever it was he'd been experiencing.

"This is the case of *State v. Joseph Owens*, docket number 34773-C," Judge Hinton announced. "The defendant is charged with two counts of malice murder and one count of armed robbery at the Harrington Diner in Harrington, Georgia. We're here on a motion by the defense to close pretrial proceedings in this case to the public and to the media."

She called on Owens's attorney, Noonan County Public Defender Michael Delaney.

"Judge, we can't have the media in here during pretrial motions involving potential evidence that we believe will be inadmissible at trial," Delaney said. "The thing is, Judge, if you rule certain evidence won't be admissible at trial, or prohibit certain testimony, potential jurors who see news reports about this hearing on television or read about it in the newspaper will learn about the excluded evidence. Some of it is, well, rather gruesome. My fear is that once they hear about it, they won't be able to forget about it if they're selected to serve on the jury."

"Thank you, Mr. Delaney," Judge Hinton said, cutting him off. "I've reviewed your brief and I understand your position. I see that Gregory Williams and Elena Samuels of the Fox Stern firm have filed a brief on behalf of Channel 3 News. Do either of you want to be heard this morning?"

"I'd like to speak briefly, Your Honor," Elena said.

"Ms. Samuels, you may proceed."

Elena took a quick look at Greg, whose eyes remained fixated on Owens. She shook it off, for the moment at least, and rose, literally and figuratively, to the occasion.

"Your Honor, since we've already submitted a brief that addresses the Supreme Court's nearly absolute ban on closed courtrooms in criminal proceedings, I'll keep this short. In a democracy such as ours, it's critical for the courts to have the public's confidence and support. There's no better way to ensure continued public confidence in the judiciary than to let the people see for themselves what takes place in the courtroom."

"Ms. Samuels, I take your point. But let's cut to the chase," Judge Hinton said. "What about the defendant's constitutional right to a fair trial? Let's say that, after this hearing, I decide to prohibit the state from introducing certain evidence. If your client broadcasts news reports that include mention of that evidence, isn't the defendant's right to a fair trial placed at risk? I mean, as Mr. Delaney pointed out, what good does it do for me to prohibit the state from introducing a piece of evidence if potential jurors have already heard about it in your client's news reports?"

"Your Honor, you have many options to protect the defendant's right to a fair trial without barring media coverage, such as allowing the lawyers additional time to question prospective jurors about their knowledge of the case, whether from news reports or otherwise. If that's not sufficient, the Georgia Supreme Court has held that, rather than excluding the media from pretrial hearings, you are required to move the trial to another part of the state where there hasn't been as much news coverage of the case."

Elena waited a moment to see if there was another question. But Judge Hinton had heard enough.

"I agree with Ms. Samuels. I deny the motion to close the courtroom. Mr. Delaney, you may raise the issue again as the trial approaches if pretrial publicity is still a concern and I'll consider other options to protect your client's right to a fair trial. If there's nothing else, we will adjourn."

Elena put her notepad into her briefcase and was ready to leave when she looked at Greg, who hadn't budged. His eyes remained locked on Owens as the two deputies led the prisoner out of the courtroom.

"C'mon, Greg," Elena said as she grabbed his arm. "We need to get out of here and have a talk."

CHAPTER EIGHT

Nine months later

Judge Hinton gazed out into the courtroom as fifty-seven pairs of eyes stared back from uncomfortable wooden benches. Some looked bored. Others were attentive, but leery about serving on a jury.

"Truth be told, I'm nervous about presiding over my first murder trial," Hinton had told her law clerk shortly before walking into the courtroom that morning. "And why'd it have to be a capital case?"

"Y'know," her clerk responded, "Georgia law puts the life-or-death decision in the hands of the jury, not the judge."

"That's true," Hinton shot back. "But my rulings during the trial, especially on the admission or exclusion of evidence, will have a substantial impact on how the jury views the case. So there's no ducking it."

"Fair enough," the clerk replied. "But one step at a time."

"The court will come to order," Hinton announced after startling dozing jurors with a sharp bang of her gavel.

"The prosecutor, District Attorney Paul Chastain, seated at the table to your left, will ask some questions of you first. Then Mr. Owens's defense lawyer, Mr. Michael Delaney, will do so. Please listen carefully to their questions and respond to each of them honestly and completely. All right, Mr. Chastain, you may begin."

Chastain slowly stood, buttoned his charcoal gray suit jacket, and walked to the podium, carrying only a notepad and pen. Chastain's ego told him that, as the long-time chief prosecutor in Noonan County now serving his fifth term, everyone in the courtroom knew who he was. But he played it straight.

"Ladies and gentlemen, I'm Paul Chastain, the district attorney for Noonan County. I represent the State of Georgia in this case against the defendant, Joseph Owens. This is one of the most serious kinds of cases for which any citizen of Noonan County can be called to serve on a jury, so out of fairness to the State and to Mr. Owens, I ask that you listen carefully to my questions."

Sitting at the defense table and facing the prospective jurors, Delaney had to restrain himself from expressing his disgust at Chastain's feigned concern for fairness to Owens.

"As some of you may already be aware from media reports, the State has charged Mr. Owens with the shooting deaths of Steve Tillotson and Eduardo Gonzales, and with armed robbery of Mr. Tillotson's restaurant, the Harrington Diner, in the early morning hours of September 27, before the restaurant opened. If, as the State will urge, you convict Mr. Owens of the first-degree murder of Mr. Tillotson, we will ask you to impose the ultimate punishment, the death penalty, under Georgia law."

A few gasps came from the assembled group, followed by a buzz among the potential jurors, some muttering to themselves and others turning to say something to the person next to them. The sharp rap of Judge Hinton's gavel banging repeatedly on a wooden block shocked them into silence.

"There will be no audible responses to the district attorney's statements," Judge Hinton said sternly, "unless Mr. Chastain asks a question of you individually. And under no circumstances—*no circumstances*—are any of you to address any comments or questions to other potential jurors."

Hinton sat quietly, staring at the jurors, letting her words sink in.

"Is there anyone here who does not understand what I've just said?" There was no response from any of the prospective jurors. "Good. Mr. Chastain, you may resume."

Five-feet, ten-inches with short, neatly combed black hair set off by a tinge of gray around the temples and almost as trim and fit as he was when he started his legal career as a criminal defense lawyer thirty-seven years earlier, Chastain possessed an air of authority.

"Thank you, Judge," he said. "Now, ladies and gentlemen, as I was saying, if Mr. Owens, the defendant, is found guilty of murder, it's the state's intent to ask the jury to impose the death penalty." Chastain was looking for a flinch or a squint or anything that betrayed the slightest hesitance or potential resistance to imposing the ultimate punishment.

"Let me be clear about this. I'm not here to criticize or argue with any of you who don't support capital punishment. You're each entitled to your own opinion. But if any of you think that, either as a matter of conscience, or for any reason, you could never vote for the death penalty regardless of the facts the state proves during this trial, I need you to raise your hand."

Six women and two men raised their hands. Chastain addressed each of them individually, seeking an explanation for why they would not vote for the death penalty under any circumstances. At the prosecution table, Delaney's chief deputy, Roger Maxwell, was taking detailed notes of the responses from each juror.

Almost two hours later, it was Delaney's turn. Wearing a blue blazer with gray slacks that were about an inch too long and crumpled around his scuffed black loafers, Delaney ran his right hand through his already tousled brown hair and took a quick sip of water as he stood. He removed his wire-framed reading glasses and carefully laid them on the table as he prepared to speak.

"Ladies and gentlemen, my name's Michael Delaney. I'm the public defender in Noonan County, and it's my privilege to represent the defendant, Joseph Owens," Delaney said as he stepped behind his client and placed a hand on each of Owens's shoulders, hoping to convey a sense that he knew this man, had a personal relationship with him, and trusted him. Owens was looking directly at the potential jurors, just as he'd been told to do by Delaney.

"Now, I imagine most everyone here understands that under our system of law, defendants in criminal trials like this one have a presumption of innocence. Anyone here not familiar with that concept or disagree with it?"

There was no response from any of the jurors.

"But here's the thing," Delaney continued. "With all the sensational headlines and news stories about this case in newspapers and broadcast on TV, I realize it's possible that some of you, through no fault of your own—*absolutely* no fault of your own—have heard about the murders, have heard about some of the evidence Mr. Chastain plans to introduce during this trial, and may already believe my client is guilty. Or, perhaps, even if you haven't decided, you're inclined to think that way. And I imagine you understand that, in fairness to my client, I need to know if that's the case. So I wanna start by asking if any of you already believe Mr. Owens is guilty?"

Two jurors, a woman sitting in the first row and a man sitting in the back, raised their hands. Delaney made notes and moved on.

"Now, this is a slightly different question. Even if you've not decided, are any of you inclined to think Mr. Owens is guilty?"

Four more jurors raised their hands.

Sitting near Owens, taking notes, was a psychologist, Dr. Karlise Jones-Wong, who specialized in evaluating prospective jurors in high-profile, white-collar criminal cases. Although her usual fee was $50,000, Dr. Jones-Wong typically agreed to work for free on one or two cases each year on behalf of poor defendants facing the death penalty.

Delaney did not introduce her to the jury, preferring to keep her role confidential and knowing most people in the courtroom would assume she was his paralegal or secretary. But her job was to listen to each juror's answers and to assess the likelihood that they would vote in favor of the death penalty should the jury find Owens to be guilty. Perhaps even more important was to identify any jurors who, as a matter of principle, would refuse to impose the death penalty.

After two days of Chastain and Delaney questioning the prospective jurors, five men, one of whom was of Asian descent, and seven women, one of whom was Black, were chosen to serve on the jury. Delaney was ecstatic. Dr. Jones-Wong assessed two of the women, one white and the lone Black juror, as highly unlikely to vote for the death penalty.

CHAPTER NINE

The trial began the next morning with Chastain's opening statement. After reminding the jurors of what they already knew all too well—that the case "involved the shooting deaths of two members of our community, two men in the prime of life who left behind wives and young children"—Chastain stretched out his left arm and pointed his index finger toward Owens as he vowed "to prove the defendant's guilt beyond a reasonable doubt."

A sneeze from a juror momentarily interrupted the district attorney's opening and unintentionally broke the solemn mood in the courtroom. The juror said, "Excuse me," and Delaney quickly said, "Bless you," in a voice loud enough to draw the eyes of the jurors away from Chastain and toward himself.

Chastain, annoyed at the interruption and even more at Delaney's opportunistic solicitousness, sought quickly to take back the spotlight. He moved out from behind the wooden podium on which he'd placed his notepad and took two steps toward the far end of the jury box.

"These murders," he said, "took place at the Harrington Diner in the predawn hours of September 27, soon after Steve Tillotson, a devoted husband and father of twin six-year-old boys, had arrived to prepare to open his restaurant for the early morning breakfast business. The State will prove to you, beyond a reasonable doubt, that the murder of Mr. Tillotson was planned, calculated, and carried out by this man," again pointing at Owens with his left index finger, "the defendant, Joseph Owens. As you will hear, Mr. Tillotson fired Mr. Owens just three days before the murders, after Mr. Owens repeatedly got into arguments and fights with other employees at the diner."

Most of the jurors turned to look directly at Owens, their eyes having followed Chastain's hand as he gestured toward the wooden table occupied by the defendant and his lawyer. Wearing a dark blue suit, white shirt, and a maroon-and-white striped tie that his wife, Jasmine, had purchased for him and brought to the courthouse, Owens looked directly back at the jurors, just as his attorney had coached him to do.

"Show them you have nothing to be ashamed of, nothing to apologize for," Delaney had told him. "First impressions matter. Be confident, but don't smile. And don't stare at any of them."

"These murders were especially heinous and atrocious," Chastain said. "The defendant entered the restaurant through the back door, carrying a .45-caliber pistol. After ordering Tillotson to unlock the safe, and grabbing the cash to make it appear as though this was a robbery, he took Tillotson into the dining room, forced him to sit in a chair Owens pulled out from one of the dining tables, and tied Tillotson's hands to the back of the chair.

"Then," Chastain told the jurors, "still in a rage over being fired three days earlier, Owens pointed the barrel of a .45 caliber gun at Tillotson's forehead and fired a shot directly into Tillotson's skull at very close range. The blast was so powerful that it sent blood and brain tissue all about, pieces of Tillotson's skull flying onto the table next to where he was sitting and on to the surrounding floor. That shot had its intended effect. It ended the life of a man who'd operated this popular local restaurant for many years. A man who had a deep and loving relationship with his wife of eight years, Grace Tillotson. And, perhaps most tragically, a man who left behind his twin six-year-old boys. Boys who now will have to grow up without their father."

Chastain, who had two children and five grandchildren, stopped as he uttered those words, appearing to react emotionally to his own words. None of the veterans of the courtroom—lawyers, clerks, and news media—ever had witnessed such a reaction from Chastain in his many criminal prosecutions.

Delaney, looking away from the jury, rolled his eyes. Chastain, apparently having regained his composure, turned to the second victim.

"As Owens headed to the back door to flee," he said, "the cook, Eduardo Gonzales, entered the restaurant. Knowing that Gonzales would recognize him and identify him to the police, Owens quickly raised his right arm and fired his weapon, shooting Gonzales just below the heart. Death came quickly, but as you'll hear, not instantly. Mr. Gonzales lived long enough to identify his assailant to another restaurant worker who arrived a few minutes after Owens fled the scene."

"Objection," Delaney said with a tone of urgency as he stood. "The district attorney is expressing his own opinion regarding the meaning of highly contested testimony he intends to present rather than stating facts he expects to prove."

"Counsel will approach the bench," Hinton directed.

With one hand over the microphone on the bench and speaking in low tones so the jurors wouldn't hear what anyone was saying, Hinton looked at Delaney and said, "Explain your objection."

"Judge, there's a witness the State will call who'll claim that a sound Mr. Gonzales purportedly made just seconds before he passed, which sounded like a moan—'ohhh'—was intended to identify the defendant, Mr. Owens, as his killer," Delaney said. "We've moved to exclude that testimony, because any expression of opinion by the witness about what Mr. Gonzales may have meant by that sound would be utter conjecture and extremely prejudicial to the defense. But now, Mr. Chastain effectively has preempted Your Honor's consideration of this issue not only by referring to the contested testimony, but by expressing his own opinion and vouching for it in his opening statement. It's absolutely outrageous."

"Mr. Chastain," the judge said, gazing sternly at the DA, "what do you have to say for yourself?"

"Judge, I was merely informing the jury of facts we intend to prove, which will include the witness's testimony not only about Mr. Gonzales's dying declaration, but also her perception of what he was saying, and the factual basis for her opinion that he was identifying Mr. Owens as the shooter."

"No, Mr. Chastain, you went beyond describing the testimony you expect to present. You deliberately injected your own opinion about the meaning of the sound made by Mr. Gonzales and how the jury should understand it, which you certainly know isn't permissible in an opening statement," Judge Hinton said, the anger apparent on her reddened face, as well as in her voice.

"Judge," Delaney said, "Mr. Chastain's hardly a novice trial lawyer. This wasn't an inadvertent mistake. There's no way to erase from the minds of these jurors this inappropriate expression of opinion by the district attorney. Under the circumstances, I believe the DA has so severely prejudiced these jurors at the outset of this trial that the defense must, and does, move for a mistrial." Knowing such motions were highly unlikely to be granted, Chastain stood silently for a moment, anticipating that Judge Hinton would quickly deny it.

"Mr. Chastain, do you want to respond to the defense motion for a mistrial before I rule?"

"Judge," a plainly startled Chastain said, "I sincerely apologize to the court and to Mr. Delaney if I crossed the line. It certainly wasn't my intent to do so. Mr. Delaney will have a full opportunity to present the facts from his client's perspective momentarily, and I urge the court to reserve any ruling until after he's done so, when Your Honor will be in a better position to evaluate any purported prejudice caused by my inadvertent lapse in judgment."

"We're going to take a recess for fifteen minutes while I consider the motion for a mistrial," Judge Hinton said, staring intently at Chastain.

Then, after calming herself, she informed the jurors there would be a brief recess requiring them to return to the jury room while she considered "an important legal issue that's arisen." As soon as the jurors had left the courtroom, Judge Hinton stood and quickly strode off the bench without saying another word.

CHAPTER TEN

Back in chambers, a still-seething Judge Hinton removed her robe and flung it in disgust over the back of a guest chair. "I just don't get it," she said to her clerk. "The prosecutor comes into the courtroom on the side of almighty God and the angels. He's got every advantage possible in the eyes of the jurors, and still Chastain pulls a cheap stunt like this."

"You think it was intentional?" asked the clerk, naively incredulous at the very thought.

"Does the sun rise in the east?" the judge replied. "Chastain's been around way too long to make a rookie mistake like this. No, he knew exactly what he was doing, knew how defense counsel would react, and bet I wouldn't have the nerve to declare a mistrial."

"So what are you going to do?" her clerk asked.

"I'm going to let him sweat about it while I calm down," she replied. "Then, maybe after fifteen or twenty minutes, I'll probably deny the motion for a mistrial, give the jurors an instruction to disregard any opinion expressed by the DA, and give the defense attorney some leeway to express his own opinion on the same subject during his opening statement."

When she returned to the courtroom, Judge Hinton called counsel back up to the bench. "Mr. Chastain, you're this close," she said, holding up her right index finger and thumb, which were almost touching, "this close to a mistrial. If you think I'm going to let you run roughshod over the rules or over me, you're sadly mistaken."

The color drained from Chastain's face as he realized the calculated gamble he'd taken had exploded in his face. Never had he imagined a young judge like Hinton would seriously entertain the possibility of granting a mistrial. Not only would a mistrial be an enormous embarrassment, it also would generate a lot of negative publicity just as reelection time was approaching.

"Your Honor, I sincerely apologize to the court and to defense counsel," Chastain said. "My emotions about this heinous double murder of two young men in the prime of their lives got the better of me, which I deeply regret. I'm embarrassed by my lapse in judgment, and I humbly urge the court not to subject the victims' survivors and the witnesses to the delay a mistrial would cause."

For what seemed like an eternity to Chastain, Hinton stared down from the bench at him. Finally, she said, "I'd be entirely justified in granting the defense motion here and now, and I will do so if you even come close to the line again. With some misgivings, but to move this case along, I deny the motion for mistrial."

"Thank you, Your Honor," Chastain said.

As he was about to say something more, Hinton cut him off. "Mr. Chastain, I'm going to instruct the jury to disregard your inappropriate expression of opinion regarding the meaning of the sound made by the dying victim. But if you make another mistake like that during this trial, not only will I declare a mistrial, I'll assess the costs incurred by the defense against you personally and consider whether there are other sanctions I can impose. Am I clear?"

"Yes, Your Honor. Very clear."

Then, to her surprise, Delaney asked her not to instruct the jury to disregard Chastain's statement. "It'll only reinforce that opinion for those jurors who noticed it and bring it to the attention of those who might have missed it," Delaney said.

Hinton's eyebrows shot up in surprise. "Well, all right," she said. "If that's your preference, I'll respect it."

Chastain took less than five minutes to complete his opening and to thank the jurors for their attention before sitting down.

"Mr. Delaney, you may present your opening statement for the defense," Judge Hinton said.

"Thank you, Your Honor," Delaney said as he rose. "The defense will reserve its opening statement until after the State presents its evidence."

This time, it was the judge's face that betrayed surprise. Chastain, who was leaning over to whisper something in Maxwell's ear, twisted his head toward Delaney with his eyes opened wide, plainly caught off-guard by a tactic he'd not seen in all his years as a lawyer.

"What the hell do you think he's up to?" Chastain whispered to Maxwell.

But before Maxwell could answer, Judge Hinton said, "All right. Mr. Chastain, you may call your first witness."

"Judge, if you don't mind, I didn't expect we'd get to witness testimony until after lunch, so my witness is not yet present. May we take an early lunch break and pick up with the first witness at after lunch?" Chastain asked.

"The defense has no objection to the district attorney's request, Your Honor," Delaney responded. The DA's unpreparedness suited Delaney, since it meant he would get to cross-examine the first witness immediately after his direct testimony rather than leaving it in the jury's mind unchallenged over the lunch break.

"All right," the Judge said. "The court will be in recess until one o'clock."

CHAPTER ELEVEN

"Junk, junk, junk," Greg said as he clicked the delete button on his keyboard repetitively.

"Who are you talking to?" Elena asked as she strode into his office on the 47th floor of midtown Atlanta's newest granite and glass skyscraper. The building received glowing reviews in architectural magazines and a mix of admiration and unspoken envy from the firm's competitors.

"The email gods," he replied. "I'm praying for the invention of a better junk filter." Elena smiled at Greg's meager effort at humor. "What's up?" he asked.

"Did you read the news reports about the Owens trial this morning?" she asked.

The two of them had talked about the Owens case a few times since the pretrial hearing. But Elena hadn't asked, and Greg hadn't offered to explain his mysterious emotional reaction when he saw Owens in the courtroom.

"Yes," he replied as he turned away from his computer screen and smiled at Elena. "Interesting move by Delaney yesterday."

"I don't understand why he wouldn't make an opening statement so he could tell his client's story to the jury immediately," she said. "Sounds to me like he's gambling with his client's life. The jurors could make up their minds even before he gets up to bat."

"My guess," Greg responded, "is that Delaney has something up his sleeve that he'll use to seek a dismissal from the judge at the conclusion of the DA's case, and he doesn't want to tip off Chastain. If so, he's taking a helluva gamble."

After a pause, Elena changed the subject. "Greg, we've never talked about what went on at the hearing on Delaney's motion to close the courtroom. I'm worried about you."

Greg quickly brushed it off. "Thanks, Elena," he said. "I'm fine."

"I'm not so sure—"

Just then, Clay Morrisey, the firm's managing partner and a long-time friend of Greg's, appeared in the doorway, interrupting her. "Elena, would you excuse us, please?"

"Of course," she replied.

Clay crossed the threshold into Greg's office as Elena exited and closed the door behind her. Clay took a seat in one of Greg's new brown-and-beige-striped guest chairs. "This is really comfortable," Clay said. "And it looks great in here. Nicely done."

"Thanks, Clay." Although his office furniture was stylish and comfortable, it paled compared to the furniture Morrisey had ordered for his own office on the fiftieth floor at the apex of the new office tower. Rumor around the firm was that he had spent upward of $70K, not including the museum-quality artwork, to furnish the twelve-hundred-square-foot office allocated to the firm's leader.

"Greg, I owe you an apology," Clay began. "I wasn't completely forthcoming with you two weeks ago when we had our discussion about Carrie Melton's comments following the verdict in the *Frontline Medical v. Rogers Manufacturing* case." Greg had won a jury verdict for $7.3 million on behalf of Clay's client, Frontline Medical. But Melton, the company's president, was furious that the jury hadn't awarded punitive damages.

"What do you mean?" Greg asked.

"Carrie wasn't just upset about not getting punitive damages. I'm sorry to tell you this, but she's lost confidence in you and doesn't want you handling her cases any longer, including the Maxwell Technologies case," Clay said. "So I want you to know I've asked Katherine Bergman to take over as the lead partner on that one."

Greg's face turned crimson with anger as he shot up out of his chair. "What the hell are you talking about, Clay? We *won* the Frontline Medical case. Hell, we got the client every penny it was entitled to from the defendant. *Every penny*! How on earth could she be so upset?"

"Greg, calm down," Clay said coolly, refusing to allow himself to get ruffled. "I've known Carrie for over twelve years. She's temperamental and can be irrational. But it really doesn't matter how or why she reached this conclusion. She's the client, and she pays us millions of dollars in fees each year to represent her company. I tried to persuade her to reconsider, but she was insistent."

"You have another option," Greg said in a sharp tone that seemed to startle Clay. "You could stick up for your partner and tell the client she can take her business elsewhere."

"That's *not* an option," Clay responded curtly, standing to match Greg's gaze.

"This partnership has never allowed a client to dictate a change in the lead lawyer on an existing case under circumstances such as this," Greg said. "Until this moment, we've always had each other's backs. This is an enormous embarrassment to me."

"Times, unfortunately, have changed, Greg," Clay responded, again speaking softly, trying to dial down the temperature. "Be reasonable. Think about how the other partners would react if I allowed a client who pays us millions in fees each year to walk out the door just to keep one partner from getting his nose out of joint."

"Well, I guess that's where we disagree," Greg said in a derisive tone. "I think they'd respect you. They'd realize you'd do the same thing for them. Instead, now I'm going to be known as the first lawyer in the firm's history to win a $7.4 million verdict and get fired by the client."

"C'mon, Greg, don't take it so hard. Everyone at the firm knows you did a great job on the case," Clay said as he headed to the door. "You've got nothing to worry about."

CHAPTER TWELVE

"I don't know if I can do this," Elaine Jessup pleaded as she wiped tears from her eyes. She was in the witness room that adjoined the courtroom and was about to be the first witness called by the prosecution.

"Elaine, I know this is going to be tough, but you need to think of Steve and Eduardo. Do this for them," Chastain said. "Do it for Grace Tillotson and the twins. Do it for Camila Gonzales and her daughter. Keep them in mind and draw your strength from them."

The horror of finding the bodies had terrified Jessup for weeks afterward, depriving her of a sound night's sleep. As the trial approached, the nightmares returned.

"For them," she thought to herself. "I need to do it for them." Minutes later, Jessup was sitting on the witness stand and keeping her eyes focused on Chastain.

"Ms. Jessup," he asked as he gestured toward the defense table, "do you recognize the man in the blue suit sitting at that table?"

"Yes," she said, "that's Joseph Owens."

"How do you know him?"

"He worked at the Harrington Diner as a busboy for about three, maybe four weeks," Jessup said as she dabbed her eyes.

"When was that relative to the murders of Mr. Tillotson and Mr. Gonzalez?"

"Until three days before the murders."

"Did you observe Mr. Owens during the time he worked at the diner?"

"Yes, I did."

"Did he get along with the other employees?"

"Some days he was okay. Not friendly, but he minded his own business. Other days, he got into arguments and even a couple of fights with other workers. That man's got a violent streak in him."

"Objection," Delaney said, as he rose to his feet.

"Sustained," the judge said without waiting for Chastain to respond. "Ms. Jessup, just answer the question that Mr. Chastain asked without adding your own opinions about the defendant's character." Jessup nodded.

"Ms. Jessup," Chastain said, "did you ever witness the defendant commit any violent acts against other employees or customers at the restaurant?"

"Objection," Delaney said. "This line of questioning is over broad, irrelevant, and amounts to trial by character assassination. It has nothing to do with the crime for which Mr. Owens is on trial."

"Judge," Chastain replied, "the defendant's propensity to become angry and violent is directly relevant to the murder of Mr. Tillotson, which the State contends was an act of revenge. As the witness has already testified, the murders of Mr. Tillotson and Mr. Gonzalez took place just three days after Mr. Owens was fired."

"I overrule the objection," Judge Hinton said. "The court reporter will read back the last question and the witness will answer it."

After hearing the question read back, Jessup, now sitting up straight and looking directly at the jurors, told them, "Yes, sir. Several times."

"Please describe each of the incidents you witnessed?"

"Yes, sir. I think it was the second week Mr. Owens was working at the diner. I heard him yelling and turned toward the drive-thru window, where he was shoving Malcolm Smithson against the wall. Just as Mr. Owens was about to take a swing at Malcolm, Mr. Tillotson stepped and broke it up."

"Who is Mr. Smithson?"

"He's a young fella—a senior in high school, I believe—who works part time to earn some spending money. Usually he'd relieve Mr. Tillotson at the drive-thru window as soon as he'd arrive around seven."

"What happened when Mr. Owens shoved Mr. Smithson?"

"Mr. Tillotson was just a few feet away and rushed over to pull Owens off Malcolm. Then he took Owens to the storage room."

"Did things calm down after that?"

"Well, I guess you could say that. All I know is that, a few minutes after Mr. Tillotson took him to the storage room, I saw Owens leave through the back door. He didn't come back till the next day."

"Were there any other instances of violence involving Mr. Owens that you witnessed?"

"Yes, I saw him lose his temper with a waitress while he was wiping down tables in the dining room."

"Do you know why Owens got angry with the waitress?"

"No sir, I don't. But later the waitress told me—"

"Objection," Delaney said. "Hearsay."

"Sustained," Judge Hinson said.

"Let me try the question again, Ms. Jessup. How did you know that Mr. Owens was angry?"

"Because he raised his voice and called the waitress a stupid bitch, then he flung down his wet cleaning towel on the table so hard it startled everyone in the dining room. The waitress was stunned and crying as Owens stormed off toward the kitchen. So I tried to calm her down."

"And what happened after that?"

"A few minutes later, Mr. Tillotson came into the dining room and apologized to all the guests. He told them the employee had been 'dealt with'—those were his words—and that everyone's meals were on the house."

"Were you present at the restaurant on September 24, the day Mr. Owens was fired?"

"Yes, sir. I'd arrived early that day to have breakfast at the diner, as I usually did, and then to start getting the dining room ready to open at six thirty."

"Was Mr. Owens there when you arrived?"

"He was supposed to be there by six, when the drive-thru window opened, but I didn't see him until he came in through the back door around six forty."

"What did you witness Mr. Owens say or do that morning?" Chastain asked Jessup while looking at the jury.

"Well, Mr. Owens collected the trash from the kitchen and the drive-thru window and went outside where the trash bins are located. After a few minutes, he hadn't come back inside, and I heard Mr. Tillotson say he was going to look for Owens. Of course, I couldn't see what was going on out there, but before the door closed behind him, I heard Mr. Tillotson yell for Eddie to come outside quickly."

"Who's Eddie?"

"The cook, Eduardo Gonzales," she said.

"What happened next?"

"I saw Mr. Gonzales come back inside with Mr. Guerrero, whose face was a bloody mess. Mr. Gonzales took him to the bathroom to clean up."

"What did you see after that?"

"I saw Mr. Tillotson come inside, holding Owens by the arm, and leading him into the storage room."

"Were you able to hear what either Mr. Tillotson or Mr. Owens said to each other in the storage room?"

"No. But after a few minutes, Mr. Tillotson came out of the storage room and went back to the bathroom where Guerrero was still cleaning himself up. Then Tillotson went back to the storage room and, a minute or two later, Owens stormed out of the storage room, shoved open the back door, which leads to the parking lot, and left. Everyone in the place, including the customers, jumped when they heard the back door slam against the wall," Jessup said. "It took little imagination to realize what had just happened."

"Ms. Jessup, I'd like you now to focus on the morning of September 27, three days after Mr. Tillotson fired Owens. Please describe what you saw when you arrived for work that morning?"

Jessup closed her eyes and sat quietly for a few seconds. Chastain walked over to his table, poured a cup of water, and offered it to her. After taking a sip, Jessup looked up.

"I parked in my usual spot and saw that Mr. Tillotson's pickup truck and Eddie's car were already there," she said, and then closed her eyes for a moment before continuing. "As I got out of my car, I noticed that the back door wasn't completely closed. That was unusual, since the back door is always supposed to be kept closed and locked. Only employees with keys could get in unless, like with food vendors, they used the intercom to get someone to open the door for them."

After another sip of water, she continued. "I thought I heard a sound, so I pulled the door open just enough to look into the restaurant. I saw someone lying on the floor just a step or two inside the back door. It wasn't until I went inside that I saw it was Eddie. Then I saw the blood around his chest and neck and…," she said as she burst into tears and bowed her head as she held a tissue to her eyes.

"Do you need a break?" Judge Hinton asked Jessup.

"No, thank you, Judge. I'll be okay. I'm sorry."

"No need to apologize, Ms. Jessup. Continue when you can."

Moments later, Jessup resumed. "I saw the blood under Eddie's body and called his name, over and over, but he didn't respond. Then I kneeled down by his head and started pleading with him to tell me who had done this to him."

"Ms. Jessup, do you recall the exact words you used at that moment?"

"I was crying and I could see that he was still breathing, although not like regular. It was more like quick, repeated gasps. I leaned down close to his face and said, 'Eddie, please, tell me who did this to you. Who shot you?' Then I saw his left eyelid move, opening ever so slightly, and he made a sound."

"Can you describe the sound?"

"It was like, ohhh. Just that sound, and then he was...," as her voice trailed off.

After giving her a moment, Chastain asked what she did next.

"Before I could stop and think, I got up and called out for Steve. He didn't answer, and I started looking for him. Then I turned around and saw there was someone else on the floor in the dining room. I went over there and realized it was Steve. He lay on the ground, tied to a chair that had fallen over. And there was...," Jessup again paused to regain her composure. "There was a hole in his forehead, and there was a hole in the side of his skull." Her voice was breaking and tears flowing as she spoke. "I remember becoming very light-headed and thought I was gonna faint."

Chastain waited as Jessup struggled to regain her composure. Then he asked, "Do you recall what you did next?"

"No. It appears from what I've been told that I called the police, but honestly, I don't have any recollection of making that call."

"Do you recall anything else from the morning the shootings took place at the restaurant?"

"Nothing until I was sitting in a booth with a police officer who was asking me about what I'd seen when I arrived."

"Did you later learn who the officer was?"

"Yes. It was Captain Gerald Smith of the Harrington Police Department."

"Ms. Jessup, what do you recall Captain Smith saying to you or asking you?"

"He asked me whether Mr. Tillotson had any disagreements or arguments with anyone recently."

"And what did you tell him?" Chastain asked.

"Objection," Delaney said as he stood. Before he could say another word, Judge Hinton instructed the bailiff to take the jury out of the courtroom. When they were gone, she allowed Delaney to continue.

"Your Honor," he said, "this is exactly the testimony I was anticipating in my earlier objection to the district attorney's opening statement. The witness is about to testify that, when Mr. Gonzales made the sound, 'oh' just before he died, he intended to identify my client as the shooter. This is utter speculation by the witness. It's without any factual basis and extremely prejudicial," he said. "I have no objection to the witness making the sound she heard. But I ask the court to prohibit the witness from speculating on what the deceased meant by that sound."

Judge Hinton turned to Chastain, who said, "The witness's testimony is perfectly consistent with a reasonable interpretation of Mr. Gonzales making a dying declaration, which the jury may accept or reject after having the benefit of Mr. Delaney's cross-examination."

Hinton considered for a few seconds.

"I believe there's a sufficient testimonial basis for the witness to form an opinion on what Mr. Gonzales was saying," Judge Hinton said with some tentativeness in her voice. "Mr. Delaney, as Mr. Chastain has pointed out, you can cross-examine Ms. Jessup on this and all aspects of her testimony. And each of you can argue to the jury about the reasonableness of Ms. Jessup's interpretation of the sound made by Mr. Gonzales. I overrule the objection and deny the motion for a mistrial."

As soon as the jury came back into the courtroom, Chastain said, "Ms. Jessup, how'd you respond to Captain Smith when he asked whether you recalled if Mr. Tillotson had any disagreements or arguments recently?"

"That's when I remembered Owens storming out the back door after Steve had fired him a few days earlier. At that instant," Jessup said, "I realized Eduardo wasn't just moaning and making the sound, 'oh.' He was trying to answer my question and say the name Owens."

Chastain announced he had no further questions for Ms. Jessup.

"Cross-examination, Mr. Delaney?" Judge Hinton asked.

"Yes, Your Honor, thank you," Delaney responded as he rose from his chair. He walked to the podium without taking a notepad.

"Ms. Jessup, you did not see who shot Mr. Tillotson, correct?"

"No, but—"

"Thank you," he said. "And you also didn't see who shot Mr. Gonzales, correct?"

"No," Jessup said.

"You didn't see any cars pulling out of the restaurant parking lot as you approached it that morning, right?"

"That's right."

"Other than the victims' cars, which you recognized, there weren't any other cars in the parking lot at the diner when you arrived the morning of the shooting, correct?"

"That's true."

"And you certainly didn't see Mr. Owens at the restaurant that morning, right?"

"No, I did not," she whispered, her eyes cast down.

"Excuse me, Ms. Jessup, I'm not sure the jurors could hear your last answer. Did you see Mr. Owens at the restaurant when you arrived there on the morning of the murders?"

"No."

"Do you know what type of car Mr. Owens drove at the time?"

"It was a small, white car. Maybe a Ford. But I'm not sure."

"You didn't notice a white car leaving the parking lot or on the streets around the restaurant as you approached, did you?"

"Not that I recall."

"In fact, from the day Mr. Tillotson fired him until the moment you walked into this courtroom today, you'd not seen Mr. Owens. Isn't that true?"

"Yes."

"One last question, Ms. Jessup. Regardless of how you interpreted or now understand what you thought you heard, the sound that Mr. Gonzales made was something that sounded like the letter O. Nothing more, correct?"

"Well," she said, and then hesitated.

"Mr. Gonzales did not speak the name Owens, did he?"

"No, but I know what he meant."

"One more time, Ms. Jessup. Setting aside how *you* now interpret what Mr. Gonzales said or what *you* believe he may have meant, your testimony here today is that he uttered something that sounded like the letter O, not the name of my client, correct?"

"He did not speak the full name," she conceded. "But I believe that's what he meant."

"When people are sick, injured or hurting, it's not unusual for them to moan and make a similar sound, such as 'Oh,' wouldn't you agree?"

"I s'pose so," she grudgingly acknowledged.

"Thank you, Ms. Jessup. Nothing further for this witness."

CHAPTER THIRTEEN

Greg was reading in the living room of his condo when his girlfriend came out of their bedroom with a jacket on and a suitcase in each hand.

"I'm leaving," she announced.

"Okay. I didn't realize you had a trip coming up. When will you be back?"

"I won't," she said. "We're done."

"What?" Greg said as he bolted out of his chair. "What's the matter?"

"You've changed," she told him. "All you seem to care about are your cases. I care about my work, but there's more to life than being a lawyer."

"Y'know, you could've said something. We could've seen a counselor. I think I deserved at least that much consideration after almost three years."

When she stared at him without responding, the light went on.

"Is there somebody else?" he asked.

"Have a good life, Greg," was all she said as she walked out the door, but the flash in her eyes when he asked the last question told him all he needed to know.

Greg was stunned. After lying awake most of the night, he headed to the office shortly after 5:00 a.m. and spent hour after hour with his door closed, staring out the window at nothing in particular and getting no work done. Two days later, having not seen or heard from Greg, Elena knocked at his office door. There was no response.

"Is he in there?" she asked Greg's assistant.

"I think so, but I have no idea what he's doing," Gail said. "He hasn't come out since I arrived at eight.. There have been no visitors and, as far as I can tell, he hasn't been on the phone."

Elena knocked again. When he still didn't respond, she opened the door slowly and poked her head inside. Greg's head was on his desk, resting on top of his arms, with his eyes closed.

"Greg, are you ill?" she asked. "Can I get you something?"

He didn't respond.

"Greg, I'm worried about you. Are you okay?"

He lifted his head and looked at her, but said nothing.

"Greg, what's the matter?"

His lower jaw jutted out as he shook his head slowly, and ever so slightly, but still said nothing.

"How about taking a walk with me to the coffee bar downstairs?" Elena asked. He stood and silently accompanied Elena down the hall and into the elevator lobby. As the elevator descended, he stared at the floor with a lifeless expression on his face, almost as though he didn't care where he was going or why.

"Two large double-shot lattes with skim," Elena told the barista. "Grab that table in the corner, Greg. I'll be there as soon as the drinks are ready."

He did as he was told.

"I hope you don't mind my asking," Elena said as she sat down, "because I know it's none of my business. But your face bears a striking resemblance to an old hound dog I had as a child. Do you want to talk about it?"

"Not really," he said.

"Let's just say not only am I concerned, so are many of your friends and colleagues."

"I'm really not so sure I have any friends right now. My personal life is in shambles and my professional life feels like it's circling the drain. And the funny thing is, I don't know what I've done to deserve any of this."

"Do you want to talk about it?"

Greg looked up and stared at Elena for a few seconds. "I haven't talked about this to anyone, and I'd appreciate it if you would keep it to yourself."

"Of course," she said reassuringly.

"The two people I trusted most in the world each have betrayed me in ways that aren't just painful, but that make me question who I am as a person and as a lawyer. I'm devastated, to tell you the truth. And I'm wondering what exactly I'm doing with my life. I think it may be time to make some big changes."

"What happened?"

"My girlfriend, who I thought was about to become my fiancé, walked out on me last Sunday," he said. "There's somebody else."

"Oh, Greg, I'm so sorry."

"And despite our victory in the Frontline case, Clay Morrisey transferred Carrie Melton's other case to Katherine Bergman without even discussing it with me first. Can you imagine being treated like that after decades of being not just partners, but close friends?"

Elena took it all in and sat quietly for a few moments before she spoke. "Perhaps you're focusing on the wrong things. Or at least, the wrong people."

Greg looked at her with a puzzled expression on his face.

"Why are you allowing your self-worth to be measured by what a faithless, cheating woman did to you or by how a clueless ingrate of a client treats you? Neither is worth the loss of a single minute of sleep. Thank God you hadn't already married her when she cheated on you."

"Perhaps you're right about her. But Clay Morrisey has been my friend and law partner for more than twenty years. We attended law school together and grew up as lawyers, working side-by-side. We built our careers together and helped build this law firm into one of the largest and most profitable in the city. But rather than stand up to a client who wouldn't know an excellent lawyer if she came face-to-face with Clarence Darrow, he tossed me on the junk heap without a blink." Realizing it was important to let Greg get all of this off of his chest without any push back, Elena took a sip of her latte.

Then, without thinking about what she was about to do, she reached out and placed her hand on top of his, looked him in the eyes, and said, "My minister taught me, as a young woman, not to judge or condemn myself based on the opinions of others. 'If you do,' he said to me, 'you will have times when you're disappointed in yourself. Have faith in God and define success, in whatever you undertake in your life, for yourself.' I've lived by that advice ever since."

"You're wise beyond your years."

"I'm not that much younger than you," Elena said with a laugh. "It just took me seven years of teaching elementary school to realize I'd rather work around adults. So that's when I went to law school."

"And now, I expect, you realize you're still surrounded by a lot of children," Greg said as a smile emerged on his face.

"We'd better head back up before people wonder where we went off to," Elena said as she removed her hand from Greg's. At home that evening, Greg felt something stirring in him, but he wasn't quite sure what it was. The dark cloud in his head lifted, and he looked forward to the next day for the first time in weeks.

CHAPTER FOURTEEN

"Mr. Guerrero, do you see Mr. Owens in the courtroom?" Chastain asked the former assistant cook as the second day of testimony began.

"That's him." Guerrero pointed to Owens, sitting at the defense table next to Delaney. Owens stared directly at Guerrero and smiled, which visibly unnerved Guerrero. He seemed to recoil at the smile, then squinted at Owens and shook his head slowly.

"Are you okay, Mr. Guerrero?" Chastain asked.

"Yeah, I'm fine."

"Did Mr. Owens ever attack you?"

"I was preparing the lunch specials one day when Owens came up behind me and said something about not feeding my cooking to his dog. I looked at him and asked what I'd ever done to him. He started shouting some foul crap at me about lazy Hispanics—that was not the word he used—and I told him to stay away from me."

"Did Mr. Owens make physical contact with you or hit you?"

"He tried. Twice."

"When was the first time?"

"About two weeks after he started work at the restaurant. I noticed he was glaring at me one morning. Then, out of nowhere, he took a swing at me. Mr. Gonzales, who was standing nearby, grabbed Owens's arm and told him to walk away and to focus on his job."

"And what about the second time?"

"It was on the day they fired him. I had parked in the back, where all the employees park, and was walking in when Owens came at me from near the dumpster. He tackled me, and we rolled around on the ground swinging and kicking at each other, until Mr. Gonzalez pulled him off me."

"Did you do anything to provoke the attack?"

"Absolutely *not*! He's a violent lunatic."

"Objection," Delaney said, knowing his objection wouldn't do any good, since the jury had already heard Guerrero's last words. But he hoped, at least, to convey to the jury his belief that those words were unjustified and inappropriate.

"Sustained," Judge Hinton said, without any protest from Chastain. "The jury will disregard the witness's last statement."

"That's all the questions I have for Mr. Guerrero," Chastain announced.

"Any cross-examination?" the judge asked, turning to Delaney, who stepped quickly to the podium.

"Mr. Guerrero, have you ever started a fight with anyone? Delaney asked.

"I suppose so," Guerrero replied, looking a bit surprised by the question.

"Let me ask you, sir, on the day Mr. Owens was fired, isn't it true you attacked him from behind rather than the other way around?" Delaney asked.

"No, sir," Guerrero replied.

"You arrived at the restaurant early and waited in the dark, hoping to catch Owens there so you could blame him for the fight *you* started. Isn't that true, sir?"

"No, sir, that's absolutely not true."

Delaney turned and looked directly at the jury rather than at the witness. He kept his focus there, remaining silent until he was certain each of the jurors was focusing on him, rather than on the witness.

"In fact, Mr. Guerrero, you'd mentioned your plan to one of the other employees at the diner a few days earlier, hadn't you?"

After a short, but awkward, silence, Judge Hinton directed Guerrero to answer the question.

"Who told you that?" a seemingly incredulous Guerrero asked Delaney.

"I'm asking the questions here," Delaney responded.

"The witness will answer the question," Judge Hinton said testily. "Don't make me tell you again."

"No, that's not true."

Delaney didn't press the issue since Guerrero's hesitancy to answer until the judge directed him to do so twice did enough to undermine his credibility. "No further questions," he said.

As he sat down at the defense table, Owens leaned over and whispered in Delaney's ear. "How'd you find out about that?" he asked.

"Lucky guess," Delaney replied. "I was just hoping to plant a seed of doubt. But Guerrero's hesitancy turned it into a home run."

Owens seemed startled. Then he smiled and said, "You're okay, man."

Malcolm Smithson, the drive-thru window attendant, was the next prosecution witness. He testified Owens grabbed him forcefully by the arm and spun him around, away from the window where he was taking a customer's order.

"I didn't know what was going on," Smithson said. "I hadn't said a word to Owens and suddenly he's shoving me and screaming some gibberish I couldn't understand. Then I see him pull his arm back and his fist coming toward my face."

"Did he hit you?" Chastain asked.

"He would've, except that Mr. Tillotson was only a few steps away. He ran over and grabbed Owens's arm. If it wasn't for Mr. Tillotson, I would've had my face smashed in."

Chastain asked Smithson whether he recalled doing anything or saying anything to Owens that might have provoked the attack.

"Absolutely not. We'd never really had anything to do with one another. I don't think we'd said ten words to each other since Owens started working at the diner."

"No further questions," Chastain said.

"Cross-examination, Mr. Delaney?" the judge asked.

"Mr. Smithson," Delaney said as he rose from his chair, "you were aware of Mr. Guerrero's plan to jump Mr. Owens in the parking lot, weren't you?"

"No, sir," Smithson replied.

"In fact, you encouraged Mr. Guerrero to do that after your plan to get Mr. Owens fired by starting a fight, but blaming it on him, failed?"

"No, sir."

"No further questions for this witness," Delaney said.

"It's now eleven thirty," Judge Hinton said, "and I have an urgent matter in another case on which I've agreed to meet with counsel at noon. So we'll take the lunch break now and return at one o'clock. The court is in recess."

When Judge Hinton hadn't returned to the courtroom by one thirty, Chastain asked the court reporter to go back to the judge's chambers to see if she would resume the trial soon. A few minutes later, the court reporter returned and conveyed the judge's apology. "She said it'd be a while longer. She's still meeting with the lawyers in the other case about some kind of restraining order." The judge finally returned to the courtroom shortly before two thirty and immediately instructed the bailiff to bring the jury back into the courtroom. Moments later, the bailiff returned by himself.

"Judge, there's a problem. A juror has become sick," he said. "According to other jurors, she's been in the bathroom for a long time. She finally came out, but she just put her head down on the table and kept moaning. I tried talking to her, but she wouldn't respond."

"Why don't you see if she'll allow you to escort her into the courtroom so I can speak to her?" Judge Hinton said. A few minutes later, the bailiff returned with the juror, who was bent over and clutching her stomach. Delaney's heart skipped a beat. It was one of the two jurors his consultant had identified as being unlikely to vote for the death penalty. Worse yet, she was the one Dr. Jones-Wong had referred to as "Owens's insurance policy."

After asking the juror a few gentle questions, Judge Hinton asked the bailiff to escort her out into the hallway and to stay with her while she decided how to proceed.

"She appears to need medical attention," Judge Hinton said. "I don't get any sense that she's pretending to be ill in order to get off the jury. Is there any objection to dismissing her and substituting the first alternate?"

"No objection from the State," Chastain said.

Delaney's mind had been racing to consider the alternatives. If the juror was truly sick, he had no choice. Delaney also worried that, even though the judge told the jurors not to discuss the case, some loose talk may have caused this juror to sense the mood of the other jurors moving toward a guilty verdict, and she wanted to get out now.

"What about it, Mr. Delaney?" Hinton asked.

"Judge, it's midafternoon," he said. "I'm reluctant to change the composition of the jury at this stage of the proceedings. May I suggest we send the juror for medical attention at the emergency room and delay a decision until the morning, when we might have a better sense if her illness necessitates a replacement?"

Hinton seemed irritated, but recognized that Delaney was well within his rights to seek a brief delay in the trial under the circumstances. Although she could encourage him, she knew it wasn't her place to second guess his judgment on replacement of the juror, at least at this point. She instructed the bailiff to bring the jurors back to the courtroom, then announced that the trial would not resume until the following morning, while the ill juror received medical attention. "One way or the other," she assured them, "the trial will resume in the morning. The court will be in recess until 8:00 a.m. tomorrow."

CHAPTER FIFTEEN

"Members of the jury, I apologize for the delay in getting started this morning," a chagrined Judge Hinton said when court resumed at ten fifteen the next day. "Unfortunately, we've just been told by her doctor that the ill juror cannot continue serving on the jury, so we will have to replace her with the first alternate. Mr. Chastain, call your next witness."

Chastain called Lieutenant Randall and began by having him describe his expertise in ballistics. Then he asked, "Lieutenant Randall, did you examine the shell casings found at the Harrington Diner on the morning of the shootings there?"

"I did," Randall replied.

"What did you observe?"

"The two shell casings recovered at the diner after the shooting were both from a .45 ACP cartridge."

"Are you familiar with that weapon?"

"Very familiar. I'd describe it as a weapon of choice for the military and many police departments because of its capacity to stop a human target with a single shot. For the same reason, unfortunately, it's popular among certain criminal elements."

"Thank you, Lieutenant. Nothing further for this witness."

Delaney quickly stepped to the podium and looked to score a big point with his first question. "Lieutenant Randall, isn't it true that you didn't find any of my client's fingerprints on the shell casings recovered at the scene?"

"Counselor, it's very difficult to recover fingerprints from used casings because of the heat and gases to which they're exposed when fired."

"Lieutenant, did you have the casings checked for fingerprints? Yes or no?"

"Yes, sir, I did," Randall responded.

"And did you find even a partial fingerprint on either of the casings?"

"No, sir, we did not."

"Thank you, Lieutenant," Delaney said. "No further questions."

Chastain then called Lieutenant McKee, a forensic specialist. Originally from Savannah, McKee had been with the Harrington Police Department for seven years and had led the forensic investigations team for the past two years.

"Detective, did you take part in the investigation of the murders at the diner?" he asked.

"Yes, sir, I was in charge of the forensic investigation."

"Would you explain the process you followed?"

"Well, together with two other members of the forensic team, we made a thorough search of the entire crime scene. This would include the point of entrance, being the rear door used primarily by employees and vendors, the area inside and outside of the rear door, the storage room, kitchen, and dining room. Of course, we paid very careful attention to the areas where the bodies of the victims were found."

"Please explain to the jury what you and your colleagues on the forensic team would've been looking for during this search?"

"Yes, sir. We were looking for any type of evidence that could help us identify any individuals who'd been at the scene, such as fingerprints, as well as blood, body fluids, or hair, which could provide DNA evidence. Also, because both victims were shot, we searched for the bullets used in each of the murders so we could identify the weapon used by the assailant."

"Did you find any bullets?"

"Yes, sir, we found two bullets and the shell casings. Unfortunately, we could not recover any latent fingerprints from the casings, which is not unusual."

"Did you find any fingerprints in the restaurant that you could identify as those of the defendant, Joseph Owens?"

"Yes, we found fingerprints matching those of Mr. Owens in two locations. Do you want me to discuss where those were found?"

"Yes, please."

"Fingerprints matching the defendant's left thumb and a partial print matching his left index finger were found on the inside doorknob of the rear door. In addition, we recovered four prints—the thumb and next three fingers of his right hand—from the top slat of the chair to which Mr. Tillotson had been tied."

"What, if anything, did you surmise from finding the defendant's fingerprints on the doorknob and chair?"

"The position of the prints on the top slat of the chair showed it had been gripped from the rear. That would have been consistent with someone pulling the chair back from the table, such as to place it in a position in which a person could sit down in it. The prints on the inside doorknob of the back door were consistent with someone gripping the doorknob from the inside in order to exit the building."

"Were you able to tell how recently the defendant's fingerprints were left on the chair and doorknob?"

"No, I can't tell you precisely when Mr. Owens placed his hand on the chair or the doorknob, Mr. Chastain. However, given the frequent use of the door over the course of an ordinary day, it's almost inconceivable that Mr. Owens's prints would've still been so clearly detectable if he'd not been at the restaurant since being fired three days earlier.

"Similarly, wiping down the chairs and tables was a routine part of the cleaning process at the restaurant. So, while not impossible, it seems improbable that we could recover clean prints three days after Mr. Owens's termination. But that was not the case. The prints we lifted from the chair slat were clearly those of the defendant."

"Thank you, Lieutenant. Nothing further for this witness," Chastain said.

Delaney recognized this was the most damaging testimony yet. It was the only testimony that purported to place Owens at the scene of the crime on the morning of the murders.

"It's not unusual, is it, Lieutenant, to find fingerprints at a crime scene that have been there for three days or more, true?" Delaney asked.

"No, it's not unusual."

"Fingerprints on non-porous services, such as metal doorknobs, actually can remain there for months or even years if not wiped away, correct?"

"That's true."

So far, so good, Delaney thought.

"You testified, did you not, Lieutenant, that one of Mr. Owens's fingerprints you lifted from the inside doorknob of the back door was a partial print?"

"Yes, sir, that's correct," she replied.

"Do you know why there was a partial print on the doorknob?"

"Yes, sir. We found another print on top of Mr. Owens's print."

"Does that mean someone else exited through that same door on the morning of the murders?"

"It appears so."

"And were you able to identify the print of the person who touched the handle after Mr. Owens?"

"No, sir."

Delaney smiled to himself. He'd found the basis for reasonable doubt. "If that partial was that of a Harrington police officer, would it have shown up in the database?"

"Yes, absolutely. We fingerprint all our officers before they're hired."

"So, Lieutenant McKee, let me ask you this," Delaney said as he turned and faced the jurors. "If, as the district attorney alleges, Mr. Owens shot Mr. Tillotson and Mr. Gonzales in the early morning hours of September 27 and then fled the scene through the back door, can you tell me who placed his or her hand on the rear doorknob *after* the DA contends Mr. Owens fled the scene and left the print that partially covered Mr. Owens's print?"

McKee, recognizing the trap she was in, looked to Chastain for help, and he took the cue.

"Objection, Your Honor," Chastain said. "The question calls for speculation."

"It does nothing of the sort, Your Honor. I'm only asking the witness if she knows who placed a fingerprint over that of my client's fingerprint. It calls for a simple "yes" or "no" answer."

"I overruled the objection. The witness will answer," Judge Hinton said.

"No, I've not been able to identify whose print that is, Mr. Delaney."

"But you would agree, would you not, that the unidentified print means somebody other than a police officer had been inside the restaurant, and exited through the rear door, after the shootings, but before the police arrived?"

"Yes, sir. I'd have to agree with that."

"And as you sit here today, you do not know who that fingerprint belongs to, right?"

"That's correct."

"No further questions, Your Honor," Delaney said. He walked back to the defense table and gave Owens a wink as he sat down.

"Any redirect by the State?" Judge Hinton asked.

Chastain sat in his chair for a few moments, contemplating whether to ask McKee anything more.

"No, Your Honor," Chastain said. "But the State reserves the right to recall Lieutenant McKee to the stand at a later time."

The next witness was Dr. Karen Reed, the medical examiner who had performed the autopsies on Tillotson and Gonzales. "Dr. Reed, I'm handing you two diagrams. Can you identify them for us?" Chastain asked.

"Yes," she replied. "These are diagrams I prepared to illustrate the fatal injuries sustained by Mr. Tillotson and Mr. Gonzales."

"Dr. Reed, please explain what each diagram shows."

"As you can see, a single shot at Mr. Gonzales penetrated his chest right below the heart, nicking the descending thoracic aorta and resulting in a substantial loss of blood. Death would've occurred in no more than ten to fifteen minutes, possibly sooner, without immediate medical attention. And even then, I'm not sure he would have survived."

"And what about Mr. Tillotson?"

"The bullet fired into the front of Mr. Tillotson's head caused massive damage to his skull, and to the temporal and occipital lobes of his brain, before exiting out the back of his skull. The force of the blast caused a fragment of the skull to separate and land a few feet from the spot where the shooting occurred," Dr. Reed testified. Pointing to the diagram of a skull, she said, "This is where the bullet entered, and this is where it exited Tillotson's skull. He would've experienced massive swelling of the brain and a swift death."

"How long could he have survived?" Chastain asked.

"Perhaps ten to fifteen minutes, at most," Dr. Reed testified.

"That's all the questions I have for Dr. Reed, Your Honor," Chastain said.

"Cross-examination, Mr. Delaney?" the judge asked.

"I'll be brief, Your Honor," Delaney said as he stood at the defense table. "Dr. Reed, just for the benefit of the jury, you're not expressing any opinion about who fired the shots that killed the two victims, correct?"

"That's correct," she replied. "My testimony relates strictly to the medical cause of the deaths of the two victims. I'm a doctor, not a police detective, and have no opinion regarding who carried out the killings of these two gentlemen."

"Thank you. Nothing further for this witness, Your Honor."

"That was indeed very brief," Judge Hinton said. "That will conclude the testimony for the day. Jurors and counsel will be back here at 8:00 a.m. sharp."

CHAPTER SIXTEEN

"The State calls Captain Gerald Smith of the Harrington Police Department as our next witness," Chastain announced when court resumed in the morning.

"Captain, how soon after Ms. Jessup called 911 did you arrive at the Harrington Diner?"

"Oh, I'd say about thirty-five or forty minutes," Smith said, "but I was in constant radio contact with Lieutenant Randall all that time."

"Were the bodies of Mr. Tillotson and Mr. Gonzales still there when you got to the scene?"

"Yes, sir."

"Did you notice any signs of life in Mr. Tillotson?"

"No. He'd expired by the time the first officer arrived on the scene."

"And did you speak with any witnesses while you were there?"

"Unfortunately, there were no witnesses to the murders. The woman who found the bodies and called it in, Ms. Jessup, was there, and I spoke with her at some length."

"Captain, what did you learn from Ms. Jessup?"

"She was still very emotional, Mr. Chastain. She'd been close to both of the victims. She talked about each of them and how they would treat each employee like family."

"Did you ask Ms. Jessup whether she had any idea who might've committed these murders?"

"Yes sir. At first, Ms. Jessup had no idea who might've shot the two victims. But when I asked her to think if there was anyone either of the victims recently had a disagreement or an argument with, she 'bout jumped out of her chair and told me about the defendant, Mr. Owens, being fired by Tillotson a few days earlier."

"Did you also ask her whether, to her knowledge, Mr. Owens had any reason to shoot Mr. Gonzales?"

"No. It was pretty clear, based on the location of Gonzales's body, that he wasn't an intended target. Unfortunately, he arrived at the restaurant that morning just as Owens was fleeing the scene. My focus was on Tillotson rather than Gonzales because of the manner in which Tillotson was shot."

"Please explain what you mean by that."

"We believe Owens shot Tillotson with a .45 caliber handgun, at a range of no more than an inch from his forehead, just above his right eye. The bullet traveled from the victim's right to left, exiting out the back of Mr. Tillotson's skull, and causing him to topple over backwards and to his left."

"What does the direction the bullet traveled tell you?"

"It tells us that, most likely, the assailant held and fired the gun with his left hand."

"Have you determined whether Mr. Owens is right-handed or left-handed?"

"Yes, I observed Mr. Owens when he filled out some paperwork as he was being booked. He's left-handed."

"Did you make any other observations about the murder scene, Captain?"

"Yes sir," he replied. "The force of the blast caused Mr. Tillotson to fall back and to his left side. There was some spatter of blood and tissue from Mr. Tillotson's skull on the table and floor near where Mr. Tillotson had been sitting."

"Captain, what do you make out of the manner in which the shooting occurred?" Chastain asked.

"Mr. Chastain, in my experience, killing a person in this manner is highly unusual. It's not routinely seen, certainly not here in Noonan County. In fact, I've never seen anything like it. Second, I don't believe robbery was the motive here. No, sir, I don't. I think it's much more likely the assailant acted out of a belief that he had been egregiously wronged in some fashion by Tillotson and committed the killing as an act of revenge."

"Please explain to the jury why you believe this was a revenge killing."

"Well, first, if this was just an ordinary robbery, it wouldn't have happened in the early morning hours before the restaurant even opened. Later in the day, such as just after the restaurant closed, there likely would've been a whole lot more money in the cash register or in the manager's possession. So I reckon that taking the money here was just intended to throw us a curve ball by making it look like a robbery and an incidental shooting. But I don't buy it. No, sir, I believe this was a planned murder that the assailant tried to make look like a robbery."

Chastain paused for a moment to let the jury digest Captain Smith's testimony. Then he asked, "Captain, based on your investigation, did you determine whether the defendant, Mr. Owens, had any reason to seek revenge against Mr. Tillotson or Mr. Gonzales?"

"Well, we know he'd been fired by Tillotson a few days earlier for repeatedly arguing and starting fights with other employees. Our investigation also revealed that Mr. Owens had been fired from a series of other jobs over the last year and had become increasingly aggressive and violent during that time period."

"Objection," Delaney said as he stood. "May we approach the bench?"

Judge Hinton waved the lawyers up to the bench. Speaking softly so the jurors couldn't hear his comments, Delaney said, "Your Honor, I move to strike the last statement about my client having been fired from other jobs and to prohibit any further evidence not directly related to the murders at issue here as hearsay—and irrelevant hearsay, at that—and also as unduly prejudicial."

"Your Honor, we believe the testimony about prior incidents goes to the defendant's history of losing his temper and to his escalating propensity to engage in physical attacks against coworkers," Chastain said. "It's close in time and consistent with his conduct here as alleged by the State and thus relevant to the jury's consideration of the defendant's innocence or guilt."

"I'm going to overrule the objection," Judge Hinton said, "but, Mr. Chastain, do not overplay your hand. I don't want you to think my patience here is unlimited."

"I understand. Thank you, Your Honor."

"Captain, did your investigation uncover any evidence that suggested Mr. Owens had the knowledge or means to carry out murders such as those that took place at the diner?"

"Yes, sir. A check of the National Crime Information Center database revealed that Mr. Owens had one prior arrest six years ago in New Jersey. It was in connection with a raid at a pawnshop where he'd worked that was owned by an organized crime family operating in the northeast."

"Objection," Delaney shouted as he jumped to his feet. "May we approach the bench one more time, Your Honor?"

Judge Hinton once again waved the lawyers up to the bench.

"Judge, the very mention of organized crime is utterly irrelevant and extremely prejudicial. There's not the slightest suggestion that my client was acting or operating on behalf of any organized crime elements in connection with the murders for which he's on trial here today. I renew my motion for a mistrial, since I don't believe the prejudice created by this reference to organized crime can be overcome."

"Mr. Chastain," Judge Hinton said, "is it the State's contention that the defendant was part of an organized crime ring when he allegedly committed these murders?"

"No, Judge, that's not what we're saying."

"So where are you going with this?" an increasingly frustrated Judge Hinton asked.

"First, we'll prove through the testimony of Captain Smith, together with testimony we intend to present from a New Jersey law enforcement officer, that while Mr. Owens was working for a New Jersey organized crime syndicate he was present at the scene of a similar killing.

"Second," Chastain continued, "we'll establish that Mr. Owens was the manager of a pawnshop owned by the same crime syndicate where he was arrested during a police raid. Missing from the inventory at the pawnshop, and never recovered thereafter, was a .45 caliber handgun matching the type of weapon used in the murders of Mr. Tillotson and Mr. Gonzales."

"Oh, c'mon," Delaney said, "this is nothing but rote speculation. There are millions of .45s out there. Unless the prosecution is going to connect the weapon used in these murders to the one that mysteriously went missing in New Jersey, this is as irrelevant and as unduly prejudicial as anything I've ever seen in a courtroom."

"Mr. Delaney," Judge Hinton said, "I'm going to deny your motion for a mistrial, and overrule your objection to the proffered testimony regarding the gun, for now. You're free to raise it again, if you so choose, should the prosecution continue to pursue this line of questioning. Mr. Chastain, you're walking a fine line here. If you cannot link up this testimony to the murders of the victims in this case, you may well find yourself on the losing end of a motion for a mistrial. Do you understand?"

"Yes, Judge," Chastain replied. "I understand."

"Captain Smith, to your knowledge, did the defendant cooperate with the New Jersey authorities following his arrest in connection with the pawnshop raid?" Chastain asked.

"It appears he did. New Jersey court records I've reviewed reveal that, eighteen months after agreeing to a plea deal, the judge entered an order dismissing the charges against Mr. Owens. That's when he moved to Georgia."

"Thank you, Captain," Chastain said. "Now let's turn to the second victim. Was the shooting of Mr. Gonzales carried out in the same manner?"

"No, sir. We believe Mr. Gonzales was just in the wrong place at the wrong time, arriving for work before Mr. Owens could make his escape. Based on the location of Mr. Gonzales's body just inside the rear door of the restaurant, we believe he'd taken one or two steps into the store just as Mr. Owens was attempting to flee the premises through that door. Realizing that Mr. Gonzales would recognize him and identify him to the police as the assailant, Mr. Owens shot Mr. Gonzales in the chest, resulting in his death."

"Alright. Your Honor, that concludes the direct examination of Captain Smith."

"Cross-examination, Mr. Delaney?"

"Yes, Your Honor," Delaney said as he rose and stepped to the podium, carrying his notepad, and placing a binder of exhibits on the corner of the defense table nearest the podium, within his easy reach in case he needed to refresh Smith's memory about any details of the police reports on their investigation. Then he turned to the witness.

"Apart from the questionable fingerprint evidence discussed yesterday, there is no evidence—*none*—that places Mr. Owens at the Harrington Diner on the morning of the murders, correct?"

"That's correct, counselor, if you want to ignore the fingerprint evidence."

"There were no video cameras inside the restaurant, were there?"

"No."

"But there was a video camera outside the convenience store located across the street from the diner, correct?

"Yes, sir, that's correct."

"The video taken by that camera showed the front of the diner and traffic moving along the road between the two businesses on the morning of the shootings, didn't it?"

"Yes, sir. We looked at video retrieved from the service station across the street from the diner. Unfortunately, because the two buildings aren't directly across the street from each other, the camera didn't provide a view of the driveway leading to or from the diner's parking lot."

"Is that the same service station where there was an armed robbery and murder of the attendant a few weeks before these murders?"

"Yes, sir, that's the same place."

"The video of that robbery and murder, if I recall properly, showed the assailant jumping into a black car and racing away from the scene toward I-75, isn't that true?"

"Correct."

Delaney turned to look at the jury. "Have the police identified or arrested any suspects in the service station shooting?"

"No, we haven't, but our investigation is continuing."

"By the way, the car used in the service station shooting was a black 2012 or 2013 Camaro, correct?"

"That's right."

"Captain, you've searched Mr. Owens's car. Please tell the jury what kind of car Mr. Owens drives?"

"It's a 2008 Ford compact—a Focus, I believe."

"What color is it?"

"White."

"Did the police obtain any video footage of traffic in the vicinity of the Harrington Diner at or about the time of the shootings?

"Yes."

"Was there a white Ford Focus visible in any of that footage, sir?"

"No, there was not."

"So Mr. Owens's automobile did not appear on any video of the area around the restaurant on the morning of these murders, correct?"

"That's correct, but again, there was no video available showing the restaurant driveway. Unless the assailant turned right out of the parking lot and passed in front of the restaurant, the camera at the convenience store across the street wouldn't have picked it up on video."

"As part of the investigation, you impounded Mr. Owens's vehicle and police lab technicians went over it with a fine-toothed comb, correct?"

"Yes, sir."

"Captain, if, as you testified, the shooter was standing very close to Mr. Tillotson at the time of the shooting, you'd expect to find some spatter of blood or human tissue on the shooter's hands and clothing, right?"

"That'd be likely, yes, sir."

"And if the shooter got into a car within minutes of the shooting, it's also likely, isn't it, that the spatter of blood and human tissue on his hands or clothing would've been transferred to the door handle, the steering wheel, the driver's seat, or the floor area around the driver's seat. True?"

"That's possible."

"It's not just *possible*, Captain, it's virtually unavoidable unless the perpetrator took the time to change his clothes and shoes and to wash off his hands before getting into the car, right?"

"That's hard to say, Mr. Delaney. It'd depend on how much spatter landed on the shooter and where it landed. So, yeah, it's possible, but I wouldn't go so far as to say it was unavoidable."

"Well, if the shooter was standing next to Mr. Tillotson when the shot was fired, don't you believe the shooter would have been covered in a substantial amount of spatter?"

"I don't know. It also would depend on the angle of the shot. If Mr. Owens was standing to the victim's right, and fired the shot with his arm fully extended, it could well be that most of the spatter went away from him."

"Well, the search of Mr. Owens's car conducted by your officers as part of the investigation didn't turn up any evidence of blood or human tissue, did it?"

"That's correct."

"And that's despite the use of luminol, a chemical that illuminates when sprayed on a surface such as a car steering wheel or leather upholstery, where there's any trace of blood, correct?"

"That's correct."

Delaney took a moment to review his notes before turning his gaze back to the jury.

"By the way, Captain, did you find the murder weapon, which I believe you described as a .45 caliber handgun?"

"No, sir, we've not located it yet."

"Your officers didn't find it when they searched Mr. Owens's home?"

"No, sir."

"And they didn't find it in Mr. Owens's car, correct?"

"That's correct."

"In fact, the murder weapon remains missing to this very day, correct?"

"Correct."

"Nothing further, Judge," Delaney said as he cast one more glance at the jury and returned to the defense table.

After a lunch recess, Chastain called Harrington Police Sergeant J.T. Pooler, who testified about the scene at the Owens home when she responded to a 911 call on the day Tillotson had fired Owens.

"When I arrived," Pooler testified, "I saw broken dishes in the kitchen and some that even hit a wall in the living room. Mrs. Owens plainly was afraid for her life when she called 911. I've listened to the recording of the call and you could hear it in her voice as she reported her husband was throwing pots and dishes at her head. By the time we arrived—about twelve minutes after the call came in—she had calmed down. She said her husband had been in a rage after being fired and had thrown the dishes and pots at her. But she declined to sign a complaint for assault against her husband. I wish she'd signed one so I could've arrested Mr. Owens and gotten him the counseling he needed, but that's never a simple thing for a wife to do."

Delaney's cross-examination comprised a single question.

"Sergeant, you were not involved in the investigation of the shootings for which my client is on trial here today, correct?

"Correct," Pooler answered.

The last witness for the State that day was Detective Sergeant H. M. Jones of the New Jersey State Police, who testified that a .45 caliber handgun was missing from the pawnshop inventory where Owens worked at the time he was arrested there, and remained missing. Anticipating, and looking to blunt, the impact of a likely cross-examination question, Chastain asked Sergeant Jones whether he knew what happened to the missing handgun.

"No, sir," Jones replied, "but there were only two people working at the pawnshop between the date the handgun went into inventory and the date we discovered it was missing."

"Was the defendant, Mr. Owens, one of those two people?"

"Yes, sir."

"Finally, Sergeant, did you take part in the investigation in which Mr. Owens was arrested in New Jersey following the raid on the pawnshop?"

"Yes, I worked directly with the lieutenant who headed that investigation."

"In the course of that investigation, did you learn anything about the organization that owned and operated the pawnshop?"

"That group had been on our radar for a long time. Their activities were well known and were being monitored under certain warrants the state attorney's office had obtained in connection with an ongoing investigation into organized crime."

"Objection," Delaney said. "This line of questioning is irrelevant and immaterial to the case against my client and is being introduced to prejudice him through innuendo."

Judge Hinton instructed the bailiff to take the jury out of the courtroom while she considered the objection. Once they were out of hearing, she looked at the DA and said, "Mr. Chastain, is there going to be a connection to organized crime made to this case or would you like the jurors to tune in to an episode of *The Sopranos* this evening?"

"Judge, if you'll bear with me for a minute, you'll see the connection to this case. I intend to ask only two more questions of this witness to establish that Mr. Owens was present at one such execution."

Delaney was outraged. "Your Honor, even if my client *was* present at such a shooting, it doesn't make him more likely to have committed the killing of Mr. Tillotson. There are enormous gaps in the prosecution's argument. Even if Owens was allegedly present at the place where such a killing was carried out, that doesn't mean he actually witnessed the killing or that he had any propensity to commit murder, let alone that he used the same type of gruesome technique years later to kill Mr. Tillotson."

"Any response, Mr. Chastain?"

"Your Honor, this type of killing does not come naturally to people. It's an uncommon style of murder that must be learned in some form or fashion, typically through observation or participation in organized crime or other gangs. Because of that, we submit that evidence of Mr. Owens's presence at a similar shooting is relevant because it gave him the opportunity to observe and learn this method of killing."

Judge Hinton pondered the argument, weighing the relevance of the testimony against the prejudice it would likely cause to Owens. It was, she thought to herself, a very close call. Even though her gut told her the testimony was a step too far by the State, she allowed it, but with a caution to Chastain.

"I'm going to allow it," Judge Hinton finally said. "Mr. Delaney, your objection is in the record and you can pursue it on appeal if necessary. Mr. Chastain, you are on a short leash, a *very* short leash, and I will not hesitate to yank it in front of the jury if you go an inch too far. Bailiff, bring the jury back in."

Once the jury was back in their seats, Chastain turned to the witness and said, "Sergeant Jones, there's been testimony in this case describing the shooting of one of the victims as being carried out at very close range while he was tied to a chair. Was this a technique that the New Jersey crime organization was known to employ?"

"Yes, without a doubt, and on multiple occasions."

"To your knowledge, was Mr. Owens known to have been present when a killing was carried out in this manner?"

"Yes, sir, our investigation revealed that he was present for at least one such execution-style shooting."

"No further questions for the witness."

"Cross-examination, Mr. Delaney?"

Delaney stood at counsel table and looked at the witness. "Sergeant, it's fair to assume that if the New Jersey State Police had *any evidence whatsoever* that Mr. Owens was involved in such a shooting, he would've been arrested and charged with murder or with being an accomplice to murder, right?"

"Yes, sir."

"And yet, he wasn't arrested or charged by the New Jersey State Police in connection with the shooting at which you claim he was present, correct?"

"Correct."

"So the police must've concluded he was nothing more than an innocent bystander, right?"

"Oh, I wouldn't go that far. It could've just been a case of having insufficient evidence to charge him."

Delaney sat down and silently kicked himself for asking that last question.

CHAPTER SEVENTEEN

"Your Honor, the State has an urgent matter that we need to discuss with the court before the jury returns," the district attorney announced after the break.

"What's this about, Mr. Chastain?" Judge Hinton asked skeptically.

"The police informed me during the break that they've identified and located another witness who we'd like to call to the stand," Chastain said.

"Mr. Chastain, there had better be a very good explanation for this," Hinton said as her face reddened and her eyes flashed. "I don't much like trial by ambush."

"I apologize to Mr. Delaney and to the court that this person wasn't on our witness list, but while we had reason to believe such a witness existed, despite diligent efforts, the police had neither identified him nor, of course, interviewed him until last evening. I now have a witness statement that I'm handing to Mr. Delaney, and I request the court's permission to call the witness to the stand."

Delaney asked for a moment to review the witness statement. As he did, his face went from pink to red to crimson.

"Your Honor, I strenuously object to this last-minute witness identification," Delaney said. "The State's been aware of the existence of this witness for many months, but claims it's only now identified him. It's simply not credible. Allowing a surprise witness to testify when we have had no opportunity, let alone adequate opportunity, to interview the witness, to investigate the witness's testimony, to prepare for cross-examination, or to identify other witnesses who might refute the testimony—would be the grossest kind of violation of my client's right to due process and a fair trial."

"Your Honor, if defense counsel is not aware of this witness's proposed testimony, it's only because the defendant apparently failed to mention to his lawyers that, while sitting in a bar on the day he was fired by Mr. Tillotson, he had a conversation with another bar patron. In the course of their investigation, the police interviewed the bartender who told them he recalled observing Mr. Owens sitting at a table next to another patron, but the bartender didn't know the other man's name since he wasn't a regular and had paid in cash.

"That patron, our newly identified witness, will testify that Mr. Owens told him about having just been fired and swore that he would get revenge on the man who'd fired him. The police had no way to identify or interview the witness until, by sheer happenstance, the bartender called 911 shortly after 7 p.m. last evening to report the man was sitting at the bar. Police immediately went to the bar and interviewed the witness. I only received a copy of the witness's sworn statement minutes ago. Captain Smith is available to take the witness stand to verify all of this if the court or defense counsel would like him to do so."

"Anything else from defense counsel?" Judge Hinton asked.

"Your Honor, the defendant's right to due process and a fair trial is of the utmost constitutional importance. Allowing this testimony to be introduced under these circumstances will eviscerate my client's constitutional rights. Even assuming the police are blameless for this delay—which we certainly don't concede—the price they're asking my client to pay in order to introduce this testimony is outrageous. Without time to interview this proposed witness and to investigate the veracity of his testimony, as well as his character and credibility, the only way to refute his testimony would be for Mr. Owens to take the witness stand. But doing so would subject him to cross-examination and thus deprive him of the constitutional right to remain silent. I urge the court to deny the State's request."

"All right, counsel. We're going to take a recess while I do a little research of my own," Judge Hinton said. "I'll be back as promptly as I can."

Seventy-five minutes later, she returned to the bench.

"I'm of the view that the State used appropriate diligence in seeking to identify and locate this witness, and in the interest of justice should be permitted to present the witness's testimony. However, Mr. Chastain, I caution you that the law is far from clear on this issue, so the State's taking a not insignificant risk of reversal on appeal should Mr. Owens be convicted. Do you still wish to call the witness?"

"Yes, Your Honor."

"Bailiff, bring the jurors back in."

"The state calls Kevin Gordon to the witness stand," Chastain said as soon as the jurors took their seats.

"Do you know the defendant in this case, Joseph Owens?" Chastain asked as he gestured toward the defense table.

"I didn't know him by name, but I recognize him from a brief encounter a year or more ago, at the McGinnis Tavern, a few blocks from here. He was sitting at the table next to me and looked very despondent," Gordon said. "So I asked him if he was okay and he said, 'No, man, I've just been fired, and I don't know what I'm gonna do now.'"

"Did you respond to Mr. Owens?"

"Yeah, I asked why he was fired, and he said his boss was blaming him for fights other people had started. I just said something like I was sorry to hear that and wished him good luck finding a new job."

"Did Mr. Owens say anything else to you?"

"He did. And I've not been able to forget it. He stared at his beer for a few moments, but then looked up at me and said, 'Oh, don't be sorry for me, man. Be sorry for him. I'm gonna teach him a lesson for firing me.'"

"No further questions for this witness, Your Honor," Chastain said.

"Mr. Delaney, if you would like a brief recess to review your notes before proceeding, that would be acceptable to the court," Judge Hinton said.

"Thank you, Judge, but I'm ready to proceed," Delaney replied as strode to the lectern.

"Mr. Gordon, were you already at the pub when Mr. Owens arrived?" Delaney asked.

"No, sir, he was there when I sat down," he said.

"Do you recall what time you arrived?"

"Not precisely, but I think it was around 11:45 a.m."

"How do you know it was around that time?"

"Well, I live in Atlanta and come up this way on business occasionally, and I usually stop at the McGinnis Tavern for lunch. I like their food and the atmosphere is pleasant in there."

"Do you know how long my client had been there by the time you arrived?"

"No, sir."

"Do you know how many drinks my client had consumed before you arrived?"

"No, sir."

"Did Mr. Owens appear to be intoxicated at the time you arrived?"

"Yes, I'd say moderately so."

"What did you observe that leads you to say he appeared moderately intoxicated?"

"Well, his head was sort of hanging down, his eyelids were droopy, his eyes appeared to be bloodshot, and his speech was slurred."

"Did you take his comment about teaching his boss a lesson as a threat of physical violence?"

"Y'know, in that moment, I don't recall what I thought about it. I guess I didn't take it all that seriously, seeing that he seemed, y'know, to have had a few too many."

"Did you report your conversation to the authorities?"

"What authorities?"

"The Harrington Police Department or the Noonan County Sheriff's Office, for example?"

"No."

"Did you even bother to mention it to the bartender or to your waiter?"

"No."

"If you had thought Mr. Owens was making a credible threat of violence against his boss, as a responsible citizen, you certainly would've reported it to the authorities. Isn't that true?"

"Sure."

"No further questions."

"Any redirect, Mr. Chastain?" Judge Hinton asked.

Chastain, who appeared to be engaged in an intense conversation with Captain Smith, either didn't hear the judge's question or chose to pretend he didn't. A few seconds later, the judge, plainly annoyed at Chastain, said in a sharp tone, "Mr. Chastain, do you have any redirect for this witness, or may he be excused?"

"I apologize, Your Honor. Nothing further."

"It's four thirty and we've had a long day," Judge Hinton said. "This may be a good time to adjourn. Mr. Chastain, how much more testimony does the state intend to put on?"

"Actually, Judge, if you'd permit me to recall Captain Smith to the stand for a few very brief questions, the State is prepared to rest its case."

"Well, that's good news, Mr. Chastain. Captain Smith, please return to the witness stand." As he took his seat, Judge Hinton reminded him he was still under oath.

"Captain Smith, were you in the courtroom to hear the testimony of Lieutenant McKee yesterday afternoon?" Chastain asked.

"I was, Mr. Chastain."

"Have you taken any steps to identify the fingerprint that was placed over that of Mr. Owens on the inside doorknob of the rear door of the restaurant?"

"Yes, sir. After yesterday's testimony, I spoke to Lieutenant McKee and advised her that a news reporter who has a police radio in his car made it to the restaurant just as the first officer to respond entered the building. The reporter followed him inside. Officer Donner instructed him to leave immediately and observed him as he exited through the rear door. We've now requested the reporter to allow us to fingerprint him so we can determine if, as I suspect, the print is his."

"Nothing further, Your Honor."

"Do you wish to cross-examine?" Hinton asked Delaney.

"Yes, thank you, Your Honor. Lieutenant, sitting here today, you don't know if that reporter touched the doorknob on his way out or not, correct?"

"That's true."

"If the door was left ajar, he could've pushed it open without touching the doorknob, correct?"

"I suppose so."

"Nothing further, Your Honor."

"Your Honor, the State rests its case," Chastain said.

"Very good," Hinton said. "Court is adjourned. We'll resume at 9:00 a.m. tomorrow, rather than the usual eight, because of a prior commitment I have first thing in the morning."

CHAPTER EIGHTEEN

"Greg, do you remember that case up in Noonan County where Elena represented the station against an effort by the public defender to close the courtroom for pretrial proceedings?" Karen Cepeda of Channel 3 News had called early to be sure and catch Greg as soon as he arrived at the office.

"Sure do, Karen," he said. "I've been keeping an eye on your news reports about that trial. Sounds like a bit of a weak case to me. If it was being tried in Atlanta, I think would be thrown out of court before getting to a jury. But in Noonan County, who knows? They're a bit more—shall we say, deferential—to the police and the prosecutors than the judges here in Fulton County."

"Interesting, I guess we'll find out before too long. It sounds like the case is getting close to wrapping up, which brings me to the reason for my call."

"Oh?" Greg said, puzzled by Karen's comment.

"Our reporter thinks it's unlikely the defense will put up any witnesses, especially since, in her view, the State's case seems pretty weak. If so, the judge likely will go straight to closing arguments, and after that, she'll give the jury its instructions."

"Very interesting. But surely this isn't why you're calling. So what can I do for you?"

"Well, it is, and it isn't. I was hoping you might attend the closing arguments and give our viewers some perspective on how the lawyers did, what their chances are, and how long the jury might deliberate. That sort of thing."

"You mean you want to put me on the air as a legal expert?"

"Exactly."

"Karen, I'm flattered, but I'm not a criminal law expert. In fact, I've never tried a criminal case, so I wouldn't have much credibility."

"We'll pay your hourly rate while you're up there."

"It's not about the money. I just don't have the legal expertise you need. But tell you what. How 'bout if I make some calls and find you a lawyer with criminal experience who might want the exposure and would do this for you?"

"I suppose that'll have to do," Karen said. "But I need somebody quickly."

"I'm on it."

An hour later, Greg called Karen to tell her he'd come up with someone well qualified and willing to serve as Channel 3's expert commentator.

"Who is it?

"Her name is Sharon Johnston. Have you heard of her?"

"Isn't she the lawyer who got the so-called 'Lord of the North Georgia Underworld' acquitted in that big racketeering trial a year or so ago?"

"Bingo."

"Good work, Greg. You're off the hook."

On the way out the door, Greg swung by Elena's office to let her know about Karen's unusual request. "You would've been great at that," Elena said. "And, who knows? You might've become a media star."

"No thanks. But I have a light day tomorrow, so I'm thinking about taking a drive up to north Georgia tomorrow morning and perhaps wandering into a certain courtroom, just as an observer, not as a television expert. Any interest in going with?"

"Sure, but I'll have to stay late to finish up a brief I'm drafting. What time are you planning to leave?"

"Around 7:30-ish. It's only about a 90-minute drive to Harrington, but I'd like to leave a little early in case there are any traffic problems. We can meet here or I can pick you up at your place if it's more convenient for you."

"Greg, I don't want to bring up something that may be painful to you, but. . ."

"It's okay, Elena. I know what you're going to say, and I'll be fine," he assured her.

"You sure?"

"Yep."

"Okay. Sounds good then. I live in a condo just off Lenox Road, and it'll save me some time if it's not out of your way to pick me up there."

"No problem. Text me your address."

CHAPTER NINETEEN

Greg's concern about potential traffic problems was prescient. They were in their seats for less than five minutes when Judge Hinton gaveled the courtroom to order and immediately called on Delaney. "Does the defense wish to make a motion?" she asked.

"Yes, your honor. The defense moves to dismiss the State's case," Delaney said. "There's not nearly enough evidence for any reasonable juror to conclude that my client, Mr. Owens, committed the murders for which he's charged. Not only are there no eyewitnesses, but there's also no evidence—*none*—that places Mr. Owens at the scene on the morning of these murders beyond a couple of fingerprints the State has failed to prove were made on the date of the murders. There's also no murder weapon or evidence my client has ever possessed such a weapon.

"Without such proof, the State's case cannot, and does not, meet the applicable test, which is that the State must prove its case beyond a reasonable doubt. Frankly, the evidence presented by the State *doesn't even approach* that standard, let alone meet it. It's simply outrageous for the State to prosecute a case, especially one in which it seeks the death penalty, on such scant and vaporish proof. We ask that the court put an end to this charade of a case right now."

To Delaney's shock and Owens's dismay, Hinton denied the motion without even inviting Chastain to respond.

"She should've granted that motion!" Elena whispered in Greg's ear. When he didn't respond, she noticed Greg was concentrating on Owens.

"Are you okay?" she asked as her eyes widened with concern.

Greg nodded.

"Look at me and tell me you're okay," Elena demanded.

"It's harder than I thought," he managed to say. Then he broke the stare and turned to look at her. "I'm okay. Maybe not good, but okay."

"Do you intend to present any evidence?" Hinton asked Delaney.

"No, Your Honor."

"So there's no need to present an opening statement, which you reserved at the commencement of trial, correct?"

"Correct. We can go straight to closing arguments."

Judge Hinton ordered the jurors brought back into the courtroom.

"Ladies and gentlemen, the defense has elected not to present any evidence, which is its right, so we'll now have closing arguments." The eyebrows of several jurors shot up. Elena, sitting in the back row on the aisle nearest the jury, let out a gasp when she observed two of the jurors exchange quick glances. Each had a smirk on his face.

"Did you see that?" she whispered in Greg's ear.

"See what?"

"Those two guys in the back row of the jury box, the bearded ones sitting next to each other, smirked when Judge Hinton announced there would be no more evidence presented."

"So what? You don't know what they're thinking. Could be they understand the State's case is so weak that Delaney doesn't need to put on any evidence."

"Wanna bet?" Elena asked with a tone of certainty that startled Greg.

"You'll now hear closing arguments from both sides," Hinton told the jurors, starting with Mr. Chastain."

As Chastain rose, he turned to look at the victims' widows and Steve Tillotson's mother, who were sitting in the front row, just behind him. Chastain had assured them he would do everything in his power to bring the murderer to justice. Now was the time to deliver.

"Steve Tillotson did not have an enemy in this world," he began as he turned toward the jurors. "Not one, until he very understandably fired Joseph Owens for starting fights with several employees at the Harrington Diner, the popular restaurant he'd owned and operated for five years. Mr. Tillotson was a businessman with a passion for good food, for taking care of his customers, and for taking care of his employees.

"It was his sense of duty to his employees that led Tillotson to fire Owens, a malcontent since the day he was hired. You heard testimony about how his temper repeatedly flared at the restaurant, leading to disruptions, confrontations, and fights with several employees. It was only after giving Owens a second chance and urging him to change his ways, that Tillotson himself observed Owens in a fight with another employee. At that point, he had no choice but to fire Owens in order to protect the rest of his employees and his customers. For that, Steve Tillotson paid with his life and the life of his close friend and cook, Eduardo Gonzales.

"The killing of Mr. Tillotson was a cold, calculated, and brutal act of revenge. It's what you heard the police refer to as an execution-style killing. It's certainly not something police see every day of the week. As the New Jersey officer who testified told you from the witness stand just yesterday, Joseph Owens was present when such an execution was carried out during his time working for the mob in New Jersey. He knew how it was done. And, as we established, Owens also had access to a .45 caliber handgun—the type of weapon used in these shootings—which had gone missing under mysterious circumstances from the pawnshop in New Jersey that Owens had managed.

"We also know that Owens was angry about being fired and planned to get revenge. Kevin Gordon, a businessman from Atlanta who sat near him at the McGinnis Tavern in Harrington just hours after he'd been fired, testified that Owens vowed to get revenge against Mr. Tillotson. Mr. Owens's counsel tried to discredit Mr. Gordon's testimony by suggesting that he didn't take the comment seriously enough to report it to the police. I deeply regret that Mr. Gordon didn't do so, but it doesn't change the fact that Owens made the threat.

"He took that revenge, as we have proven, a mere three days after being fired, in the same brutal manner he'd witnessed a few years earlier in New Jersey. He tied Mr. Tillotson to a chair and held a .45 caliber revolver up to of his face, in what had to be a moment of sheer terror for a good and decent man, a husband and a father of twin, six-year-old boys.

"The killing of Mr. Gonzales, on the other hand, resulted from unfortunate and tragic timing. Had Mr. Gonzales arrived at the restaurant just a few minutes later," Chastain said, "he would still be alive today to help his wife, Camila, raise their infant daughter. Now, Camila Gonzales and Grace Tillotson must raise their young children on their own, without their husbands by their sides.

"But Mr. Gonzales lived long enough to identify his killer. As you heard from Elaine Jessup, the waitress who found Mr. Gonzales laying on the floor after being shot in the chest. She asked Mr. Gonzales who had done this to him and it was only then—in response to Ms. Jessup's question—that he roused long enough to utter a sound, 'ohh!'" The defense wants you to disregard that sound as nothing more than a meaningless moan. *But Eduardo Gonzales wasn't moaning or making sounds before Elaine Jessup asked that question!* He only made that sound when he heard his friend and co-worker ask, 'Who did this to you?'

"You also heard testimony about Owens's propensity to become violent, even toward his own wife. Called to their apartment by neighbors who were concerned about screaming and the sound of objects crashing against their walls, Harrington Police Sergeant Pooler testified that Jasmine Owens reported she narrowly escaped injury when her husband threw a pot and a dish at her, one object narrowly missing her head. That took place soon after Owens left the McGinnis

Tavern, where he had told another patron, Kevin Gordon, that he intended to take revenge against Mr. Tillotson. Just three days later, he did so.

"The State's evidence proves that Joseph Owens is a violent and dangerous man, who had the motive, opportunity, and premeditated intent to murder Steve Tillotson. Ladies and gentlemen of the jury, it's your duty to weigh all the evidence and, when you do, I believe you'll find the defendant guilty of the murders of Steve Tillotson, the man who fired him, and Eduardo Gonzales, who, sadly, came face-to-face with Owens just as Owens fled the restaurant after making good on his vow to take revenge on Tillotson.

"In the name of the State of Georgia, we ask you to do your duty by returning a verdict finding the defendant, Joseph Owens, guilty— *guilty*—of murder in the first degree of Steve Tillotson, guilty of murder in the second degree of Eduardo Gonzales, and guilty of armed robbery. Thank you."

"Mr. Delaney, you may present the closing argument for the defense," the judge said.

"Ladies and gentlemen of the jury, you have a solemn obligation before you," Delaney said. "It's your responsibility to determine the guilt or innocence of my client, Joseph Owens. One thing the judge will tell you is that the State bears a heavy burden of proof in criminal cases such as this one. Under the law, Mr. Owens is presumed innocent—let me say that again, he is *presumed to be innocent*—unless the State introduces credible evidence that establishes his guilt beyond any reasonable doubt.

"That's a very high standard, which we submit the State has utterly and completely failed to meet. The crimes committed here were violent, brutal, and tragic. Terribly tragic. Of that, there is no doubt. But if, as we contend, the State has failed to prove my client's guilt beyond a reasonable doubt, it's your solemn obligation under the law to find him not guilty. *Not guilty.*"

Delaney paused for a moment to let his point sink in.

"I'm going to review the evidence with you, after which I believe you'll agree that the evidence falls short—far short—of establishing my client's guilt beyond a reasonable doubt. In fact, it's so inconclusive that a verdict of not guilty is the only possible result."

Delaney then began methodically walking the jury back through the testimony of each witness, focusing on what he called the "most important questions, the ones left unanswered." Chief among those, he said, was the absence of proof that Owens was present at the scene of the crime.

"You'll recall that, in his opening statement, the district attorney told you that had Eduardo Gonzales, the second victim, arrived just two minutes later, Owens would have been out the back door, in his car, and racing away from the diner. Those were the words of the district attorney, Mr. Chastain, when he told you in his opening statement what the State's evidence would prove.

"But where's the proof—*any proof*—that Mr. Owens was at or near the restaurant that morning? The best the State could do was point to two fingerprints on the interior doorknob of the back door, one of which was partially covered by an unidentified person's fingerprint. Please take a moment to think about that. The State's forensic expert, Lt. McKee, admitted she didn't know when Mr. Owens's fingerprints were left on that doorknob. If, as Mr. Chastain contends, Mr. Owens left those fingerprints while fleeing the restaurant soon after shooting the victims, the question remains: whose fingerprint was found on top of his?

"The State's fingerprint expert admitted it didn't belong to any of the police officers investigating the murders. Who else was in the restaurant that morning?" Delaney asked rhetorically. "Somebody was, but Mr. Chastain has no answer or explanation for that fact, other than speculating about a news reporter, but presenting no *evidence* to prove the reporter touched the doorknob. The reporter did not testify, and the State did not even attempt to prove the overlaying print was that of the reporter. What does that tell you?

"Common sense suggests a much more likely explanation for that fingerprint," Delaney continued, "which is that Mr. Owens left his prints on the doorknob three days before the murders, shortly after being fired. There would've been plenty of time for someone else— another employee, or a vendor, perhaps—to leave through the back door over the course of those three days and just happen to touch the very same spot on the doorknob that Mr. Owens had touched.

"Another major hole in the prosecution's case is the absence of any witnesses who place my client at the diner on the morning of the shootings. The closest they could come was based on an encounter that took place in a pub in Harrington, several hours after Mr. Owens was fired, which was *three days* before the murders took place. That witness not only admitted Mr. Owens was heavily intoxicated and bleary-eyed, but he also didn't take the statement seriously enough to report it to the police, or even to mention it to the bartender. If the witness didn't take that comment seriously, neither should you.

"So I ask you, where's the State's proof that Mr. Owens actually went to the restaurant on the morning of the killings? Very simply, it has none. Despite recovering video from cameras across the street from the restaurant and from cameras at various locations between the restaurant and Mr. Owens's house, you heard Captain Smith admit there are no images—*none, absolutely none*—of a white Ford Focus, let alone one with Mr. Owens at the wheel, on *any* of the video recovered by the police from the early morning hours of September 27. So how'd Mr. Owens supposedly get to the restaurant from his house? It certainly was too far to walk. The State doesn't even suggest that as a possibility. And how'd he get back home before the police showed up to search his car and his house? Again, the State offers no evidence to explain that gaping hole in its proof."

Delaney paused again for a few moments to let that last point sink in.

"Nor, as you'll recall, did the police find any trace of Mr. Tillotson's blood on Mr. Owens's clothing, shoes, or in Mr. Owens's car when they searched it. You heard Captain Smith admit that such blood spatter almost certainly would have landed on Mr. Owens if, as Mr. Chastain contends, my client committed the murder of Mr. Tillotson while standing next to him. Captain Smith also acknowledged the spatter likely would've been transferred to the inside of Mr. Owens's car, which they contend he used to flee the scene.

"But no such spatter was found in Mr. Owens's car, in his house, or on his clothing. The State offers no explanation for this additional—and again, absolutely critical—hole in its case."

Then, knowing it might make or break the defense, Delaney paused, took a sip of water, and faced the jury again as he dealt with the most damning evidence in the State's case.

"Ms. Jessup, bless her grieving heart, means well with her testimony, but she knew and worked with Mr. Tillotson and Mr. Gonzales for many years. Over those years, Ms. Jessup came to know the wives and children of both Mr. Tillotson and Mr. Gonzales. Not having a family of her own, she considers all of them to be her family. On the other hand, she only worked with Mr. Owens for only about three weeks, and during that time, what she witnessed was a troubled man who couldn't control his temper."

After another momentary pause to make sure he had the attention of all the jurors, Delaney continued. "Ms. Jessup's emotions were understandably raw after she came across this horrendous crime scene. It's certainly understandable that, given the emotions she felt that morning, she concluded that the sound of the letter O uttered by Mr. Gonzales was meant as an identification of Mr. Owens. But nobody can honestly say they know what Mr. Gonzales meant, if he even meant anything at all. It may've been nothing more than an unconscious moan. As Her Honor will instruct you shortly, under the law of Georgia, an accused is innocent until proven guilty. She'll also tell you that the burden is on the prosecution to prove a defendant's guilt by an extremely high standard known as beyond a reasonable doubt.

"With great respect for Ms. Jessup and the trauma she went through that morning, her understanding of Mr. Gonzales's last sound—*not word, not name, but sound*—simply does *not* provide a basis for any of you to conclude, beyond a reasonable doubt, that my client was *even at* the scene of the crime, let alone the murderer. Nor is there any evidence that he possessed a .45 caliber gun such as the one used in the commission of this crime. The testimony that one such gun went missing from inventory at a pawnshop in New Jersey where Mr. Owens worked four years ago—without any evidence of when it went missing or who took it—also leaves too much doubt, *far more* than a reasonable doubt, to allow for a conviction of Mr. Owens.

"Without proof that Mr. Owens ever possessed *any* weapon, let alone a .45 caliber weapon, without proof that he was anywhere near, let alone at, the Harrington Diner in the early morning hours on the day of the shootings, without proof that his car was at or near the restaurant on the day of the shootings, can any of you say that the State has proved Mr. Owens's guilt beyond a reasonable doubt?" Delaney said, moving his gaze slowly from one juror to the next. "I think we all know the answer to those questions. Your duty under the law, unquestionably, is to return a verdict of not guilty. Thank you."

As Delaney sat down, Judge Hinton asked Chastain if he had any rebuttal.

"Just two quick points, Your Honor," Chastain said as he rose and faced the jurors once again.

"Members of the jury, Mr. Delaney urged you to disregard the fingerprint evidence found on the inside doorknob of the back door because he speculates that somebody else, whose fingerprint appeared on top of Mr. Owens's print, might—*might*—have been hiding out in the restaurant and was the murderer. But allow me to remind you that Captain Smith testified about a news reporter who followed the initial police responder into the diner that morning and was quickly ordered to leave. He did so, as you heard, through the back door. So there is no need to speculate about who left those fingerprints on top of Mr. Owens's prints, as Mr. Delaney urged you to do.

"Second, Mr. Delaney wants you to discount the testimony of Elaine Jessup, who as you will recall, testified that Mr. Gonzales identified Owens as the murderer by speaking the sound 'oh' moments before he died of a gunshot wound to his chest. Mr. Delaney tried to persuade you that the sound Mr. Owens made was not an identification of the shooter, but nothing more than the moan of a dying man.

"How you interpret that sound is, of course, up to each of you. But let me remind you that Eduardo Gonzales did not just utter the sound, oh, in a vacuum. As you will remember from the testimony, Mr. Gonzales was lying silently on the floor, unconscious and unresponsive to Ms. Jessup's cries, until the moment he heard the voice of his friend ask, 'Eduardo, who did this to you?' It was only then—*at that moment, and in response to Ms. Jessup's question*—that Mr. Gonzales stirred and identified his killer by uttering the sound Ms. Jessup reasonably understood as Owens's name."

"On behalf of the State of Georgia, I urge you to do justice by convicting Joseph Owens of the murders of Steve Tillotson and Eduardo Gonzales. Thank you."

Judge Hinton told the jurors they would take the lunch break and return in an hour, when she would give them instructions on the law before sending them off to deliberate.

Once the jurors were out of the courtroom, she declared court in recess until 1:30 p.m. But as she stood to leave the bench, Hinton was surprised to spot Greg and Elena in the back of the courtroom. She hadn't been told of any issues arising regarding the media during the trial, so their presence in the courtroom puzzled her.

"Excuse me," Hinton said, stopping everyone in their tracks as they started to leave for lunch. "I see counsel for the media in the courtroom. Have any issues arisen regarding media coverage of this trial?"

"No, Your Honor," Greg said. "No issues at all. But thank you for asking."

"Ms. Samuels, would you have a few minutes to speak to me in chambers?" Hinton asked.

"Of course, Judge," she said immediately, masking the fact that she was a bit startled by the request.

Once Hinton had left the courtroom, Elena and Greg exchanged puzzled looks. "What do you think this is about?" she asked.

"I can't imagine," Greg said, "but don't keep her waiting. I'll wait right here for you."

CHAPTER TWENTY

"Judge Hinton's expecting you," the assistant said to Elena when she entered the judge's reception room. "It's right through that door. Please go on in."

"Hello, Ms. Samuels," the judge said as she rose from her chair behind a large wooden desk on which there were stacks of files. "I apologize for the clutter, but you just wouldn't believe how many crises can arise in the course of a single day."

"I understand, Your Honor—"

"I'm not 'Your Honor' in here," Hinton said, quickly cutting off Elena. "It's just Janice, please."

"Thank you, Janice," she replied. "And I'm Elena."

"Would you care for coffee or a soft drink?" Judge Hinton asked.

"Thanks. A cup of tea would be great if that's available," Elena replied.

Hinton stepped outside to ask her assistant to bring in two cups of tea. That gave Elena time to take a quick look around the office. The wood paneling on the walls was filled with diplomas, certificates, and awards the judge had received while in college, law school, and since being appointed to the bench. Behind her desk was a photo of Judge Hinton with a man Elena assumed was her husband, who was holding a bible as the judge took the oath of office from the governor.

"Please take a seat over there," Judge Hinton said, gesturing toward two upholstered chairs with a round wooden table between them. "I spend too much time behind my desk dealing with contentious lawyers and their clients, so I like to get out from there when I have time for a social visit."

"Thank you, Janice," Elena said as she settled into a chair. "This is an unexpected pleasure."

"Well," said Hinton as she stirred a packet of sugar into her tea, "I was surprised, but pleased, to see you in the courtroom this morning. I wanted to tell you how impressed I was by the brief you filed and your presentation a few months ago on behalf of your client. I'm not a big fan of the media. They seem to get much more wrong than right when they cover the courts. But the analysis of the law in your brief was on point and your argument was persuasive."

"Thank you," Elena said. "That's very kind of you to say."

"Tell me a bit about yourself," Hinton asked. "Where'd you grow up and attend school?"

"I was born in Atlanta and raised by my mother after my father died in an automobile accident," she said. "A drunk driver hit him broadside. Probably never knew what hit him. I was just five years old and an only child, so I've got some photos of him, but not a lot of memories."

"I'm so sorry to hear that," Hinton said. "That must've been terribly hard on your mother and on you."

"Well, I'll say this. If it was hard on her, which it certainly had to be, she never showed it. At least, not to me," Elena said. "She's a strong woman. A couple of months after my father died, she got a job as a teacher's aide at my elementary school and made my education her top priority.

"So after I graduated from Grady High, I attended the University of Georgia on a scholarship and received my bachelor's degree with honors in early childhood education. Then I taught elementary school for four years before deciding I wanted to become a lawyer. I took the LSAT, sent out a lot of applications, and was shocked when I was accepted at Yale, which also offered a full scholarship. Three years later, I graduated and, knowing I wanted to practice in Atlanta to be close to my mother, I accepted an offer from Fox Stern. I've been there ever since."

"That," Hinton said, "is an incredibly inspiring story. Good for you! And for your mother. Is she still with you?"

"Yes, thank you," Elena said. "Her strength is my inspiration."

"Greg Williams obviously is a supporter as well," Hinton said. "I can count on one hand the number of male attorneys who give younger, women lawyers a chance to argue an important motion in court."

"Well, he's been a mentor, not just a supporter," Elena said. "In fact, he was one of my biggest supporters when I came up for partnership last year. He's not just a terrific lawyer, he's a very special person."

Hinton smiled. She wasn't quite sure what Elena meant by her last statement. But not wanting to go there, she changed the topic.

"I'm sure you're wondering, so let me tell you why I asked you to stop by," Hinton said. "The governor has made it a priority to identify more qualified women lawyers who have an interest in serving on the bench."

Elena's eyes opened wide as a jolt shot through her.

"He's asked me to keep my eye out for women who appear in my courtroom and who display the intellect and maturity required to serve as a judge," Hinton said. "I think you meet those requirements, especially after hearing a little about your upbringing and education, and making a few inquiries of lawyers I know and respect in Atlanta. If you've any interest, I'd be very pleased to pass your name along to the governor's staff for consideration when an opening occurs in Atlanta."

"Judge, I don't know what to say. I'm so flattered that you'd be willing to submit my name to the governor. Would it be okay if I take a little time to consider whether this is a path I want to pursue?"

"By all means. There's no rush and certainly no pressure at all. I just like helping talented women lawyers advance their careers. Take all the time you need and call if you have questions or would like to discuss it further."

"So," Greg said as Elena strode out from Judge Hinton's chambers. "What was that all about?"

"Let's go get some lunch and I'll tell you about it," she said. "You're not going to believe this."

CHAPTER TWENTY-ONE

Back in the courtroom after the lunch recess, it took Judge Hinton an hour and ten minutes to read her carefully drafted instructions to the jury. "That's the law that you're to apply in this case," she said at the conclusion of her remarks. "It's your job to determine the facts that were proved by the evidence and to return a verdict on each of the charges against the defendant. You may now retire to the jury room for your deliberations."

The jury room was neither elegant nor particularly comfortable. In the back there was a long table used for coffee and muffins in the morning and for sandwiches and salads during the lunch break. "It's not exactly gourmet cuisine," one of them said to the bailiff, "but I've had worse."

The walls were painted pale green, and the floor was covered with alternating black-and-white tiles. "You'd think the county could do a little better in terms of the furniture and especially the food," one juror said.

"I think they put these chairs in here to keep us from getting too comfortable," another juror said. "And it's working. Let's get this thing over with."

After spending two hours reviewing and discussing the evidence, the jury foreperson called for an initial vote. "Let's see where we are," he said. "Write either 'innocent,' 'guilty,' or 'undecided' on a slip of paper, fold it in half, and pass it around."

The vote was 10-1 for conviction, with one juror undecided.

"Nobody has to identify themselves as the person who voted not guilty or undecided," the foreperson said. "But since we're required to reach a unanimous decision, if you're willing to speak up and to explain the basis for your vote, it might help us reach a conclusion."

The only Black person on the jury spoke up.

"It was me," she said. "And I'm glad to share the reasons for my vote."

Across the table, a burly man with a long, brown beard, wearing red, white, and blue suspenders over his blue work shirt, leaned over to an older man sitting next to him. "Told ya so," he whispered. The older man nodded.

"I'm very concerned about finding Owens guilty when there's simply no evidence he was at the scene of the crime," the woman said. "The fingerprints on the door and chair are inconclusive. The prints on the chair could've been placed there any time while Owens was sweeping and cleaning up. Y'all heard the police officer say prints can last on surfaces for a long time. And the prints on the door handle could've been placed there when he was fired.

"But what really troubles me is the absence of any video of Owens or his car at the restaurant or anywhere nearby. How did he get there? How did he leave? Even if the convenience store camera across the street didn't show the driveway at the restaurant, surely he would've shown up on at least one of the other videos of the surrounding streets the police obtained. And the fact that they didn't find any blood or — what'd they call it? — spatter, in his car . . . somebody explain that to me since the State's own witness said it most likely would be there under the circumstances of these shootings? The district attorney ignored all of that in his closing, which tells me he had no good response. To me, that's more than enough for a reasonable doubt about Owens's guilt."

"Thank you," said the foreperson. "Would anyone like to address these concerns and explain your vote to convict?"

Several members of the jury chimed in with their reasons for voting to convict. Owens's involvement with the mob in New Jersey, that a .45 caliber gun matching the murder weapon was missing from the pawnshop where Owens worked, and the threat Owens made at the tavern on the day he was fired to teach Tillotson a lesson, were weighing heavily on the minds of many of them. His temper, and the fights with several employees, were enough to persuade others of his guilt.

The result of another vote was identical to the first. After more discussion, and three more rounds of voting that turned out the same, an older man spoke up. "I'm the undecided," he announced. "But after hearing all this and praying about it, I'm gonna change my vote to guilty."

All eyes turned toward the woman who had voted to acquit. She said nothing, but looked at the foreperson and gently shook her head. On the inside, though, she was beginning to feel very alone, especially after failing to persuade the undecided juror to join her in voting not guilty, which might have helped persuade some others to reconsider.

As 6:00 p.m. approached, Delaney thought the jury must be having difficulty reaching a verdict, which he thought was a good sign. Surely, he thought, if they were all inclined to convict, a verdict would have been reached by now. What if they couldn't reach a unanimous verdict tonight? Would the judge let them work into the evening or bring them back to continue their deliberations tomorrow? The notion of a deadlocked jury no sooner crossed his mind than Judge Hinton entered the courtroom to announce there was a verdict. Chastain quickly returned from his office across the street and they brought in the jurors at 6:25 p.m.

The jury foreperson stood and read the verdict. Owens was found guilty on all counts. Silence enveloped the courtroom, save for the sound of sobbing that came from the first row of seats behind the prosecutor's table, where the widows of Steve Tillotson and Eduardo Gonzales had sat together throughout the trial.

Owens looked down and shook his head slowly as Delaney put a hand on his shoulder and said something about appealing. Joseph couldn't bring himself to look at Jasmine, who was sitting by herself in the first row directly behind him, staring at the jurors with her mouth open in utter disbelief.

"Oh, no," Owens could hear her saying. "No, no, no."

CHAPTER TWENTY-TWO

"They're going to sentence him to death," Elena declared in a solemn tone and slow cadence that bespoke certainty. Her words breached the almost hour-long silence they had observed since leaving the courtroom.

"I don't think it's a foregone conclusion," Greg said, grasping for something, anything, to help ease the pain he could hear in Elena's voice and the anger he could see on her face.

"Oh, yes. Yes, it is. Those jurors . . . they want revenge," Elena said. "They want revenge to comfort the widows and the children left behind. They want revenge to make themselves feel safer. They want revenge because they think it'll send a message that if anyone commits a murder in Noonan County, they'll pay with their own lives. Only it won't do any of those things."

"How do you know what the jurors want?" Greg asked.

"I was watching their faces as the foreperson read the verdict," she said. "They didn't look down or look away, the way people do when they're uncertain of what they've done. Several of them glared at Owens, not with any doubt in their eyes or remorse over the verdict, but to let him know they're not done with him. They were sending him a message with their eyes, telling him to prepare to meet his maker."

There were no more words until Greg pulled up on the street outside her apartment. He shut off the engine and looked at Elena, who sat quietly, her hands folded and looking straight ahead but not making any move to get out of the car.

"Do you want to go back up there tomorrow?" Greg asked.

She nodded. "If you have the time."

"Not really, but I don't think I'll get much work done wondering what's going on in that courtroom. Besides, if it's important to you to be there—and please don't take this the wrong way," he said, "then it's important to me."

She turned, and they locked eyes for a silent moment.

"Same time?" she asked.

"Same time," he said as she opened the door and stepped out of the car.

Greg watched as Elena walked to the door of her townhouse and went inside. Then he started the engine and headed for home. He wasn't sure what he was feeling. His mind was racing between the guilty verdict, Judge Hinton's offer to Elena, the sentencing hearing that would take place tomorrow, and the look he and Elena had exchanged just before she got out of his car.

Chapter Twenty-Three

Spectators and journalists packed the courtroom as the sentencing hearing got underway promptly at 9:00 a.m. For the first time since the trial started, a television camera was in the back of the courtroom to record the announcement of Owens's sentence.

"Did Karen really have to send a camera today?" Elena asked.

Greg, understanding Elena's anxiety level, took the question as rhetorical and didn't bother to respond.

Chastain called Grace Tillotson as his first witness.

"We were partners in every sense of the word," Grace said as she gazed softly at the jury, remaining poised throughout her testimony, but stopping now and then to avoid losing her composure. She lost control when she tried to describe how the sudden loss of their father had devastated their twin boys, Brian and Josh, now almost eight years old. "They couldn't understand, couldn't grasp. . ." Grace managed to say before choking up, bringing her hands up to cover her face and to muffle her sobs.

"We'll take a five-minute recess," Judge Hinton swiftly declared and then walked off the bench, feeling in herself some of the emotion that charged the courtroom. When she returned, Grace Tillotson remained on the witness stand.

"I apologize—" she said, but Judge Hinton cut her off.

"Please, Mrs. Tillotson, you've nothing at all to apologize for," Hinton said. "Nothing at all. Please continue if you feel up to it."

"Thank you, Judge," she said. "If Eduardo had survived, I might've been able to keep the restaurant operating under his supervision, since I knew Steve trusted and respected him." Grace turned to look at Camila Gonzales as she spoke. "But with Eduardo's death, I had no option but to try to salvage something out of the business. Through the grace of God and with the help of our friends, I was fortunate to find a buyer within three months, which provided us with enough money to keep me from having to go back to work for the first year or two after Steve's death."

Chastain called Camila Gonzales as his next witness. Tears ran down her cheeks as she approached the witness stand, clutching a Bible to her chest. "It was heartbreaking during the first months, after we lost Eduardo, when Lucinda looked around for her father each day after waking from her afternoon nap, calling out 'Pa-pi, Pa-pi,'" Camila said. "There was no way I could explain to her that he wouldn't be coming home—that she wouldn't see her daddy again in this lifetime."

Through a steady flow of tears, Camila said life had become a question of survival, both emotional and financial. "My job and my friends have helped tremendously, but without Eduardo, we're going to move to Florida to be close to my parents and my sister, who has two small children," she said. "Lucinda needs to be with family who'll love her and help to support her. And I need them too, because then I won't feel so alone in this world."

Elaine Jessup was next. "I can't even begin to tell you how much Mr. Tillotson and Mr. Gonzales meant to me."

"How'd you come to work at the Harrington Diner?" Chastain asked.

"It was near to where I was working at the time," she said, "so I had breakfast there most mornings. Steve recognized me after a few visits and would stop by my table to chat most mornings. Then, out of nowhere, he asked if I'd be interested in coming to work there. Said he needed a mature person to be in charge of the wait staff, and since I seemed to like the place, he thought I might be interested.

"I don't believe he thought for a moment that I'd accept," she went on. Then she sobbed as she described the joy of working with Tillotson and Gonzales for the last four years. "Y'know, I could've made a little more money elsewhere," she said, "but we don't all get a second family in our lives, and that's what I had there. That's what I lost."

The last witness for the State was Nancy Tillotson, Steve's widowed mother. Emotions were running deep as she stepped slowly to the front of the courtroom, stopping to turn and gaze at Owens for a moment, and then continued walking to the witness stand.

"Mrs. Tillotson, I know this will be difficult," Chastain said, "but please describe for the jurors how the death of your son has impacted your life?"

"I'm not sure I've got the words to describe the agony I've endured since then. Steve was the rock I leaned on after I lost my husband to a heart attack about seven years ago," Mrs. Tillotson said, dabbing a steady flow of tears from her eyes with a tissue as she spoke. "I thought I'd never again feel that kind of pain. But losing my son, my only child, has been almost more than I can bear."

"Mrs. Tillotson, how've you managed to cope with the loss?"

"It's not been easy, Mr. Chastain. For the first few months, I lived with Grace and the boys. She said she needed my help caring for the twins while she tried to sell the restaurant and settle Steve's affairs. But I knew it was more because she was worried about me and thought if she gave me something to do, it'd help me get through the pain. That woman is such a blessing, thinking about me when her own life had been shattered so suddenly, so inexplicably. But after a few months, I felt like it would be best to let the three of them have time to themselves. That's when I moved back to my apartment, so we all could get on with our lives as best we're able."

Once she had stepped down from the witness stand, Chastain rested the State's case.

Jasmine Owens took the witness stand as the defense's first witness. Delaney started by asking her if she'd been present in the courtroom during the State's presentation earlier that day.

"Yes," she replied, speaking softly.

"Please try to speak up a bit so the jurors can hear you, Mrs. Owens," Delaney said.

"Sorry. Yes, I heard it, and I'm so deeply sorry for the pain and suffering that Grace Tillotson and Nancy Tillotson, as well as Mrs. Gonzales and all their children, have had to endure. I know the jury has convicted my husband of these crimes, but that's not the man I know and love."

"Tell the members of the jury why you say that, Ms. Owens."

"My husband has his issues, especially with his temper, but he couldn't have done this. Like the officer from New Jersey testified, after his arrest there, Joseph did the right thing. He cooperated with the police and testified at the trial of the mob bosses, and as a result, he didn't have to go to prison there. But the stress of testifying against the mob made him nervous . . . very nervous. Joseph is always looking over his shoulder and worrying about whether or when they'll come to get revenge. He gets terrible headaches from the tension of what he's been through, which makes him very jumpy."

"But he hasn't accepted responsibility for the murders of Steve Tillotson and Eduardo Gonzales. So why should the jury accept what you're saying about his contrition and cooperation in New Jersey and spare his life, when he continues to maintain his innocence here?"

As Delaney coached her to do, Mrs. Owens looked at the jury as she spoke. "It's not that Joseph doesn't accept the jury's decision to find him guilty. He must. And he does. But he *cannot* admit to killing these men when he knows he didn't do these terrible things."

"So, what are you asking the jury to do here, Mrs. Owens?"

"I believe my husband is innocent, but the jury has spoken. All I can ask now is that you spare his life. If there's any doubt, just the slightest doubt, in any of your minds that he was the person who shot these men, please, I'm asking you to spare his life. He'll serve life in prison without a chance for parole, which is hard enough for me to bear, but at least I'll be able to visit him."

"That's all the questions I have for this witness, Your Honor," Delaney said.

Chastain declined to cross-examine, fearing that doing so would only give Mrs. Owens the opportunity to reinforce her testimony.

Delaney then called a series of other witnesses, including Owens's seventy-eight-year-old mother and eighty-year-old father, both of whom made emotional pleas for his life to be spared. Owens's fourth-grade teacher came down from New Jersey voluntarily to testify about her former pupil, who she described as "an average student but one with a good heart. Even though he got into some trouble now and then, what I remember is that he'd always tell the truth and admit what he'd done. I thought it was a sign of his character that he didn't try to lie his way out of trouble."

It was a powerful point that Delaney hoped would reinforce Mrs. Owens's testimony about Joseph's character. After the lunch break, Delaney called his last witness. She was a psychiatrist, Dr. Jennifer Lyons, who had examined Owens in prison.

"It's my conclusion that Owens suffers from post-traumatic stress disorder," Dr. Lyons said, "which possibly was caused by injuries he received and events he witnessed during his adolescent years working for an organized crime syndicate in New Jersey, and then testifying against the syndicate bosses in court. The diagnosis," she added, "might well explain Owens's frequent loss of temper and his propensity to turn violent when in a stressful situation at home or in the workplace. He's not capable of controlling his actions when he gets into an agitated state."

"Dr. Lyons," Chastain asked as he rose for cross-examination, "how confident are you that Owens suffered from PTSD?"

"I'm very confident," she replied.

"In how many cases have you testified on behalf of a defendant facing capital punishment?"

"I really don't know."

"Would you say more than ten cases?"

"Possibly."

"More than twenty-five cases?"

"I don't think so."

"And on each occasion, you testified on behalf of the defendant, correct?"

"Yes."

"And in what percentage of the cases in which you've testified on behalf of a defendant facing capital punishment have you testified that the defendant suffered from PTSD?"

"I have no idea, sir," she said, "but likely most of them."

"In fact, Dr. Lyons," Chastain said as he picked up several pieces of paper from his table and glanced through them, "the truth is you've *never* testified, even once, that a defendant you examined did *not* suffer from PTSD?"

"That's true," she replied as a slight smile appeared on her face.

"No further questions, Your Honor," Chastain said, as he sat down at counsel table.

"Any redirect examination, Mr. Delaney?" Judge Hinton asked.

"Just briefly, Judge. Dr. Lyons, have you ever served as an expert in a capital case and, after examining the defendant, concluded that he did *not* suffer from PTSD?"

"Yes, of course," she said, sounding a bit exasperated. "Many times."

"But Mr. Chastain asked you a moment ago whether you'd ever testified in a capital case that the defendant did not suffer from PTSD, and you said no. Can you explain that?"

"Certainly, Mr. Delaney. It's because in the cases in which I concluded the defendant was *not* suffering from PTSD, typically the defendant's lawyers don't put me on the witness stand to testify."

"So, if you don't find that their client suffered from PTSD, or another form of mental illness, your engagement ends, correct?"

"Correct," she said. "I use my independent, professional judgment to diagnose each individual. The chips fall where they may. Then it's up to defense counsel, not to me, to decide whether they want to put me on the witness stand."

"And if the defense counsel in any of those cases had called you to testify, would you have stated that their client did not have PTSD?"

"Absolutely," she said. "Which, of course, is why they don't put me on the witness stand in that circumstance. But that's their decision. Not mine."

"Thank you, Dr. Lyons. Nothing further, Your Honor."

"The witness is excused. Any more witnesses, Mr. Delaney?" Judge Hinton asked.

"No, Your Honor. The defense rests."

At 1:30 p.m., the judge gave the jury its instructions on the law and sent it out to decide Owens's fate. There was a strange silence in the courtroom as the lawyers, family members, and spectators alike started to stand and stretch. Most remained in place, but gradually a few filtered out into the hallway to use their phones or to find a bathroom. Nobody knew, or could even guess, how long the sentencing deliberations might take.

"Greg, what do you think?" Elena asked with a tone of urgency he'd not heard from her before.

"I don't have any idea," he said. "Prepare yourself for the worst, but hope for the best."

Shortly before six o'clock, the jury foreperson sent a note to the judge telling her they had reached a decision. As the jurors returned to the courtroom, Delaney was on edge. The verdict form was handed to the bailiff, who passed it to the judge.

"The defendant will rise," Judge Hinton pronounced. "Mr. Owens, it is the unanimous decision of the jury that you be sentenced to die by lethal injection in accordance with the law of the State of Georgia. May the Lord have mercy on your soul."

With her eyes fixed on the judge, Elena slid her hand over and took hold of Greg's hand, much as she had in the coffee shop almost a year earlier when he was in a deep depression. This time, though, it was she who needed the support.

After a few seconds, Greg squeezed her hand gently. Elena squeezed back. Their hands remained joined, but neither looked at the other. When Judge Hinton brought her gavel down on the wooden block and declared court adjourned, they released their grip. Silently, they walked out of the courtroom and out of the building. Back in Greg's car, he turned and saw a tear running down Elena's left cheek. He reached over and softly wiped the tear away with his right thumb, leaving his fingers pressed against her face for a few extra seconds.

"Why are you crying?" he asked.

"I'm so confused," she managed to say.

As she turned to look at Greg, he reached around her shoulder and pulled her close. When she lifted her head from his shoulder, their eyes locked, much as they had the day before as she was about to get out of his car. This time, however, Greg leaned in and they kissed.

CHAPTER TWENTY-FOUR

Greg woke the next morning with a start. It was light outside, and he needed to get to the office to make up for the last two days away. There was a draft of a brief sitting on his desk that needed to be filed on Monday, and he hadn't even read the first page.

As he got out of bed, he heard a voice say, "Where do you think you're going? Get back here."

"I need to get to work on the brief that's due on Monday," Greg said.

Elena was smiling and holding up the sheet for him to get back into bed. "It can wait. You will not have many changes to make. It's a *very* well-written brief if I say so myself. Now, get back here."

In the three weeks since the Owens verdict, they had sought comfort in each other's company. A few meals together and long conversations that lasted into the early morning hours led to a weekend at a friend's vacation home on the South Carolina coast, where their relationship had deepened.

"Okay," he said, sliding back into bed and under the sheet. "But that brief had better be good."

Thirty minutes later, Elena said, "Now you can get a shower. I'll make some coffee and then you can be on your way."

"Okay," he said. But he didn't move.

"Are you going to take a shower?"

"Just as soon as you release your grip on me," he said, kissing her on the nose.

"I guess I'll let you go, but I'll never release my grip on you."

Greg was on his way home to change clothes and then head to the office when the thought crossed his mind that he'd not been this happy in a very long time. Then he had another thought. Could they keep their personal relationship from interfering with their working relationship? Of course, he reassured himself. Nothing about their professional relationship would change.

Unless she decided to apply to become a judge.

CHAPTER TWENTY-FIVE

"So, what are you thinking?" Greg asked Elena as he served dinner at his place a few days later.

"I'm torn," she replied. "The possibility of becoming a judge is exhilarating. I honestly can say I never thought I'd have the opportunity until Judge Hinton raised the possibility."

"Why not?" Greg asked, puzzled by Elena's incredulity at being asked to think about going on the bench. "You're a smart, talented trial lawyer. You'd make a superb judge."

"Oh, Lord, this may the best gumbo I've ever tasted!" she exclaimed. "When did you learn to cook like this?"

"I'm self-taught," he said with a smile. "When you like good food, you either eat out a lot at expensive restaurants or you learn to cook. I hate eating out by myself."

"That's not a problem for you anymore," Elena said, smiling coyly. "But we don't have to go out to dinner if you can cook like this."

"Knock it off and answer my question," he said impatiently. "Why haven't you thought about becoming a judge before now?"

Elena put down her spoon and looked Greg in the eye.

"I'd love to be a judge," she began. "I've dreamed of being a judge since before I was in law school. And I think I could be really good at it. But to be a judge in Georgia, I'd have to be prepared to do something I simply could never do."

"The death penalty?"

"Yes, of course. I could never do what Janice Hinton did a few weeks ago. I couldn't enforce a law that not only is inhumane, but is applied discriminatorily against Black people like Owens. The data on that are overwhelming."

They sat silently, staring at each other.

"And if I can't do that," Elena finally continued, "I can't in good conscience take an oath to enforce all the laws of the State of Georgia. Right?"

"Right," Greg said, taking her hand in his and leaning forward to kiss her, but first wiping a few tears that spilled out of Elena's eyes as the painful reality of her decision took hold.

The next morning, Elena called Judge Hinton to thank her for her offer, but to decline.

"What did she say?" Greg asked.

"She wanted to know why I wasn't interested. I told her I was very interested, but while I didn't mean any disrespect, I couldn't do what she does."

"How'd she react?"

"She understood immediately. She asked, 'Is it about the death penalty?' I told her it was entirely about the death penalty."

"How'd she respond?"

"She asked why I opposed the death penalty. I told her it's because we're all human, all fallible, and I just couldn't live with myself if someone I'd sentenced to death was executed, and later proved to have been innocent."

"What'd she say to that?"

"She said there are parts of the job that keep her up at night, and that's one of them. Then she said she admired my commitment to my principles, wished me well, and said I was welcome to stop by whenever I'm in the area."

CHAPTER TWENTY-SIX

Chastain had graciously accepted congratulations from everyone in his office, from the receptionist to his highest-ranking assistant, following the Owens verdict. "Spectacular win," said Roger Maxwell as he shook his boss's hand. "You're a shoo-in for reelection now."

"Bite your tongue," Chastain snapped back at his chief deputy. "Never say anything like that outside of this office. The last thing I need is for the media to report that I sought the death penalty against Owens to help my reelection chances." Then he winked at Maxwell as he headed outside to hold a press conference, where he was appropriately reserved in responding to questions about the verdict and the sentence.

"The jurors did their duty, and we respect each of them for having the courage to do the right thing when called upon," he said. "It's not an easy thing for me to ask for the death sentence, and I'm sure it wasn't easy for the jurors to hand down that sentence. But the result is that, not only has justice been done for the widows and children of the victims, but criminals are also going to think twice before committing violent crimes in Noonan County."

Within minutes of the verdict, the Noonan Herald's web edition had a big headline across its digital front page proclaiming, "Chastain Gets Death Sentence Against Diner Murderer!"

"My office is always going to do everything it can to protect the citizens of Noonan County from violent crime," Chastain was quoted in the article as saying. "The jury's verdict sends a clear message that we won't coddle murderers by keeping them housed, clothed, and fed at taxpayer expense for the rest of their lives."

•   •   •   •   •

Meanwhile, Dick Shaw sighed as he watched the evening news in his campaign office. "Chastain couldn't pay for publicity like this," Shaw told his campaign manager. "This is going to fuel his run right until election day, and it will not cost him a penny. We need to come up with a strategy to keep the voters focused on his sorry overall record, not just focused on this one verdict."

Three weeks later, Shaw was disappointed, but not surprised, to see a new poll that showed Chastain had gained significant ground on him. "We were up by fourteen points before that verdict," Shaw told his campaign staff. "Now it's neck-and-neck. We need a fresh approach that shifts the focus off the Owens trial."

Reaching into his own deep pocket, Shaw unleashed a new media campaign highlighting his own work as a police officer before heading to law school, after which he had developed a highly successful criminal defense practice. "I faced off in the courtroom against Paul Chastain twelve times during my career as a defense lawyer," Shaw said as he gazed into a camera in front of a digital image of a bookcase filled with law books. Then the scene shifted to the Noonan County Courthouse steps, which were empty. Shaw's voice is heard saying, "Paul Chastain never had a press conference on the courthouse steps after a trial against me. Because he doesn't talk to the public or to the press about his losses."

Coming so soon on the heels of the DA's success in the Owens case, Shaw's aggressive advertisement backfired. Chastain quickly struck back. "I've been representing the people of Noonan County as their prosecuting attorney for almost sixteen years," he said on a television ad that started running one week before election day. "Unlike my opponent, I'm more interested in speaking to a jury in the courtroom than in front of a television camera. That's why the voters have elected me five times.

"I promise the voters only one thing. If you reelect me again, I'll continue to do everything in my power to protect every man, woman, and child in this county from violent crime. And if you don't reelect me," Chastain said, gazing solemnly into the camera, "I'll thank every one of you for the privilege of having been your district attorney for the last two decades. It's been the honor of my life."

When the results were tallied on election night, Chastain swept to victory by a stunning margin of sixteen points. He celebrated with friends and family that evening, accepted a concession call from Shaw with grace, and was back in his office at 8:00 a.m. the next morning.

"Now," he said to Maxwell, "what's going on with Owens's appeal?"

PART TWO

CHAPTER TWENTY-SEVEN

"This is just unimaginable," Elena said angrily as she walked into Greg's office with a copy of the Georgia Supreme Court's fifty-seven-page order on Owens's appeal. "It's a unanimous affirmance. I thought for sure they'd *at least* reverse the death sentence, if not the conviction. What a travesty of justice!"

"This isn't good," Greg said repeatedly as he read through the opinion. "I think Delaney is going to have a lot of trouble getting this overturned. He's an okay lawyer, but I don't think he has much, if any, federal court experience, let alone any experience with the US Supreme Court."

"Do you think we could offer to help?" Elena asked.

"No. Out of the question," he quickly replied. "I sympathize with Owens, but the firm would never allow us to take on something like this."

"What happened to your commitment to *pro bono* legal work?" Elena asked. "All lawyers are supposed to volunteer to represent people who can't afford to pay. Or is that something the management committee thinks is just for our first- and second-year lawyers to do?"

"C'mon, Elena, be reasonable. I support *pro bono* work as much as anyone here, for partners and associates. But it's one thing to take on a civil case for free since that's the kind of work we do. It's another thing entirely to get involved in a criminal case, especially one where the client's been convicted of murder and his conviction's been affirmed by the Georgia Supreme Court. It's not like we have any experience with that sort of thing."

"So let me make sure I understand," Elena said, her eyes focused on Greg with a discomforting, penetrating stare. "Are you saying we can't get involved in a criminal *pro bono* case because the issues are just too complicated for us Ivy League lawyers to grasp, or are you concerned about soiling the firm's reputation by representing a convicted murderer, even though you and I both know he's innocent?"

Greg's eyes met Elena's. There had been a few spats between them over the last few months, but they were about small, personal matters, and nothing that hadn't been worked out with an apology and a kiss. This was different. It not only was their first significant professional disagreement, but he also knew Elena held the moral high ground, and she would not back down.

"Okay, look, I'm sorry. Give me some time to think this through," he said. "Perhaps I reacted too quickly. Can we discuss it over dinner this evening? Because I really need to get ready for a hearing this afternoon in a securities fraud case I'm handling."

He saw her gaze soften and then, slowly, her grimace gave way to a slight smile.

"Depends," she said. "Where are we going?"

"How about François's Bistro?" he asked, knowing how much she loved the place. It was where he had taken her on their first romantic dinner date.

"Deal," she said. "But don't think you can buy me off with their Coquilles St. Jacques."

"The thought never crossed my mind," he said with a touch of mock indignation in his voice.

Elena stared at Greg for a moment. "I'm serious about this, Greg," she said softly.

"I know, Elena." The smile disappeared from his face. "I know."

Chapter Twenty-Eight

The next morning, Greg walked up the grand, circular staircase that led from the firm's reception area on the forty-fifth floor up to the fiftieth floor. Once there, he walked toward the northwest corner office, past a striking collection of black-and-white photography by some of the world's best-known photographers. The firm's office was a veritable museum, having received mention once in a prestigious London photography magazine for the collection. The best of the best of the firm's collection, not surprisingly, was located outside Morrisey's office.

"Clay, the Georgia Supreme Court just handed down its decision on the Owens appeal," Greg said. "They affirmed the conviction and death sentence."

"Surely that doesn't come as a surprise to you?" Clay said. "The justices aren't particularly sympathetic to convicted murderers, are they?"

"No, they're certainly not," Greg conceded. "But this one surprises me. Elena and I were in the courtroom for several days of the trial, and I have to tell you, the DA got away with murder. No pun intended."

"So what's the point, Greg?" Clay asked. "You represented the media, not the defendant. Why are you still interested in this case?"

He stared out of Clay's office windows for a few moments, taking in the distant view of the north Georgia mountains on a picture-perfect spring day. Turning back to Clay, he said, "Elena stopped by my office this morning, and she was very upset about the court's opinion. She thinks it's filled with errors of a constitutional magnitude."

"So?" Clay said, drawing out the word as he turned his palms upward.

"She's very concerned that the public defender representing Owens is too overwhelmed with work to devote the time he needs to the case, especially now that he's going to have to file an appeal directly to the United States Supreme Court," Greg said. "Given the unbelievable caseloads that most public defenders are required to handle, and the limited financial resources available to them, I think her concern is well justified."

"Greg, for Pete's sake, get to the point. Why are you talking to me about this?" Clay asked impatiently.

"Elena would like the firm to work with Owens's lawyer on the appeal to the Supreme Court."

"She wants the firm to represent a convicted murderer in the United States Supreme Court?"

"In a word, yes."

"In a word, no," Clay said emphatically. "First, the amount of work that would go into a brief of that magnitude would take tens of thousands of dollars in billable time, for which we wouldn't be paid. Second, I have to say I'm not wildly enthusiastic about the firm being listed on the brief as representing a man convicted of a brutal double murder. Third, if I understand this properly, the guy already has lost at trial and in front of the Georgia Supreme Court. What makes you think the United States Supreme Court will even give you the time of day?"

"I thought that would be your reaction," Greg said as he stood to leave. "Y'know, there's more to being a successful lawyer than charging the highest hourly rates in town so the partners can have seven-figure distributions. Sometimes, it's more about fighting the good fight for someone who desperately needs our help, even if the odds are heavily against him."

"Greg, I'm going to ignore that only because of our long friendship," Clay said. "*Pro bono* is important to all of us, so don't go trying to claim the high ground here. But *pro bono* only works when lawyers are competent to handle the work they undertake. Neither you nor Elena has any criminal defense experience, so this is a non-starter."

"If only it was a civil case, you'd be okay with it. Is that what you're saying?" Greg asked.

"Well, I still might not be wildly enthusiastic," Clay responded. "But yes, bring me a *pro bono* civil case with important constitutional and societal issues, and you'll have my support."

"Okay," Greg said. "Fair enough."

As he walked out of Clay's office, Greg passed Katherine Bergman, the litigation partner to whom Clay had shifted the Frontline Medical work. Although it was awkward between them for a short while afterwards, Greg knew she had no part in making the decision, so they remained on good terms.

"Hello, Katherine," Greg said with a wide smile on his face.

"Hi, Greg," she replied. "You look like the cat that just ate the canary. What's up?"

"Oh, nothing," he said with a smile. "Nothing at all."

CHAPTER TWENTY-NINE

François's Bistro was busy when Greg and Elena arrived shortly before seven. It was the best French restaurant in the city and had been for a decade. Getting a table was challenging on any night, but especially so on Friday nights in springtime, when the azalea bushes and dogwood trees were blooming all over the city.

They were welcomed back by Monsieur Jacques, the maître d', who recognized them from a recent visit. He escorted them past several tables filled with diners, a few of whom were speaking French and all of whom appeared to be enjoying their meals. An elegant, deep-red fabric wallpaper, and linen tablecloths embroidered with a blue fleur-de-lis motif, set an elegant tone.

Monsieur Jacques seated them at the corner table Greg had requested, in the rear of the dining room with a view of Peachtree Street. On the table was a simple white vase containing three red roses, adding a touch of romance to the elegant setting. "The roses are lovely," Elena said with a smile. "How come I don't see them on any of the other tables?"

"Because I ordered them just for you," he said, returning the smile.

"Thank you, sweetheart. What's the occasion?"

"Does there have to be an occasion for me to give you roses?" he asked with a look of mocked offense.

"Certainly not," she said. "But I get the feeling you're trying to soften me up for something. Is this your way of preparing me for news I'm not going to like?"

"Actually, I've got some good news for you."

"Greg, we're going to help Delaney with the Supreme Court brief?"

"No, I'm truly sorry, but we really can't do that."

"Why not?"

"For some very good reasons. First, as Clay properly pointed out, we're not criminal defense lawyers. The brief to the Supreme Court will require a thorough understanding of criminal law, which we don't have and don't have time to learn. Given the limited time for filing the brief, we actually would do Owens a disservice to try to insert ourselves into the case at this point."

"Okay. I get it. But you said you had good news. How's that qualify as good news?"

At that moment, they were interrupted by the waiter, who arrived with a bottle of Dom and an ice bucket. They remained silent as the waiter unwrapped the wire holding the foil-wrapped cork in place and then expertly removed the cork. The hissing sound drew a few turned heads, and smiles from a pair of elderly diners at the next table, who perhaps were being reminded of the romantic days of their youth.

"Look at it this way," Greg said. "Delaney is stuck with the trial record and, as a result, he's likely to fail. On the other hand, assuming the Supreme Court rejects the appeal, which is almost certain, we then could volunteer to serve as Owens's counsel in his habeas corpus proceedings."

With that, Elena's eyes opened wide.

"And in the habeas case, we can use our imaginations to raise every constitutional violation we can find in the trial record or through our own investigation, including those committed by Chastain, Delaney, the judge, or the police," Greg said. "In fact, because Delaney's own performance can provide the basis for seeking relief, he's not able to serve as Owens's habeas lawyer."

It took just a few seconds for Elena to process what Greg was telling her. Then her face lit up. "You've got the firm's approval for us to handle the habeas case?" she asked.

"Sort of."

"Sort of? What does that mean?"

"It means that in return for dropping the request to assist on the criminal appeal, I got Clay's assurance that he'd support our handling a substantial and complex *pro bono* case, so long as it's a civil rather than criminal proceeding. And even if Clay doesn't realize it just yet, habeas corpus cases—even those resulting from criminal trials—are civil lawsuits."

"Well done," Elena said with a smile as she lifted her champagne glass. "I'll pray Delaney is successful with the appeal to the Supreme Court. But I'll sleep better tonight knowing that we can take on the habeas case if needed." They clinked their glasses and drank to Delaney's success on appeal.

Just then, their waiter arrived and presented them with an amuse-bouche of blinis with caviar and tart crème fraiche. "From the chef," the waiter said. "It pairs beautifully with the champagne."

The dinner, which lasted late into the evening, only got better from there. They took their time enjoying each course, finishing their meal by sharing a crème brûlée with their coffee. Then, they went back to Elena's apartment and made love until, exhausted, they fell asleep in each other's arms.

CHAPTER THIRTY

The next morning was Saturday, so there was no need to jump up and get ready to go to work. As they lay facing each other with the morning sun illuminating the bedroom, Elena broke the silence. "There's something I've been meaning to ask you."

"What about?"

"It might be sensitive," she said.

"Try me. I can't imagine anything you could ask I'd be sensitive about. You know pretty much everything about me by now."

"Alright. But if you don't want to discuss it now, that's okay."

"Go ahead," he said, puzzled by where she was heading with this.

"The day we went up to Noonan County for the first time, when you accompanied me to the hearing on excluding the media, I couldn't help but notice how hard you were staring at Owens in the courtroom. You couldn't take your eyes off of him. I tried talking to you, asking what the matter was, but you didn't respond."

Instantly, Greg separated himself from Elena and turned on his back, staring at the ceiling for a few minutes, saying nothing.

"And when we went back for the trial, the same thing happened, even though you assured me you would be okay. It's worried me ever since," Elena continued, "and I've been trying to find the right time to bring it up, because it was obvious something about Owens deeply affected you. Now that we're talking about taking on his habeas case, I need to know if there's something that might hold you back from fully participating. And apart from that, I just want to know if you're okay. Can we talk about that now?"

Greg remained silent, staring at the ceiling, for several more minutes.

"Oh, sweetheart, I'm sorry," Elena finally said. "This isn't a good time. It's okay. I'm so sorry."

"No, no, it's okay," Greg said, reaching out and taking her hand in his, pulling it to his lips to kiss, and resting their clasped hands on his chest. "You've every right to ask, and I've wanted to talk to you about it. I just wasn't sure when or how to bring it up. It's about when I was a television news reporter in Florida three decades ago, before I went to law school. I covered one of the final court hearings in a case involving the death penalty. The judge rejected the inmate's appeal and my boss told me to see if he'd agree to an interview."

"The judge?" she asked.

"No. The condemned inmate."

"Oh, that must've been hard to do, especially considering how young you were then. Had you ever been inside a prison before that?"

"No, and it didn't thrill me to go inside then. I actually hoped the guy would turn me down. But sure enough, I got a call from the warden's office the next morning telling me he'd agreed to the interview, and off I went to the prison. When I got there, instead of being taken to the visitor's room, they took me to an empty cell and told to wait there by myself.

"I said to the sergeant, 'I'm interviewing him in here?' He said it would be fine. But I almost freaked out. A few minutes later, the sergeant brings the guy into the cell, removes his handcuffs, and locks me in the cell with him."

Greg went silent again, lost in unspoken memories. All Elena could hear was Greg taking in deep breaths and then letting them out, very slowly. After a few minutes, as he remained silent, she snuggled close and gently pulled his head against her shoulder.

"That's enough for now," she said, softly caressing his face with her hand. "We can talk about it again, later on, when you're ready."

CHAPTER THIRTY-ONE

A few days later, Greg walked into Elena's office and handed her a brochure he'd received in the morning mail. "You should sign up for this seminar on habeas corpus proceedings in death penalty cases."

"Are you planning to attend?" Elena asked.

"No. I'm going to be in depositions that day. I was hoping you could attend, take good notes, and get the written materials they'll provide. It'll be a big help if Owens loses his appeal in the Supreme Court."

"Aren't you surprised the decision is taking this long? It's been more than seven months since the appeal was filed. Seems like it wouldn't take this long if they were just going to deny his claims."

"Don't get your hopes up, Elena," Greg pleaded, and not for the first time. "The Supreme Court is flooded with cases, so the passage of time simply means nothing. You know the odds are heavily, heavily against him."

"I know, but it just seems that, if all they're going to do is to say, 'Appeal denied,' it would've happened by now."

"Please, sweetheart, do not—"

"Greg, don't you call me that in the office," Elena said emphatically. "We've talked about this. We need to keep our personal lives separate from our professional lives. If someone hears you call me that, they'll stop thinking of me as a competent lawyer and start thinking I'm only where I am because I slept with you. And you know how fast that would spread around the firm."

"I'm so sorry," he said. "It just came out without thinking. I'm really sorry."

She flashed a quick smile to let him know all was forgiven.

"But as much as we go out together, surely it's not a surprise that we've been noticed.

"No, that's fine, Greg. I'm not surprised and I'm not trying to keep our relationship a secret. All I mean is, when we're in the office, we keep it professional."

"I understand and agree. Now, I do think this seminar will be very helpful if we end up taking on Owens's habeas case. Rebecca Masters, an attorney who recruits volunteer lawyers for these cases, will be one of the seminar leaders. I've seen her speak, and she's just brilliant. The rest of the faculty is first rate as well."

"I think I can attend," Elena said as she flipped through the brochure. "But Clay will need to approve. What do I say if he asks why I want to attend a program like this?"

"He won't even notice it. But if he does, explain to him it's an excellent opportunity to learn about constitutional law from the best and the brightest lawyers and law professors in the country. Which, by the way, is true."

Two days later, Elena walked into Greg's office and said, "Good news. Clay approved the seminar request."

"See. I told you there wouldn't be a problem."

"Well, he did ask me to come by his office. When I got there, he asked why I wanted to attend a capital habeas program, and I answered just the way you suggested. Then he asked whether a program about habeas in the criminal context had any relevance to the types of civil cases we handle."

"And what'd you say?"

"I told him that habeas corpus cases are civil proceedings," she said with a smile. "It took him a second. But then I saw the light come on and he muttered, 'Oh, shit,' under his breath." They both laughed at Clay's revelation. "Guess he figured out what's coming," Elena said.

"Only if Owens loses his appeal."

"I don't suppose you're recommending I attend this seminar just for the intellectual stimulation."

"Hope springs eternal. But no, I'm not optimistic about Owens's chances in the Supreme Court. So let's get prepared."

CHAPTER THIRTY-TWO

Six weeks later, the decision in Owens's case was handed down by the Supreme Court. It denied the appeal.

Before going to see Clay to seek the firm's formal permission to take on the case, Greg placed a call to Masters. "Greg, you were on my list to call," she said. "I was so pleased to meet your partner, Elena, at the seminar a few weeks ago. She's very impressive."

"I agree! And she came back really fired up about working on a capital habeas case. So I'm calling you about the Owens case."

"Well, that's exactly why you were on *my* call list. Are you familiar with his case?"

"We are. Elena appeared at a preliminary hearing on behalf of one of our media clients to argue against a defense motion to close the courtroom to the public during a pretrial hearing," he said.

"Does that give you a problem in terms of a conflict?" Masters asked with a touch of anxiety in her voice.

"No. That had nothing to do with the merits of the case. It was strictly a first amendment issue, which we won, and we've had no further involvement in the case, except as spectators."

"I'd really love it if you and Elena could take this one on. Would it be helpful if I sent a copy of the case file to you overnight so you can review it and then decide?"

"Yes, very helpful. But please keep in mind that, even if Elena and I are interested, we'll have to get the firm's approval. Although I'm hopeful, I'm not completely confident the management committee will agree."

"Understood. I'll send the entire file by overnight delivery. Look it over and call me with questions. And remember, there'll be a lawyer from the federal defender's capital unit assigned to work with you if you agree to take the case."

After Masters hung up, Greg quickly called Elena. "How's your schedule for tomorrow?"

"I'm just trying to finish up on a summary judgment motion in a fraud case I'm defending in federal district court. What do you need?"

"Rebecca Masters is sending me the file on Owens's case," he said. "I think we each should review it and discuss the best way to approach Clay about getting the management committee's approval."

When the overnight delivery arrived the next morning, Greg had a copy made and took it to Elena's office. She wasn't there, so he left it in her chair. Thirty minutes later, his phone rang.

"Got it," she said. "When do you want to discuss it?"

"How about over dinner tonight?"

"At François's Bistro?" she asked hopefully.

"I was thinking more about at Chez Elena."

"Fine," she replied, her voice tinged with disappointment. "But the food isn't nearly as good."

CHAPTER THIRTY-THREE

The file sent by Masters included copies of the indictment, Delaney's post-trial motion to set aside the verdict, and a background memo about the case Masters had prepared, identifying possible legal issues to explore. Greg called Rebecca after reading through the materials.

"Rebecca," he said, "this is even more daunting than I'd expected. We're not experienced at criminal investigations, let alone murder investigations, and I'm not sure where we should start."

"Remember what I told you," she replied. "The assistant federal defender assigned to the case will help with all of that. Her name is Liz Wilkes. She's terrific and a lot of fun to be around. I suggest you call her and set up a meeting as soon as possible. She'll have good suggestions on the people you'll need to hire to help with preparing the case."

"What people?"

"Like a private investigator to review the police work. Usually a retired detective is best. As the case proceeds, you'll also want to think about retaining other professionals, such as a psychologist, to evaluate whether your client was mentally competent to stand trial or to be subjected to the death penalty."

Greg called Wilkes as soon as he hung up. "Liz, my name is Greg Williams and I'm the lawyer who's considering volunteering for the Owens habeas case."

"Hey, Greg," Wilkes said. "I can't talk right now because I have to pick up my kids at school and I've got a brief due in another case by midnight that I've barely started."

Greg, who typically wanted briefs completed days before they were due to be filed, was aghast. But he restrained himself. "Okay, Liz, I understand. Can we talk tomorrow?"

"How 'bout if I come over to your office tomorrow around one?"

"Why don't you come at noon and we can have lunch? I can ask Elena Samuels to join us since she'll be working on the case as well."

"Sounds good. See you then."

Greg heard the click of the call being disconnected and hung up the receiver. Then he called Elena.

"Elena, I just had a very brief call with Liz Wilkes, the federal defender who'll be working with us on the Owens case. I hope she's not nearly as flighty and disorganized as she sounded on the phone."

"That doesn't sound promising," Elena replied.

"Well, she's coming to the office for lunch tomorrow just so we can get acquainted. I've reserved a private dining room. Are you available?"

"I've got another lunch on my calendar, but I can reschedule it. This takes priority."

CHAPTER THIRTY-FOUR

At 12:15, just as Greg was beginning to wonder if Liz was going to show up, the receptionist called to tell him she'd arrived. Stopping at the door to Elena's office, Greg told her Liz had arrived, and they walked down the stairs to the reception area together.

"Hi, Liz. I'm Greg and this is Elena," he said.

"Sorry I'm running a bit late," Liz said with a grin on her face. "I'm not very good at being on time. Between getting the kids off to school and dealing with the baby, mornings are a little rough around my place."

"How old is the baby?" Elena asked.

"Three months. And she's a handful."

"How on earth do you have time to work on habeas cases?"

"I just find the time where I can and rely on our nanny to show up when she's supposed to, which is more wishful thinking than reality," she said, laughing. "Elena do you have any children?"

"No, I'm not married."

"That doesn't seem to be a requirement anymore, now does it?"

"It is for me," Elena said firmly.

Realizing she may have touched a nerve, Liz quickly changed the subject. "This is such a beautiful building, and your reception area has incredible views of the city. I love the firm's photography collection."

"Thanks. We've only been in this space for a few months. I'm still getting used to everything. If we have time after lunch, I'd be glad to show you around. The photography is really something."

"Where do you want to go for lunch?" Liz asked.

"Oh, I guess I wasn't clear," Greg replied. "The firm has a dining room on the next floor."

"A firm dining room? Nice!" Liz exclaimed. "Lead the way."

As they reached the next floor, Liz stopped for a moment to gaze at more of the collection of black-and-white photographs lining the hallway. "Not too shabby. You do know your office is an art gallery, right?"

"That's how I feel," Elena said.

"Through here," Greg said as he opened the door to the dining room. "It's a self-serve buffet. Once you've fixed your plate, we're going into the private dining room through those doors at the other end."

"This is a really sweet setup!" Liz exclaimed as she looked at the buffet offerings. "And look at those desserts! I'd put on a ton of weight if I worked here."

Once they all had their lunches, Liz asked whether either of them had any experience with capital habeas work. The awkward stares from Greg and Elena told Liz everything she needed to know.

"We're fast learners," Greg said.

"Okay. No problem. I'll send over some pleadings and briefs from other cases to give you a feel for what these cases are like. But the most important thing to know is that every claim we raise *must* be based on a violation of Owens's state or federal constitutional rights. Those are the only types of claims that a habeas judge can consider."

"So, can you give us some examples of the types of claims that are typically raised?" Greg asked.

"We can assert claims for police violations, such as failure to read the defendant his Miranda rights before questioning, due process violations by the prosecutor, or incompetent representation of Owens's trial counsel, to name just a few possibilities."

"Sounds like we've got an enormous job in front of us," Greg said. "Where do you suggest we begin?"

"You'll need to read the pretrial and trial transcripts very carefully," Liz said. "In fact, I suggest you read them several times. Take careful notes of anything that looks remotely questionable to you, and we can discuss it. The quickest way to get the transcripts is from Owens's trial lawyer, Michael Delaney. Call him. I think he'll be cooperative. Also, you need to serve a subpoena on the district attorney, Paul Chastain, for his records relating to the Owens case."

"Good idea," Elena said. "This is just a hunch, and perhaps I'm going out on a limb here, but I have my suspicions about Chastain."

"What do you mean?" Liz asked.

"Well, I noticed he was reelected a few months after the Owens trial. And for the first time in many years, he was facing a very serious challenger. To me, it doesn't take much imagination to conclude that, whether consciously or unconsciously, Chastain's decision to charge Owens so quickly after the murders—and to seek the death penalty— was aimed at bolstering his image as being tough on crime. Not surprisingly, the case generated a lot of free publicity for Chastain during the campaign."

"Are you saying that if this didn't occur until after the election, Chastain wouldn't have sought the death penalty?" Greg asked.

"We'll never know, Greg. What we do know, though, is that his strategy worked. Owens was convicted just three months before election day. The amount of publicity the case received in Noonan County was enormous. And even though the early polls had Chastain lagging his opponent by double digits in the months before the trial, he ended up being reelected by a pretty wide margin."

Greg was impressed by Elena's analysis of what may have motivated the DA. It resonated, especially in light of what he thought was a weak and entirely circumstantial case. "Okay, Elena. But first things first. Let me talk to Clay," Greg said. "I think he'll approve our taking on the case. Perhaps reluctantly, but he'll approve, although he'll have to take it to the management committee before we get the green light."

"Who's Clay?" Liz asked.

"The firm's managing partner," Greg replied.

"You don't have your firm's approval yet?" Wilkes asked, a bit startled by this revelation.

"No, but Clay is aware of our interest in taking a habeas case, so this won't come as a surprise. I'm going to see him this afternoon and will let you know what he says."

As soon as Wilkes left, Greg headed up the circular stairs to the top floor and found Clay in his office with the door open. "I'd been expecting this ever since I signed the approval for Elena to attend that seminar," Clay said when Greg told him why he was there. "Do you understand what you'll be getting yourself into if we approve this?"

"I think so. Elena and I had lunch today with an assistant federal defender who'll work with us if the firm approves taking on the case."

"I'll poll the management committee and I'll support you. But you should assume there are others in the firm, perhaps some on the committee, who won't want us to represent a convicted murderer, let alone do it for free."

"I get it," Greg said. "But if firms such as ours don't step up and take on these cases, who will?"

"Are you sure you'll have enough lawyers volunteer to work on the case?" Clay asked. "You and Elena are good, but you're going to need help if we approve this."

"We have two other lawyers who've offered to devote 50 percent of their time to the case. And I've got no doubt others will step up to help with legal research and other tasks that arise as the case progresses."

Shortly before six, Clay called to say the management committee had approved. "There was some debate, but only one member voted against your request."

"Thanks, Clay. This means a lot to me."

"Keep me informed on how it's going. And keep in mind I'll expect you to do everything you can to get this over with as quickly as practical."

"Nothing happens quickly in a capital habeas case," Greg replied. "But we'll do what we can."

CHAPTER THIRTY-FIVE

"The very first thing you need to do is to seek an extension of the deadline to amend the habeas petition," Liz told Greg the next morning. "Right now, the amended petition is due next week, which is *beyond* impossible. You're going to need a minimum of four months—probably more like six to nine months—to investigate the case thoroughly."

Greg filed a motion the next day and emailed a copy to the chambers of the judge assigned to the case, Alvin Parsons. Two days later, before the State had even filed a response, Judge Parsons denied the motion.

He phoned Liz straightaway. "I don't understand it. Judge Parsons has denied our motion for an extension," he said.

"Wait," Liz said, "you just filed it two days ago, and the State hasn't even filed a response, right?"

"Right."

"Please tell me you're joking."

"Do you want me to email a copy of the order to you?"

"Oh, my God! You're serious, aren't you? This is just unbelievable. Send me a copy right now. I'm going to make some calls, but in the meantime, you'll need to get to work on a motion for reconsideration that lays out the consequences to our client of the court's refusal to allow sufficient time for us to investigate and to identify claims."

"What happens if the judge refuses again?" Greg asked.

"If we don't get an extension," Wilkes cautioned, "we'll have to seek permission from the Georgia Supreme Court to appeal immediately. If we can't get more time to investigate and file an amended petition, Owens is as good as dead."

Wilkes's last words sent Greg into an emotional tailspin. Sitting in his office, his mind flashed back to Owens as Greg first saw him, in an orange prison jumpsuit, his hands and feet shackled and his eyes vacant, being led into the courtroom for the pretrial media hearing. Then his mind went blank. The next thing he knew, Elena was standing beside him, calling his name and gently shaking him on his shoulder.

"What are you doing?" he asked when he finally realized what was happening.

"Your assistant called me," Elena said. "Gail came into your office to ask you a question, but you were just staring into space and wouldn't respond to anything she said. She was afraid you were having a stroke or something."

"But why'd she call you?" Greg asked, his mind still not completely clear.

"Do you think she's blind and deaf?" Elena asked. "We seem to spend a lot of time in each other's offices, and it appears our relationship is becoming common knowledge around here."

"I guess so."

"So what happened? Is this about the time you were a reporter?"

He looked down and remained silent.

"Greg, you need to see a counselor about this. I'm worried about you, and if you can't talk to me about it, you'll need to talk to someone else, especially now that we've signed on to represent Owens. You can't go on this way."

"Can we discuss it this evening?" he asked.

"Yes, but did the Owens case trigger this?"

He told Elena about Judge Parsons's order.

"Oh, Lord," she gasped.

"I spoke to Liz. She says we need to draft a motion for reconsideration describing all the tasks that are required for us to be effective as Owens's lawyers and explaining the time needed to accomplish all of it. She'll help with the details. We also need to make it clear, without saying so expressly, that if the judge doesn't grant us additional time, he's going to run a high risk of being reversed on appeal."

"Okay. I'll take care of it. But you go home and try to relax. I'll be there as soon as I can." Greg looked up from his chair and stared at Elena. She leaned down and kissed him on the lips. "I thought we weren't supposed to do that sort of thing in the office," he said.

"We're not," Elena said, as she leaned down and kissed him again. "Now, go home. I'll be there as soon as I can. And then," she paused, "we're going to talk."

CHAPTER THIRTY-SIX

Driving home, Greg could think of nothing but the coming conversation with Elena. She was right. He knew that. He'd repressed the memories for so long. But there was no getting around it now. If this relationship was to progress, he had to tell her what was haunting him.

When he got home, he pulled his laptop out of his briefcase, poured a glass of wine, and settled on the sofa with the laptop on the coffee table. It took him a while to find the file containing the video. He thought maybe showing it to Elena would spare him the pain of speaking the words himself. He hadn't watched it in years. But when he opened the file and saw his younger self looking back at him, everything came flooding back.

•   •   •   •   •

Gazing up at Judge Bernard Cook from the front row at the federal courthouse in Jacksonville, Florida, 23-year-old television journalist Greg Williams observed a rare moment of unguarded emotion cross the aged judge's face.

Stoic throughout the testimony of witnesses pleading with him to prohibit the state from strapping Malcolm Ford into 'Old Sparky,' the gruesome nickname for Florida's electric chair, Cook displayed, for just a moment, an ever-so-slight wince, his eyes squinting and his cheekbones rising slightly. He was listening to Jacksonville Police Officer Rosa Lupo graphically describe the gruesome, bloody murder for which Ford was convicted and sentenced to death.

"How'd the hearing go?" Mike Dearing, the news director at Channel 3 News in Jacksonville, asked his young reporter.

"He's a dead man," Greg opined. "Cook is gonna fry him."

"How do you know?"

"You should have seen the look on the Judge's face as Ford's lawyers argued for a stay," Greg replied. "He was totally disinterested. He walked off the bench as soon as they concluded their presentation without asking a single question."

"Did he hint at how long it would take him to issue a ruling?" Dearing asked.

"Only that he would get his decision out as quickly as he could. I've no idea what that means, but I suspect it'll be sooner rather than later. Maybe later this week. Probably by the end of next week at the outside."

Two days later, Williams walked into Dearing's office and tossed a copy of the judge's ruling upholding Ford's death sentence on Dearing's desk. "As predicted," he said.

"So where does he go now?" Dearing asked.

"His lawyers tell me they'll file an appeal with the circuit court of appeals and seek an emergency stay of execution. But they didn't seem very confident. If the circuit court sends them packing, the Supreme Court is Ford's last stop before he's escorted into the execution chamber."

"Greg, why don't you see if Ford will talk to you?"

"You mean I should ask for an interview?" he replied, a bit startled at the prospect. "I don't know if the prison will allow it, or Ford would agree to it."

"Well," Dearing shot back wryly, "there's only one way to find out. Make the call. Now."

The next day, Greg walked up to Dearing in the newsroom and said, "Ford agreed to the interview."

"That's great!" After a pause, Dearing said, "You don't look very excited. This story could make your career. Do it right, get him to open up, and you'll make a name for yourself. When's the interview?"

"Tomorrow at eleven."

"Don't worry, kid. He'll be on the other side of the glass talking over a telephone. Keep your eyes on his face. No matter what he says, that'll tell you more about how he really feels about meeting his Maker. Have you done your research?"

"Yeah," Greg said. "They found Ford at the scene of a bloody murder when police responded to a call from the night manager at a fleabag motel in Tallahassee. His hands and shirt were drenched in blood, and Ford didn't deny the killing. A few days later, after meeting with a public defender, Ford claimed he had been acting in self-defense when his male traveling companion viciously attacked him after Ford refused his demand for oral sex. But the jury, which heard and saw police photographs of the victim's skull having been smashed beyond recognition with a concrete block, wasn't buying Ford's story."

"Sounds like a prince," Dearing said. "Have fun."

The next morning, after a restless night, Greg found himself on his way to Florida State Prison in Starke, less than an hour's drive from Jacksonville. He was shocked Ford had agreed to be interviewed and, truth be told, he was apprehensive about coming face-to-face with a convicted murderer, even on the other side of a glass partition.

After Greg entered the prison and passed through the screening process, he was met by Sergeant Harold Pierce. "Follow me," Pierce said. As they walked past a door with a sign that said, "Visitor Meeting Rooms," Greg asked Pierce where they were going. "We can't bring him out here, so you're gonna have to go to him."

"What do you mean, I'm gonna have to go to him?" Pierce didn't respond, but a moment later, they went through an iron gate that led into a cellblock. "Take a seat in here," he said, gesturing to a cell with the door propped open. "I'll go get Ford."

"I'm interviewing him in a cell?" a visibly startled Greg asked.

"Yep," Pierce said nonchalantly. "Don't sweat it. You'll be fine."

Shocked by the unexpected interview setting, Greg's nerves frayed as his senses filled with the sights and sounds of the prison block. The cell next to him was empty, but others along the block were occupied. Shouts and screams rang out, and metal doors clanged. Greg's pulse was pounding, and he was struggling to regain control of his emotions, while awaiting Ford.

Less than five minutes went by before Pierce returned with Ford. Greg immediately recognized him from the mug shot taken at the time of his arrest, which was used in his news reports on the case. Ford's thick, wavy, black hair with a streak of gray running through it, deep-set black eyes, and angular face were unmistakable.

"Turn around and face into the cell," Pierce ordered. With Ford now gazing directly at him, Greg watched as Pierce removed the handcuffs that had secured Ford's hands and said, "In there." As soon as Ford sat down, Pierce closed and locked the cell door. Then he looked at Greg and said, "You've got thirty minutes," before disappearing around the corner.

The two stared silently at each other for about ten seconds before Greg overcame the shock of being locked in a cell with a condemned man without any guards in sight. "Thanks for agreeing to see me," he finally said.

"Sorry you came all this way," Ford said. "After I agreed to talk to you, my lawyers told me not to talk to any reporters. They said it might hurt my chances in court. But that was late yesterday afternoon and there wasn't any way to get word to you not to come."

Greg's mind raced as he processed Ford's calm demeanor, which surprised him, and the news Ford had conveyed. He was struggling to convince Ford to go ahead with the interview. "I just want to ask you a few questions about the case, but nothing that relates to the legal issues your attorneys are pursuing in court."

Ford stared at him, squinting as he pondered what Greg had said. He didn't understand the legal issues being raised by his lawyers, but he decided to stick with their advice. "I'm really sorry. I can't."

"Okay," Greg replied. "I understand. But it's going to be another twenty-five minutes until the sergeant comes back to get me. So how 'bout if I just put down my notepad and pen, and we can just talk for a while."

"Yeah, I guess that's okay," Ford said. "But not about the case."

For the next twenty-four minutes, Greg kept his word and asked nothing about the murder or the legal case. Instead, keeping the conversation casual and never touching his pad or pen, he asked Ford about his life as a child growing up in a small Texas town. He asked about his schooling (there wasn't much), his friends (there weren't any), and his parents (there was only one, his mother, who struggled to find work so she could pay the rent and buy groceries).

The story Greg told on the air that evening was better than the story he had expected to tell. Rather than talking about legal issues, his report was a powerful and disturbing portrait of an only child who grew up in abject poverty in a small Texas town.

·   ·   ·   ·   ·

Greg had just finished watching the video when Elena walked in. "What are you looking at?" she asked.

"It's something I should have shown you long before now. But I just haven't been able to bring myself to do it. In fact, I haven't even looked at it for a very long time."

"It's entirely up to you whether you show it to me," Elena said as she sat next to him. "How about if you just start by telling me what it is?"

"Does the name Malcolm Ford mean anything to you?"

"No, sorry. Who is he?"

"He was a death row inmate in Florida executed thirty years ago. I'd reported on the case when I was a television journalist in Jacksonville, fresh out of college. Then, one morning, my boss told me to go to the federal courthouse to cover a hearing that was pretty much Ford's last chance to avoid the electric chair. When I told him the judge refused to delay the execution, my boss immediately ordered me to see if Ford would agree to an interview."

Elena gasped. "Oh, Greg, I had no idea."

"And to my shock, Ford agreed. The interview was scheduled for the next day."

"Greg, how old were you at the time?"

"Twenty-three. Less than one year out of college. Honestly, I prayed Ford would refuse to be interviewed. But when he said yes, I had no choice but to go through with it."

Elena reached out and took Greg's hand in hers. "Do you want to tell me about the interview?"

"Maybe I should just show you the report I filed when I got back to the station that night." He turned the laptop screen so Elena could see it and clicked the play arrow.

"Our reporter, Greg Williams, is outside of Florida State Prison," the news anchor said, "where he's just interviewed condemned killer Malcolm Ford, who is now just four days away from his scheduled execution. Greg, what did Mr. Ford have to say?"

"Ford didn't want to discuss his appeal, but he opened up about his family," Greg reported. "Growing up in rural south Texas, Ford never knew his father and wouldn't talk much about his mother. He was a chronic school truant and spent time in a state juvenile home twice. During the second stint there, he escaped and decided to get out of Texas.

"That's when his troubles really began. Ford ran into an older man who befriended him and together they hopped a freight train headed east. Uncomfortable and hungry, they jumped off near New Orleans, where they dodged gangs and police while panhandling for enough money to get something to eat. Then they hitchhiked through Louisiana, Mississippi, and Alabama, picking up a few dollars by doing odd jobs on farms and in a car salvage yard. A couple of weeks later, they found themselves with enough cash to get a couple of burgers and a six-pack of beer, which they took back to their room at a fleabag motel in Tallahassee. Before midnight, Ford was in the Leon County jail, charged with the murder of his traveling companion.

"As time was running out and sensing that we'd made some kind of connection, I took a chance," Greg told his viewers, "and asked Ford if he spent any time thinking about the possibility the state would execute him soon. Ford just stared at me—or maybe right through me, I'm not sure—for what seemed like an eternity. My heart was pounding as his head tilted to one side and his body swayed slightly from side to side. His eyes squinted, as though deep in thought, and then opened wide as though observing something horrific. It sent shudders up and down my spine. Then, without any warning, Ford lurched forward and shoved me so hard my chair toppled backward as he let out a scream. The back of my head hit the concrete floor. I was in a daze, but remained conscious, looking up at Ford as he bent over to grab the lapels of my jacket.

"At that moment, I heard the jangle of keys. Then I heard Sergeant Pierce yell out for help as he pulled Ford away from me. Almost instantly, I saw two more prison guards helping Pierce as he forced Ford to the ground face down, pulled his arms behind his back, and handcuffed him before dragging him out of the cell.

"Once Ford was secure, Pierce turned back to me and, as he helped me up, asked if I was okay. I told him the back of my head hurt, and he told me to sit down and wait while he sent for the prison doctor to look at me. As I sat back in the same chair I'd been in, I saw Ford being led away by two prison guards, with his legs shackled. Ford looked in my direction for just a second, still seemingly lost inside his mind, his head still swaying from side to side.

"I came away with an unmistakable sense that Ford does not comprehend what is happening to him and what may await him a few days from now, let alone why. And I believe he's neither expecting, nor prepared, to die. This is Greg Williams, Channel 3 News, outside the Florida State Prison in Starke."

Greg closed his laptop and looked back at Elena, whose right hand covered her mouth as tears filled her eyes.

"That's what happened. I haven't shown that video to anyone, or talked about it, since the day of the broadcast. Ford was strapped to the electric chair four days later, and it haunted me for years. I thought I'd finally put it behind me," he continued, with his eyes focused on the floor, "but the moment I saw Owens walk into the courtroom in that orange prison jumpsuit, I started reliving the Ford episode all over again. It happened again when you asked me to go back to his trial, but maybe because I expected it, it wasn't so bad. Then, when Liz said that if we can't get an extension, Owens is all but dead, well . . ." but he couldn't finish the sentence. He didn't need to.

I'm worried," Greg said, still staring at the floor. "We've taken on this case, and I thought I could handle it, but . . ."

"Look at me," Elena said, but he kept his gaze on the floor. "Sweetheart, look at me." Slowly, Greg lifted his head and he could see the love, compassion, and determination in her eyes.

"You're not doing this alone," she said. "We agreed to handle this case together, and we'll be at each other's side every step of the way."

Greg nodded slowly.

"But you need some help to deal with these painful memories. You need to see a psychologist, Greg. This is not optional. I'm worried about your mental health. Will you do that for me," she pleaded, "if not for yourself?"

Again, Greg nodded. "Yes. Yes, I will."

CHAPTER THIRTY-SEVEN

Two days later, after a brief telephone call with a psychologist recommended by his physician and making an appointment to see her the following week, Greg went back into the office. "Thanks for calling Elena the other day," he said to Gail, who stepped into his office moments after she saw him arrive.

"When I saw the look on your face, I didn't know what to do or who else to call," Gail replied. "She seems to care about you a lot."

"Yes, she's a very good friend," Greg said.

"Is that all?" Gail asked with a questioning smile on her face. "Just a good friend?" Greg blushed. Nobody in the office had been so direct with him about their relationship, and he wasn't sure how to respond.

"Okay," he said. "It's more than that, but please don't talk about it around here. I don't want us to be the subject of office gossip."

"Oh, good for you!" Gail said. "She's so lovely. And I hope you're feeling better. Is there anything you need today?"

"Just close the door and keep the wolves away," he said, grinning at her. She smiled back and closed his door as she left.

While reviewing Elena's draft of the motion for reconsideration, he received another order by email from Judge Parsons's chambers. To his surprise, this one struck a very different tone.

"On its own initiative," the latest order stated, "the court has reconsidered its earlier order denying the motion for an extension of time to file an amended petition. Now that new counsel has entered an appearance for Petitioner Owens, and in the interest of justice, the motion for an extension of time is GRANTED." Rather than allowing the four-month extension Greg had requested, Judge Parsons gave him six months.

"I don't know what happened," Greg said to Elena as he handed her a copy of the order. "I'm mystified." Then he called Masters, who was equally stunned.

"Wow," she said, "that's great news. Do you have any idea how it happened?"

"No, not at all," he said. "And I don't really care. I'm just glad we'll have an opportunity to help Owens."

The next call was to Wilkes, who just laughed. Her response baffled Greg. "Why are you laughing?" he asked.

"I thought the motion for reconsideration you were planning to file would be granted, but I didn't expect the judge to change his mind even before you filed it," she said.

"Why'd you think the motion would be granted?"

"Just a hunch."

"C'mon, Liz, you're holding back on me. Spill the beans."

"I really don't know. Truly, I don't. But the order denying your motion without even waiting to see if the State would oppose it was beyond outrageous. By not giving you any time to investigate the case and prepare for the hearing, Parsons almost certainly would have been reversed on appeal, which would've been a huge embarrassment to him and a massive waste of time for everyone involved, including the Attorney General's Office."

"So you think the AG's office quietly suggested the judge reconsider his order?"

"I've already said more than I should. Let's just leave it at that."

"Liz, I need to understand what happened."

"No, you really don't. Bye."

CHAPTER THIRTY-EIGHT

"Habeas school," as Liz liked to call it, began the next Monday. Besides Greg and Elena, four other Fox Stern attorneys and a paralegal, each of whom had volunteered to work on the case, attended the sessions, which went for two full days.

"I'm not going to sugarcoat this," Liz began. "This is going to be tough. Remember that, in order to win, it's *not enough* to prove that the judge, the prosecutors, or the defense lawyers violated Owens's constitutional rights."

"We will have to prove that, but for those mistakes, Owens wouldn't have been convicted, right?" Elena asked.

"I'm impressed!" Liz exclaimed. "Where'd you learn that?"

"A capital habeas seminar."

"Oh, yeah? Who was the instructor?"

"Rebecca Masters," Elena replied.

"Well, she's the best. That certainly gives you a leg up. But here's the most important thing to keep in mind. As you review the record of Owens's pretrial hearings and the trial itself, and as you interview potential witnesses, such as the police detectives who investigated the case, *take nothing anyone says at face value.*

"Look at everything and everyone with a critical eye, especially the police investigation records and the DA's files. Do not assume that

Chastain will play fair, because, trust me, he won't. I've dealt with him on other cases. He'll promise to cooperate, but he'll fight you tooth-and-nail about turning over anything in his files."

"How do we force his hand?" Greg asked.

"This is a civil case," Wilkes reminded them. "The same rules apply as in any other civil case. You can issue subpoenas to obtain documents and to compel everyone, including Chastain, to testify under oath at a deposition or at trial. But the first thing you need to do is to read the pretrial and trial transcripts to identify potential issues that you'll want to pursue through discovery. Read them, and then read them again. Delaney will have those in his files. Start by calling him and asking for his entire file."

"Will he turn all that over without a subpoena?" Greg asked.

"Y'know, some defense lawyers won't cooperate with habeas counsel because they're afraid of being made into scapegoats and having their reputations ruined. Delaney's never had a client sentenced to death before this one, so I've no idea how he'll react now that he could be a target of your investigation. He knows you almost certainly will base some of Owens's claims on errors he made, so don't be surprised if he seems defensive at first. But he's a square dude, so I think he'll cooperate in the long run."

Greg made the call to Delaney the next day. "Mike, this is Greg Williams at Fox Stern. How are you doing today?" Delaney remembered Greg and Elena from the hearing on his motion to close the courtroom to the media early in the case.

"What does your television client want this time?" he asked dismissively. "An interview with the losing lawyer?"

"Actually, I'm not calling on behalf of Channel 3 News," he said. "My partner, Elena Samuels, and I have volunteered to represent Joseph Owens in his habeas corpus proceedings."

There was a pause on the other end of the line. "That's very good of the two of you to do," Delaney finally said. "Joseph needs good lawyers to help him. Have you done this kind of work before?"

"No, but we're getting a lot of guidance from the federal defender's office, and we're doing our homework. Looks like we're going to need to review your files, so I was wondering whether you'd have them copied and sent over."

"I can have the pretrial and trial transcripts, and all the pleadings, copied and sent over within a couple of days. Will that do?"

"It's a good start, but we're also gonna need copies of your entire investigation file, including your notes and any memos you wrote. We need pretty much everything you have relating to the Owens case."

"Let me think about whether I can give you all of that, since some of it might be privileged. I'll see what I can do."

"Mike, let me just remind you that the attorney-client privilege belongs to your former client, Joseph Owens, not to you. And now Owens is *our* client. So we're going to need to get copies of everything, privileged or not."

"I'll need a few days to go over the files and make sure there's nothing I need to hold back," Delaney replied, sounding a bit defensive.

"Let's see. Today is Tuesday," Greg said. "I'll need to hear from you by the close of business on Thursday. If I don't hear from you by then, or if you decide not to give us a complete copy of everything in your files, including your notes from throughout the case, we'll serve you with a subpoena on Friday. Fair enough?"

"Understood."

It only took until Wednesday morning for Delaney to call back. "Greg, I apologize for my reluctance to cooperate fully yesterday. I guess I've never been this position before, and I just needed a little time to think it through. I'll get everything together and have it delivered to you within two or three days."

"The entire file?"

"Everything, including my notes. And I'll be ready to talk to you whenever you want about questions you may have with my representation of Joseph.

"That's great, Mike. I'd hoped you'd reach that conclusion. I know it might not be pleasant to have another attorney come behind you and second-guess decisions you made under fire. But as you know, that's what we're required to do in order to identify every possible claim."

"I understand," Delaney assured him. "Do whatever you need to do. And thank you for volunteering to do this. It's an enormous commitment."

True to his word, two days later, Delaney had six large boxes delivered to Greg's office.

"Let's get everything copied so we have control over a complete set of Delaney's records. Then get a couple of paralegals to organize one set of the documents chronologically."

"Why chronologically?" Elena asked.

"Because in complex cases like this one, I've always found that emails and correspondence can seem meaningless until they're viewed in sequence with other documents created at about the same time," he explained. "If you read 'em out of order, a lot of the documents make no sense. Put 'em in order, and you'll be surprised at how documents that at first looked meaningless suddenly take on great importance."

Chapter Thirty-Nine

"You're not going to believe this," said Deputy Attorney General LaToya Palmer when she walked into the office of Chief Deputy Elizabeth Austin. Palmer was referring to the new order from Judge Parsons granting Owens six months to investigate his claims and to file an amended petition. "Somebody got to Parsons. I just don't believe he had such a tremendous change of heart on his own."

Austin's office adjoined that of the attorney general and, although not fancy by private law firm standards, was considerably more comfortable and spacious than the offices provided to the deputy AGs, such as Palmer. On the wall behind her desk and credenza, Austin proudly displayed her law degree, with honors, from the University of Georgia and her undergraduate degree from Spelman College.

"LaToya, that initial order was indefensible, and you know it," Austin said dismissively. "I don't have any idea what caused Parsons to issue it. I'm actually glad he reconsidered because he was going to be reversed on appeal, right?"

"I guess so," said Palmer, a tenacious young lawyer who fought her opponents tooth-and-nail at every step along the way and who didn't take even minor setbacks lightly.

"Judge Parsons probably calmed down and realized he didn't want to be reversed, so he fixed it himself," Austin said.

"I guess so," LaToya said.

"And by the way, I've been meaning to talk to you. I know you care mightily about your cases, but you're getting something of a reputation for being, shall we say, ungracious to opposing counsel on unimportant matters, such as refusing to agree to reasonable requests for modest extensions of deadlines. At some point, you'll be the one overwhelmed by deadlines and in need of a courtesy from the other side."

"Did somebody complain that I wasn't courteous?"

"Several somebodies."

"Who?"

"If you really want to know, you need to ask her," Austin said as she nodded her head toward the attorney general's office. "She's the one who gets the complaints, and I'm the one who has to deal with them. But my advice is not to ask her, because all you'll accomplish is to put your face to the complaints."

Palmer was a bit shaken by Austin's comments, but took her advice to heart. Two weeks after the conversation, she had her first face-to-face encounter with Elena at an initial scheduling hearing in front of Judge Parsons. The hearing took place in the old, brick courthouse in Harrington, which was built in 1939 and was badly in need of maintenance. The tile floors were scuffed from years of shoe traffic and the walls had wainscoting on the lower half with pale green paint above. Historic photos of the courthouse and portraits of all the judges who had presided in Noonan County Court since the late nineteenth century filled the walls.

Elena walked down the hall to the judge's chambers on the second floor and entered through a heavy, oversized wooden door with frosted glass on the upper half. Perpetually terrified of being late for any appointment, let alone a judicial hearing, she had arrived thirty minutes early and introduced herself to the judge's assistant, who invited her to take a seat in one of the upholstered armchairs in the reception area.

"You must be Elena Samuels," said a woman who walked in shortly before the hearing was scheduled to begin. She looked to be in her early thirties, dressed professionally in a blue suit and white blouse, and carrying a large briefcase. "I'm LaToya Palmer. We've spoken on the phone, but it's very nice to meet you in person."

They spent the next few minutes getting to know each other a bit, discussing where they had gone to school and where they had worked since graduating from law school. The pleasant conversation ended when the large, wooden door to the judge's chambers swung open and Judge Parsons, who appeared to be in his late fifties or early sixties with a head full of white hair and a pleasant smile on his face, stood in the doorway.

"Please come inside, counsel," Judge Parsons said softly. "I do appreciate each of you coming to my chambers this morning rather than insisting on doing this in the courtroom. It's a lot more comfortable in here, and I think we accomplish more at these conferences when they take place in an informal setting. Don't you agree?"

Both attorneys dutifully nodded as they entered and took their seats in the upholstered wingback chairs across the desk from the judge. However, as Elena recounted to Greg once she returned to the office, LaToya had a complete change of personality as soon as the hearing began. "I tell you what," Elena said to Greg that evening when she got home. "LaToya is a force to be reckoned with."

"What do you mean?" Greg asked as he poured two glasses of Sauvignon Blanc and handed one to Elena.

"Well, while we were waiting to see Judge Parsons, she was as friendly as she could be. She wanted to know all about me, my background, and also about you," Elena said. "She told me about growing up in a small town in south Georgia where there were more rattlesnakes than people. Understandably, I would say, she was desperate to get out of there, so she studied hard, hoping education would be her way out. When she was admitted at the University of Georgia with a full scholarship, she said, in her words, 'I thought I'd died and gone to heaven.'

"Then we were invited into Judge Parsons's chambers, and it was like somebody threw a switch. LaToya tried to get the judge to reconsider the amount of time he gave us to investigate the case and file an amended habeas petition. When the judge refused, she immediately asked him to enter an order limiting us to five depositions of no more than three hours each."

"What'd you say to that?"

"I didn't have to say anything," Elena said with a laugh. "Judge Parsons immediately said he knew the two of us could work out an agreement on the number of depositions, as well as reasonable time limits for each side to ask questions, and submit a consent order for his signature. Seemed obvious to me he's had LaToya in his court before because he looked at her a bit sternly and said, 'Now, Ms. Palmer, I want the State to be reasonable here. A man's life is at stake, and I'm going to allow his lawyers the time they need to investigate their case fully.'"

"That's great. Sounds like regardless of whatever caused him to be upset when the case began, he's had a significant change of heart since. Maybe one day we'll find out how and why that happened."

Two weeks after the hearing before Judge Parsons, LaToya moved to dismiss the habeas corpus petition as "frivolous, because it alleges no legally sufficient basis for the court to grant the relief sought by Owens." The relief Greg and Elena had requested in their petition was to have Owens's conviction vacated and for him to be set free. Judge Parsons eventually denied LaToya's motion, but only after Greg and Elena spent many hours preparing a detailed response.

"That was a clever motion for LaToya to file," Elena said to Greg the evening after they received Judge Parson's ruling. "There's no doubt she didn't expect to prevail, but she forced us to spend hundreds of hours on our response."

"It was a lot of work, for sure," Greg said, "but y'know, LaToya may have done us a favor by filing that motion."

"Why do you say that?" Elena asked with a puzzled look.

"She's handled a lot of these cases for the State," Greg said, "but this is our first rodeo. By filing that motion, she forced us to focus intensively not only on the law, but on the evidence we'll need to succeed on each claim, and to think about where or from whom we might get it. Now we have a roadmap, so to speak, about how to go about developing and presenting our case."

"Oh, good point," Elena replied with a smirk on her face. "Seeing as how I was the one who had to do all the work on our brief, I'll be sure to thank LaToya at the next hearing."

Greg chuckled as they walked out onto the terrace of the thirty-fourth-floor condo they'd recently bought together. It was in Buckhead, a toney section of Atlanta not too far north of their Midtown offices. Well known for its high-end shopping and five-star restaurants, including François's Bistro, Buckhead also had sprouted towering condominiums along Peachtree Street and gated mansions with beautifully manicured yards on the side roads. The northwest view from the terrace gave them a magnificent look at the deep red and orange hues spreading through the broken, puffy white clouds on the western horizon as the sun was setting.

"I could sit out here with you watching the sunset forever," Greg said.

Elena took his hand and gave it a squeeze.

CHAPTER FORTY

"Truth be told, I'm a little uneasy about my first appointment with the psychologist," Greg said to Elena over breakfast the next morning. "I've been feeling pretty good for the last week or two, so I'm not sure I really need to do this."

"Yes, you really do need to do this," Elena said gently, but firmly. "There's no shame in seeing a psychologist. If you had a heart problem, you wouldn't hesitate to go to a cardiologist. You have a serious psychological problem, Greg, and you need the help of a professional to get past it." Greg nodded reluctantly in acquiescence.

Dr. Elizabeth Morrow's office was in a medical building on West Peachtree Street, not very far from the Fox Stern offices. It was two blocks east of the Connector, a term used by locals to describe a seven-and-a-half-mile stretch of highway in which Interstates-75 and -85 merge into ten lanes that run through the heart of Atlanta.

"Mr. Williams?" a woman at the front desk asked.

"Yes, that's me."

"Very nice to meet you. I'm Beth Morrow."

"Oh, I assumed you were the receptionist."

"Well, I am," she said, smiling broadly. "At least during lunch hour. Please follow me."

She led Greg to her office and gestured toward a small, gray leather couch. "Make yourself comfortable," she said. "Would you like coffee, tea, or some water?

"Water would be fine. Thanks."

While Morrow went to get the water, Greg looked around her office. The walls were a pale blue and filled with abstract paintings, which Greg abhorred, but thought somehow appropriate for a shrink's office. A large Persian rug covered the hardwood floors. A square, wooden table with four matching chairs apparently served as her desk.

Morrow returned with water for Greg and a mug of tea for herself, which she set on a small table next to a wingback chair across the room from the sofa where Greg had made himself comfortable. "From our brief conversation a couple of weeks ago," Morrow said, "it sounded as though you're having anxiety and other difficulties since an awful experience you had many years ago as a news reporter. Can you tell me more?"

Greg told Dr. Morrow about being sent to the Florida State Prison three decades earlier to interview Malcolm Ford, and the violent reaction Ford had to Greg's final question. "It was eerie," he said. "We'd been talking for about twenty-five minutes and it was going fine. We'd discussed his childhood, which was difficult and terribly sad. Time was running out, and I decided to ask a question about how it felt to be facing death."

Greg paused and took a sip of water. "As soon as I asked, he got this vacant look in his eyes and seemed to go into a trance. Suddenly, he leapt at me, and before I could move, he shoved me so hard my chair toppled over. Luckily, that's when the sergeant arrived, yelled for help, and pulled Ford off me."

"Do you recall what you were you feeling after he shoved you?" Dr. Morrow asked.

"I don't remember it really well," Greg said, "because I was in a daze from my head slamming against the concrete floor. I do remember being very frightened, because he was standing over me and had a bizarre, twisted look on his face. I'm not sure what would've happened if the sergeant hadn't shown up when he did."

"What's it like for you to tell me about it now?"

"It's hard," Greg said. "It forces me to relive events I'd buried long ago."

"What part of your head hit the floor?"

"The back," he said, turning slightly and gesturing toward the area just below the crown of his skull.

"Did you receive any medical attention for that?"

"The prison doctor came to see me, looked me over for a few minutes, asked me a few questions, and sent me on my way with instructions to see my doctor if I experienced any headaches or other problems."

"Did you have any headaches after that?"

"Yes. I took a pain reliever when they got bad, and that seemed to help."

"Tell me about it."

"Well, for quite a while, I'd wake up startled in the middle of the night having nightmares, and it was hard to get back to sleep."

"Can you describe the nightmares?"

"Y'know, not really. The details faded very quickly. I just recall waking in a sweat with my heart pounding."

"How long did this go on?"

"Several months, with decreasing frequency. But I still have 'em now and then. Maybe once every few months."

"Have you been able to get back to sleep?"

"It was hard, especially for the first few weeks. I'd lie down, but my mind almost immediately would go back there—to the prison, to that cell—and I'd get agitated. Then, if I couldn't get it out of my head and fall asleep, I'd put in my earphones, turn on some music, or listen to a book, until I dozed off."

"Have you ever talked to any doctor or psychologist about it?"

"Not until today."

"Do you still find yourself thinking back about what happened in the prison that day and reliving those events?"

Greg sat quietly, staring at the ceiling for a few moments. Dr. Morrow waited patiently for his response, watching as Greg furrowed his brow, as though deep in thought.

"I still have some nights, not too often, but sometimes, when I watch a movie or a television show that has a prison scene, it pops back into my mind. I try to avoid watching shows like that, but Elena likes police dramas, so she turns them on now and then."

"Tell me about Elena," Dr. Morrow said. "Is she your wife?"

"We're not married, but we've lived together for about eight months, and just bought a condo together," he said. "It's a bit complicated since she's a partner in the same law firm as me. Our relationship was purely professional until we attended a hearing in a murder case up in north Georgia."

"What was that experience like?"

"I didn't think it would be an issue, because we were only attending on behalf of a television station we represent," he said. "But as soon as the prisoner was brought into the courtroom, Elena said I became fixated on him and didn't respond to her. She says it happened again when the prisoner was led out of the courtroom after the hearing ended. But, honestly, I don't have any recollection of either of those episodes."

When their hour was almost up, Dr. Morrow looked at Greg and said, "I'm not completely certain, Greg, but I have a pretty good idea about what's going on. What you're describing sounds very much like PTSD, post-traumatic stress disorder. I believe you've been suffering from that since the time the inmate attacked you in Florida."

"That was more than thirty years ago."

"And you've been suffering from PTSD ever since, even though you didn't know it. That's what the nightmares were about. And even after they diminished, it sounds like you've had a few incidents over the years resulting from exposure, even when watching television, to crimes or criminals, especially prison inmates. But you didn't have an intense reaction until you came face-to-face in a courtroom with the inmate charged with murder in north Georgia."

"So, can you help me?" he asked.

"Well, there's not a magic pill I can give you, if that's what you're asking. But I can try to help you using therapy known as exposure therapy."

"What's involved in that?"

"In short, I will expose you, gradually, to people or settings that trigger the fear you've experienced. We'd start with less threatening situations, using photos or videos and such, and progress to more challenging ones as we go. We'll practice methods of calming your body and nervous system, such as with relaxation and controlled breathing, in order to help you quiet the anxiety when you're confronted with something or someone that triggers your fear response. All this would be in a safe environment, perhaps initially just using your imagination or through virtual reality. As you learn how to conquer your fear and feel comfortable with it, we'd move on to more challenging situations, perhaps even arrange a visit to a jail or prison."

"How long does this take?" he asked.

"That depends on you and how you react to the various stimuli you experience. It could take a couple of months or, in some cases, as long as a few years."

"It sounds okay. But there's something else I should tell you."

"What's that?"

"You remember that hearing I talked about where I went into a trance when the prisoner was brought into the courtroom?"

"Yes."

"Well, Elena and I followed the case in the media for several days, and then we actually went back up there for the last two days of trial."

"How did that go for you?"

"Y'know, it was difficult, but not as bad as the first time. We sat in the back of the courtroom, so I didn't come face-to-face with the prisoner like I did the first time we were up there. Having Elena there next to me helped. Anyway, after listening to some of the testimony and the closing arguments by the lawyers, we each came to believe the guy was innocent. But he was convicted and sentenced to death, which shocked us both. Now, we've volunteered to represent him in his post-conviction proceedings."

"I see." A look of concern came over Dr. Morrow's face. "And what exactly does that mean as far as your goals for therapy?"

"It means that, before too long, probably within the next month, we're going to have to go to the prison to meet him and talk about the case. Can you help me get through that?"

"I'll do my best to help you feel ready, and we should know more about how you're responding after a few sessions. Is there any way you can delay the meeting, even for a few weeks?"

"Probably for a couple of weeks, at the most. I'll check on it and let you know."

"Good. Let's set you up with weekly appointments for the next two months. It's also an option to meet twice a week if you'd like to move things along a little faster."

"Twice a week would be fine," Greg said.

"Okay. And I'm going to give you some reading to do before you come back next week."

"Thank you, Dr. Morrow."

"My pleasure. And please call me Beth."

CHAPTER FORTY-ONE

"I think we need to have a meeting with our client," Elena said one morning in the team meeting that took place every Monday. "We need to hear his story directly from him and see how he responds to some of the more challenging factual issues we'll have to face."

Greg nodded his agreement, but said nothing. Liz Wilkes helped them through the process by explaining how to arrange a meeting with Owens. "I've already called Joseph and asked him to add the two of you to his list of attorneys," she said. "When you're ready, you'll have to call the warden's office, identify yourselves as Owens's lawyers, and tell them you need to meet with your client. Most times you can get in the next day, but it's better if you call a few days ahead because they limit the number of visitors each day."

"Do you think you're ready for this?" Elena asked Greg as soon as soon as Liz left their offices.

"I feel like I've made progress over the last six weeks," he replied. "The breathing techniques Beth taught me do seem to help me relax, although we're still in the early stages of the therapy."

"I can go by myself," she offered.

"Thanks, but I think we both need to go. Schedule the appointment for the late next week or early the following week. That'll give me two or three more sessions with Beth before we go."

Elena made the call the next day. Twelve days later, Greg rode with Elena as she drove to the prison. The drive took about fifty minutes, which passed largely in silence. As they drove, Elena sensed Greg was becoming apprehensive. "Just remember," she said, "we're on his side. Liz said he was really grateful that we agreed to represent him."

"I know," Greg replied tersely.

"Did Beth give you any advice about how to handle this meeting?" Elena asked in a not-too-subtle effort to refocus Greg on the relaxation techniques he'd been taught. Greg nodded, but said nothing more.

Elena parked the car, shut off the engine, and looked at Greg. His eyes were closed, and he was taking slow, deep breaths through his nose and then exhaling slowly. After a minute, he looked at her and said, "Let's go." Once inside the prison, Greg and Elena first had to pass through an entry area where, much like at an airport, they were scanned for weapons and contraband. Then the guard pointed toward a small room a few steps from the screening area.

"Through there," he said.

When they entered, a gate with heavy iron bars groaned loudly as it slid closed behind them. Elena cast a quick look at Greg, who continued taking deep breaths. A guard, in a small control room behind what Elena assumed was bulletproof glass, asked if they had an appointment. After confirming the appointment, she asked for their driver's licenses and car keys, which they promptly slid through the opening at the bottom of the glass.

"You're not carrying cell phones, right?" the guard asked. "They're not permitted inside the prison." Having been alerted to this by Liz, both confirmed they were not.

Satisfied that the visitors were authorized to enter, the guard pushed a button to open a second gate, allowing the lawyers to proceed into the prison. After walking down a long, empty hallway painted a drab, institutional green and then climbing a flight of stairs, Greg and Elena encountered another guard station.

"We have an appointment to see our client, Joseph Owens," Greg told the guard. Without saying a word, the guard looked at her computer screen, and then pushed the button that opened the first of another set of iron gates. Once it closed behind them, the second gate opened. From there, it was a short walk to what looked like a visitor waiting area with orange and yellow molded-plastic chairs and a few vending machines filled with snacks and soft drinks. Three other people were sitting in the waiting area.

Greg and Elena took seats facing the gate. She looked at Greg, who had his eyes open and was continuing to take slow, deep breaths. About ten minutes passed before a guard called out the name Joseph Owens. They stood simultaneously and stepped forward. One guard unlocked the gate, then pointed to a small room on the right containing four chairs and a table. Once they were inside, the guard locked the door behind them.

"Are you okay?" Elena asked.

"Yes," he responded, although Elena wasn't so sure.

"Deep breaths," she said. "You're just here to meet a client who really needs your help."

The room had thick glass windows that provided a view of a prison hallway, where inmates wearing the standard white uniform with blue trim regularly passed by and gazed inside at the two people in business attire. Shouts, occasional screams, and clanging metal gates rang out intermittently in the distance, as if Greg needed a reminder about where they were.

Elena slipped her hand on top of Greg's and gave a gentle squeeze. Just then, they heard the door being unlocked, and she quickly removed her hand. The door swung open and Owens shuffled in. He looked heavier than he did when they first encountered him in the Noonan County Courthouse more than two years earlier. As then, he was in handcuffs and leg shackles. Elena could hear Greg silently taking in, and then letting out, long, deep breaths. Once the door was closed and locked behind him, Owens placed his back against the door, where there were openings just below waist level and near the floor, through which the guard unlocked and removed the handcuffs and shackles.

Greg was sweating and his heart was pounding as flashes of Malcolm Ford forced their way into his mind. He could see Ford rising out of his chair, coming at him. Suddenly, he felt Elena's hand on his left elbow, gently guiding him up out of his chair as he heard her say, "I'm Elena Samuels and this is Greg Williams. We're glad to meet you."

"Liz Wilkes told me you guys volunteered to be my new lawyers," Owens said as a soft smile spread across his pale face. "I didn't think nobody would help me. Thank you."

Greg's heartbeat slowed, and he started to relax. It was the tone of Owens's voice, more than the words, that calmed him. Greg managed a smile as he looked back at Owens, who was a bit shorter than him. Owens appeared to be far more in possession of his wits than he'd been when they first encountered him at the media hearing more than two years earlier in the Noonan County Courthouse.

"We're going to do everything we can to help you," Greg said. "First, though, let me ask how you're doing?"

"It's terrible in here, man," Owens said. "Bad. Real bad. I try to keep to myself, but it ain't all that easy to do, if y'know what I mean."

"I imagine it must be very hard on your nerves being locked up in here," Greg said. "Is there anything we can do to help?"

"Nah," Owens said. "They give me a pill with my lunch each day that's s'posed to keep me calm. I don't know what the hell it is, but I guess it helps."

"We're going to request a copy of your medical records from the prison, if that's okay with you," Elena said. "If they're giving you any medications that could affect your ability to remember all the details of your case and discuss them with us, we need to know about it. Okay?"

"Yeah, okay," Joseph said. "Whatever you guys want."

For the next fifty minutes, which was all the time they had remaining for their visit, Greg and Elena asked Joseph question after question about his background, childhood, family, schooling, and employment history before getting into the facts of the case.

"Ever been in trouble before this?" Greg asked.

"There was this problem I had in Jersey years ago when the cops closed down a business where I worked. At first, I was arrested and charged with something to do with having stolen property in the store, but I didn't know nothin' about that. I wasn't the one buying the stuff and there was no way I was gonna take the rap for that. My lawyer told me I'd probably be lookin' at twenty years. Maybe more. So I cooperated with the prosecutor and the charges eventually were dropped."

Each of them nodded at Owens. The question was really just a test to see how forthcoming he would be, and they had their answer.

"Joseph, tell us about the time when you worked at the Harrington Diner and the events that led up to you being fired," Elena asked.

"Well, when I started workin' there, I was happy to get the job. Not that it was the greatest job in the world, but I'd lost two other jobs, and we were running low on money. Real low. Y'know what I mean? My wife, Jasmine, started talking about needing to find a second job. I didn't want her to have to do that, so I just drove from place to place asking if they was hiring. Mr. Tillotson was standing out back of the restaurant throwing trash in the dumpster when I drove up. He told me they had just lost their busboy and asked if I was interested. That's how come I got hired."

"How soon did problems begin there?" Elena asked.

"The first week went okay," Owens said. "But early in the second week, one of the cooks was staring at me. I thought, man, this guy doesn't trust me or he doesn't like me. He's watching every move I make. It just made me nervous-like, and I told the guy to stop staring at me and mind his own business."

"What made you think he didn't trust you?" she asked.

"I dunno," Owens said. "I've had problems with my nerves ever since I testified against my boss in that trial in Jersey. Sometimes I worry they've sent someone to get me, y'know, like they're connected somehow."

"What happens when you get nervous?" Elena asked. "How does it affect you?"

"I guess I kinda stop thinking real clearly and then I clam up," he said. "I can't talk. It's like my mind gets all scrambled."

"So what went on with the cook?" Greg asked.

"He just kept looking at me kind of funny. I said something like, 'You gotta problem with me'? He pushed me away, and I shoved him back. When he came back at me, I started to throw a punch, but Mr. Gonzales came up from behind and grabbed my arm."

"What happened then?"

"Tillotson came over and pulled me aside. Honestly, I don't remember a lot of what he said. I sort of zoned out. But I remember he told me to take the rest of the day off. He wanted me to calm down and stay cool or I wouldn't be able to work there anymore. So I went home, sat on the couch, and thought about it for a long time. I decided that I'd do better. I really needed that job."

"Did you go back to work the next day?" Elena asked.

"Yeah. And everything went okay for a week or so. Then some of the other workers did things that started to get me upset. A waitress told me she didn't like the way I looked at her. I got angry and threw my cleaning rag down on her table, but I walked away without saying a word.

"A few days after that, this guy who works in the kitchen jumps me when I was out back, taking out the trash early one morning," Owens said. "I shoved him against the dumpster and he goes down. I jumped on him and got in some good licks just as Tillotson comes outside. He calls the cook, Eddie Gonzales, who runs outside, grabs me, and then Tillotson takes me to the storage room. The next thing I know is Tillotson comes in and tells me to get out, that I was fired."

"How'd you react?" Greg said.

"I was real upset," he told them. "I didn't start that fight, but he wouldn't believe me, I guess 'cause I was the newest employee and already had some problems with the other guys. I told him how badly I needed the job, but he wouldn't listen. It was like the third job I'd lost that year, and I didn't want to tell Jasmine. I went to a bar to try to calm down, had a couple of beers, and then headed home. Jaz lost it over me getting fired again and started yellin' at me. I guess I got angry and zoned out, because I don't remember much until I saw some cops come into the apartment."

"Was Jasmine hurt?" Greg asked.

"Nah, she ran outside and didn't come back until the cops showed up. She was okay," he said. "Then my brother comes over and tells me I gotta see somebody, like a counselor, who could teach me how to stay cool. He and Jaz were trying to get me an appointment when the police showed up at the apartment, busted the door down, and arrested me for killing Tillotson and Gonzales. I was like, 'for what?' I don't watch no news. I didn't know nothin' about the murders."

Although neither Greg nor Elena asked, Owens repeatedly said he was home in bed when the murders took place and didn't leave his house that evening. "Jaz was working the night shift at her job, so there wasn't nobody who could tell the DA I stayed home all night. But you guys got to believe me. I didn't do this. I've gotten into some trouble in my life, serious trouble up in Jersey, but I never shot nobody. Never."

Greg tried to trip Owens up by going back to topics they had already discussed to see if he would contradict himself, but his story remained consistent. There was a knock at the door to the interview room and a guard shouted in that they only had five more minutes. Greg asked Owens if there was anything he wanted to ask them.

"Yeah," Owens said. "They can't execute me for somethin' I didn't do, right? I mean, I didn't shoot those guys." The question and the look of desperation on Owens's face as he posed it startled Greg for a moment. Sensing from Greg's face that the question shook him, Elena jumped in.

"Joseph, we can't promise you how this'll turn out," she said. "But I'll guarantee you that we'll all work really hard and do everything we can to get your conviction overturned and to get you out of this place."

Owens nodded. "I understand," he said. "Thanks. Thanks a lot."

Greg walked over to the door and knocked. A guard called out, "You done?"

"Yes," Greg said.

Joseph moved to the far wall, away from the door. Once the door opened, Elena and Greg stepped out. Then the door was closed and locked. Owens walked over and again placed his back to the door with his hands behind him. Once the handcuffs and shackles were in place, the guard opened the door and motioned for Joseph to step out. As he did so, Joseph glanced to his left and saw Greg and Elena standing on the other side of the locked gate, smiling at him.

"See you soon," Elena said. Joseph smiled and nodded before he was led back to his cell.

Greg and Elena walked out silently, passing back through the first set of double gates, down the stairs, along the long hallway, and through the second set of gates, where the guard handed back their driver's licenses and Elena's car keys. Once outside, Greg said, "I don't know if he was being completely truthful on every point, but he certainly seemed sincere. Especially with that last question. It caught me off guard. Sorry."

"I could tell," she said. "But overall I thought you did incredibly well. Dr. Morrow must really be doing you some good."

"No question," he said. "But we've still got a way to go."

Both were lost in their own thoughts as they drove north on I-75 toward Atlanta. Elena broke the silence. "He wasn't what I was expecting."

"How do you mean?" Greg asked.

"Oh, in a good way. I sort of expected him to be a bit nervous, perhaps reluctant, y'know, to talk to people he doesn't really know or have any reason to trust. But he seemed genuinely appreciative and open with us, although obviously still anxious about the future."

"Yep," Greg said. Then, he added, "Thank you."

"For what?" Elena asked.

"For insisting I get some help. Without that push, I'm not sure I'd ever have faced up to this." Elena smiled and, without taking her eyes off the road, reached out to take Greg's hand in hers. She squeezed his hand gently and held on.

No words were needed. None were spoken for the rest of the drive back to Atlanta.

CHAPTER FORTY-TWO

Greg was reading a deposition transcript when he looked up and saw Clay Morrisey standing in the doorway.

"Hi, Clay. What's up?"

"I just wanted to see how everything's going on your death penalty case," Clay said as he lowered himself into one of the guest chairs. Greg had noticed Clay's hair had started to turn gray, and a slight frown and a troubled countenance had replaced his usual smile. It seemed to Greg that the burdens of serving as the firm's managing partner, on top of maintaining a full workload, might well be starting to take a toll on his long-time friend.

"Pretty good," Greg said. "Still in the midst of depositions, which are consuming most of my time and Elena's these days. But we're getting some great testimony that we'll make good use of at trial."

"What trial?" Clay asked.

"The trial on Owens's habeas claims for violation of his constitutional rights. It's not scheduled until March of next year, but we've got our work cut out for us to complete discovery, identify and prepare our expert witnesses, get the fact witnesses ready, and all the other stuff that goes along with a trial."

"There's going to be a trial in this case?" Clay exclaimed as his expression instantly morphed into anger. "How the hell did that happen?"

"What are you talking about, Clay?" Greg asked, astonished at the question. "Of course there's going to be a trial. How else would the judge be able to rule on our claims?"

"I guess I just assumed the judge would decide it on the briefs, sort of like a motion for summary judgment. I didn't have any idea when we approved this case that you'd have a full-fledged trial. How many days do you expect the trial to last?"

"It's a little early to know. Perhaps six or seven days. But I told you this was a civil case, and just like any other civil case, unless the judge grants a summary judgment motion—which never happens in this kind of case—or a settlement miraculously occurs, which I can guarantee won't happen here, there's going to be a trial."

"Elena will have to be there as well, I assume?"

"We'll be the two principal trial lawyers, but we'll need at least one associate, Likely Nehra Mehta, to help with witness preparation and to handle last-minute legal research. She's been working on the case and will want to attend, which will be a great learning experience for her. We'll also need to have a paralegal to manage our documents and help with the unexpected twists and turns that inevitably arise during any trial."

Clay closed his eyes for a few seconds. Then, with his face turning from pink to crimson, he lit into Greg.

"Do you have any idea—even the slightest idea—how much money the firm already has invested in this case? I'll tell you. Well over a million dollars in billable time. Do you have any idea how restless the partnership is getting as it sees more and more lawyer time and resources invested in a case many of them didn't want to take in the first place, but on which I backed you out of some, I guess, unrequited sense of loyalty?"

Greg's temperature was also starting to rise. "Dammit, Clay," he shouted. "What the hell were you expecting when we took on this case?

Did you really think we'd cut corners or leave any stone unturned with our client's life at stake?"

"No, but I also didn't expect you to deliver a deluxe defense when something less would have been more than adequate to get the job done."

"Really?" Greg shot back, incredulous at Clay's comment. "I can't even believe you'd *think* such a thing, let alone say it."

They stared at each other for several seconds, each pondering what to say next.

"What's happened to you, Clay?" Greg asked, his voice coming down almost to a whisper. "A man's life is on the line here, and you want me to cut corners? When did you lose the compassion, the sense of that special obligation of lawyers to serve the public good we learned about in law school? Is law now about nothing but making more and more money, about increasing profits per partner, so that our partner distributions can go beyond their already astronomic level?"

"Well," Clay said as he stood up to leave, "thanks for the lecture, Greg. But I suggest you grow up. This isn't law school anymore. It's real life where we play with real stakes."

"You really wanna talk to me about real life and real stakes?" Greg shot back. "Because I'm dealing with flesh and blood while you're counting dollars and cents."

"Greg, I'm telling you, both as a partner and as a friend, get this case over with," Clay said. "Our profits are down significantly this year in no small part because two partners, I don't know how many associates, and a paralegal, are putting thousands of hours of non-billable time into the Owens case each month. And now you tell me there's going to be a trial, which will be an even bigger hit to our bottom line. Under the circumstances," Clay said as he turned to look out the window, avoiding Greg's gaze, "I hope you and Elena understand your compensation is going to take a hit."

"Wait just a damned minute, Clay," Greg shot back. "We talked about this before we accepted the case. You spoke of how proud you were that we were taking this on and assured me the firm had our backs."

"I was proud of you for taking the case on. I still am. But I expected you to manage it in a way that wouldn't have such a drastic impact on our bottom line."

"You mean cut corners, do less than everything we could do to save our client's life?" Greg said, his voice once again rising and his face again turning crimson. "*That's bullshit*! You knew from the get-go that neither Elena nor I would *ever* handle this case at anything less than full speed. Now you tell us we're going to take a financial hit for doing exactly what you knew we were going to do? And what would you say if I told you some partners on the management committee—Susan Petroff, Gene Miller, Jeff Fisher—have stopped in more than once to talk about the case? All encouraging us to give this the best Fox Stern has to offer. Susan and Gene even offered to pitch in and help if we thought they might be useful."

"Easy for them to be magnanimous when they're not responsible for the bottom line."

"Hell, Clay, they're on the management committee! Of *course* they have responsibility for the bottom line."

"Don't be so naïve. They're just checking up on you. The firm has taken on a huge financial burden for the associate and staff time being devoted to this case, which you seem to use quite freely. We're also paying the fees for expert witnesses and consultants you've hired. That much was implicit when we agreed to let you take on the case. But you never asked, and I never promised, that as a partner, you'd get paid for your own time on the case."

"I never imagined I needed to ask such a question. Neither Bill Fox nor Aaron Stern ever would've contemplated or tolerated such a thing."

"That was fifty years ago, Greg, when lawyers practiced at the same firm for their entire careers," Clay said as he stood, placed his palms on Greg's desk, and leaned in. "In case you haven't noticed while you've been wrapped up in your volunteer work, the legal business has changed drastically in the last five or ten years. Partners who control a significant book of business are loyal to the firm only as long as their compensation exceeds what they can get at one of our competitors."

"That's your fault, Clay. You brought in lawyers who are driven by nothing but the size of their paychecks and who don't understand the meaning of the word 'partner,'" Greg shouted as he stood to meet Clay's stare. "We were better off without them."

"Greg, you just don't get it," Clay said, his face softening and turning from anger to incredulity. "Without bringing those folks in and increasing our profitability, we could've lost between a quarter and a third of our partners within two years. Everyone who had any meaningful amount of business was being wooed by other firms with offers of a lot more money. Chances are the firm would've had to merge into another firm or close its doors. I'll grant you the law business has changed, and in many ways not for the better. But that's the world we're in today, Greg, whether or not you like it. It's time for you to wake up and smell the roses."

"Oh, I'm wide awake, but those aren't roses I'm smelling. Now, *get out!*"

Chapter Forty-Three

That evening, Greg told Elena about the screaming match with Clay. "I don't know what's happened to him, but he certainly isn't the person I used to know."

"Sounds as though he's under intense pressure from the top partners to keep driving the firm's profits higher and higher," Elena replied. "It's like their egos are on the line if partners at one of our competitors make a thousand dollars more than them, even though they're all making a gazillion dollars. The greed at the top is just unbelievable."

"No question about that. But look, Elena, there's nothing we can do about this now. We'll deal with it once the case is over."

The next morning was the weekly team meeting, where everyone reported on the status of the work they were doing. "Y'know," Elena said, "the one thing that shocks me most is that Delaney never challenged Chastain's refusal to turn over certain documents he subpoenaed. Chastain apparently claimed the documents he withheld were "attorney work product." Delaney could've challenged Chastain on that and forced him to prove to the judge that he properly withheld the documents. But for reasons I don't understand, Delaney never did that."

"Incredible," Greg said. "Let's have a subpoena served on Chastain to force him to either give us those documents or justify his work product claim to the judge." Two days later, Chastain was on his personal cellphone when his assistant knocked and opened the door. He waved her in and gestured for her to take a seat.

"What's up?" he asked as soon as he hung up the telephone.

"This just arrived for you by courier," she said, handing the DA an envelope from the Fox Stern firm. When he ripped the envelope open and saw it was from Samuels, he handed it back to his assistant without bothering to read the document. "Send this to the attorney general's flunkies who are handling the habeas case and tell them to take care of it," he instructed.

Chapter Forty-Four

LaToya Palmer could not believe what she was reading.

"The court should order the district attorney to turn over all the documents he withheld from Delaney before the trial because he never provided Delaney with a list of those documents, as required under the court's rules," Samuels wrote in a motion seeking to force Chastain to surrender the so-called work product documents.

Palmer called Chastain immediately. "That's true," Chastain said nonchalantly.

"Paul, you know you're required to give opposing counsel a list of documents you withhold as attorney work product," LaToya said. "Why didn't you do it?"

"Because Delaney never asked for it," Chastain said. "I'm not in the business of volunteering information that defense counsel didn't request."

"C'mon, Paul, it's standard procedure to provide defense counsel with that list," LaToya said dismissively. "We're really going to look bad in front of the court when this comes up for a hearing tomorrow morning. Can you email the list to me today?"

"No, I can't," Chastain said angrily. "Since Delaney never asked for a list, we never prepared one. We're going to have to dig out the box containing the withheld documents from our storage facility. It may take a few days."

"How many days?"

"Three, maybe four."

"Get it to me as quickly as you can," LaToya said. "We have a hearing tomorrow morning. I'll see what I can do about getting us a few more days to produce the list." Then, realizing she was going to have to defend the indefensible, LaToya called Elena to explain the situation and to apologize for Chastain's conduct before the hearing.

"Elena, I'm sorry, but I had no idea before this morning that Chastain hadn't produced the list of withheld documents to Delaney," she said. "For what it's worth, in his defense, Chastain says Delaney never asked for the list."

"I'm not sure Delaney was required to ask for it, but how about emailing a copy of the list to me today, and if it's satisfactory, I'll cancel the hearing," Elena said.

"Here's the problem. I just spoke to Chastain, and he says he never created the list since Delaney didn't ask for it. He's going to get someone to pull the box from storage and create a list, but it's going to take a few days."

"Okay, but without the list or the documents, I can't cancel the hearing."

"I understand. I'll see you there, and we'll see what the judge wants to do."

At the hearing, LaToya told Judge Parsons that the State would provide Elena with the list within five business days. "Very good," Judge Parsons said. "Is Ms. Palmer's offer acceptable to you, Ms. Samuels?"

"Yes, Your Honor. But I'd ask to have our motion to compel left pending until we've received the list and reviewed it. If the documents qualify as work product, I'll notify the court and promptly withdraw the motion. If not, we reserve the right to bring this matter back to the court's attention."

"That sounds reasonable," Judge Parsons said. "Any objection from the State?"

"No, that's fine with us."

CHAPTER FORTY-FIVE

"I'm going to drive up to Harrington this morning to try to see Captain Smith," Greg told Elena as he gulped down a cup of coffee before heading out. He'd risen very early, taken a shower, dressed, and made the coffee by the time Elena came into the kitchen in her pajamas. "I've left seven or eight messages for him, and he won't return my calls. I think the only way I'll get to talk to him is to just show up in his office."

Smith had led the investigation into not just the Owens case, but the robbery and murder that had taken place across the street from the diner three weeks prior. "That convenience store shooting was just too close in time and location for police to ignore the likelihood that the same person committed both murders. But so far as I can tell, that's exactly what they've done. And I want to know why."

"Take a patience pill, Greg," Elena said with a smile.

"Better than that," he said as he grabbed Elena and gave her a hug and a kiss. "I'm taking a secret weapon."

"What secret weapon?"

But he just smiled, grabbed his briefcase, and headed out.

Greg was in his car at 7:15 a.m. and headed for the northbound entrance to I-75. Assuming no serious traffic snarls—a dangerous assumption anywhere in the metro Atlanta area during rush hour—he'd arrive at the Harrington Police Department headquarters before

9:00 a.m., even with a quick stop to grab a second cup of coffee on the way. Rather than stopping at his usual chain coffee shop, Greg pulled in at a donut shop with the words, "Fresh Hot Donuts!" lit up in the window. Besides getting a large, black coffee, he bought a dozen assorted donuts.

When Greg arrived at the Harrington Police Department, he approached the receptionist, a woman who appeared to be in her late twenties. "I'm here to see Captain Smith," he said.

"Is he expecting you?"

"He should be, but I'm not sure he realizes I'd be stopping by today."

"Does he know you?"

"Well, we've played telephone tag," Greg said, ignoring the fact that he was the only one of the two who had played the game. "But we've never met. So if you could point him out to me when he arrives, I'd surely appreciate it."

The receptionist looked at Greg warily as he reached into a bag he was carrying, pulled out a box, and handed it to her. "This is for your trouble," he said. She smiled at him and said, "I'll see what I can do," as she placed the donut box on her desk along with paper plates and napkins she took out of her desk drawer.

Twenty minutes later, a stout, slightly balding man wearing a gray suit and a tie that had been loosened—if it had ever been tied—walked in and started to turn toward a door on his right with a sign saying, "Authorized Police Personnel Only," when he noticed the box sitting on the receptionist's desk. He strolled over, peeked inside, and removed a chocolate glazed from the box.

"Thanks, Carole," the man said.

"Oh, you're welcome, Captain Smith," she replied, cutting a glance at Greg. Taking his cue, Greg jumped up from his seat on the other side of the desk. "Captain, I'm Greg Williams. I've been trying to reach you for a couple of weeks."

"You're Owens's new lawyer?"

"Yes. And I've got some questions I'd like to ask you about the investigation. Since we've not been able to connect by telephone, I thought I'd stop by to see if I could have just a few minutes of your time."

"Let me guess," Smith said. "You just happened to pass by a donut shop and decided to bring these along to build a little goodwill with Miss Carole here, so she'd alert you when I arrived."

Greg grinned. "Yeah, that's about right," he said. "I hope you don't hold it against her."

"Nah," Smith said. "She's my niece. I knew something was up when she called me 'Captain Smith.'" Greg turned and looked at Carole, who was smiling as she bit into a glazed, raspberry-filled donut, and the filling spilled out onto her chin.

"Okay, so you drove all the way up here to speak to me," Smith said. "C'mon back to my office. I can give you a few minutes." Then he grinned at Greg and said, "Grab a donut since you paid for them."

Once they settled into chairs in Smith's office, Greg cut straight to the chase. "Captain, I wanted to ask you about the other murder. Y'know, the one at the convenience store across from the diner. Have there been any arrests in that case?"

"No, not yet."

"Do you have any suspects?"

"I suppose you're hoping the answer is yes so you can try to connect the suspect to the diner murders and get your guy off. Sorry to disappoint you, but we've not identified anyone yet. We're actively working on it, though."

"Forgive me if this sounds like I'm trying to tell you how to do your job, but have you evaluated whether there might be a connection between the two cases?"

"Initially, sure, we considered it to be possible, if not probable, particularly in light of the proximity in time and location of the two incidents. But the investigation of the diner shootings took us in a different direction once we interviewed multiple witnesses who identified your client as having motive, opportunity, and a history of violence. Then we learned about his involvement with organized crime in New Jersey, and we were fairly certain we had the right man."

"Fairly certain?" Greg asked. "That seems like a helluva weak basis to charge someone with first-degree murder, let alone to seek the death penalty."

Smith stared back at him, but said nothing. Greg didn't see any point in arguing, so he turned back to his original question. "May I ask where you stand on the convenience store murder?"

"We're at a bit of a dead end. We know it wasn't Owens because he obviously doesn't match the partial view we saw on the videotape of the gunman fleeing the convenience store. We're still investigating, but we don't have any suspects yet."

"Please let me know if that ever changes."

"Sorry, Mr. Williams, but I'm not able to disclose anything to you about the progress of that investigation until we make an arrest. When that happens, it'll be all over the news. I can promise you that."

The meeting left Greg disappointed and frustrated. As he drove back to Atlanta, he called Elena, who could tell immediately that the trip had not gone well. "He seems confident that they got the right guy in the diner case even though they don't have a suspect in the convenience store killing. I'm not sure he was leveling with me. Something tells me he didn't really believe what he was saying."

"What makes you say that?" Elena asked.

"Well, Smith told me they originally were operating under the assumption that the guy who held up the convenience store struck again three weeks later at the diner, which certainly makes sense. Then, during the diner investigation, when a few witnesses mentioned Owens's temper, they investigated and found out he'd been arrested a few years earlier in New Jersey.

"When he talked to the cops in Jersey, Smith learned the arrest happened during a raid on a mob-owned pawnshop that Owens managed and, *ipso facto*, he decided Owens was their suspect. But there was just something in the way he talked about Owens that seemed unconvincing, as though Smith himself still wasn't fully persuaded that Owens was the person who shot Tillotson and Gonzales."

"But if Smith wasn't persuaded," Elena asked, "why did he charge Owens?"

"I'm not so sure Smith was the person who made that decision."

"Well, who did then?"

"Think about it for a moment," he said. "Smith strikes me as a good, smart, hard-working cop who had nothing to gain by arresting the wrong man."

"But?"

"But if you were a district attorney facing a challenger who's screaming about law and order, and there'd been three unsolved murders in your jurisdiction within three weeks, would you want all of those murders to remain unsolved leading up to election day?"

"You think Chastain jumped the gun and decided to charge Owens because they were striking out at identifying the convenience store shooter?"

"I just have a feeling Smith's holding something back. I certainly could be wrong, but I just didn't get the sense he truly believed Owens was the killer."

After a few moments of silence, Elena said, "By the way, Greg, what was the 'secret weapon' you talked about before you left this morning? It doesn't sound like it worked, whatever it was."

He laughed.

"I stopped and got some donuts to take with me to butter up the receptionist so she would point out the captain when he arrived."

"Oh, that's so tacky."

"Well, at least that part of my plan worked great," Greg said. "The rest, not so much."

CHAPTER FORTY-SIX

Five days after the hearing at which Palmer had promised to provide a list of the undisclosed work product documents, the phone rang in Elena's office shortly before eleven.

"Elena, this is LaToya. I'm calling to let you know I've reviewed the withheld documents and will produce all of them to you by the end of the day today. I can assure you that neither I nor anyone else in this office was aware of what the DA was withholding under a claim of work product."

"Okay. Thanks, LaToya. But just so we're clear, are any documents being withheld?"

"No, you'll be receiving everything Chastain withheld." It was a stunning admission that Chastain had improperly withheld documents from Delaney before Owens's trial.

Shrewdly, wanting to make sure the judge knew Chastain had engaged in unethical conduct, Elena filed a notice informing the judge that she was "withdrawing the motion to compel in light of the State's admission that none of the documents withheld by the district attorney at the Owens trial was properly classified as attorney work product and are now being produced to Owens's counsel for the first time."

The box arrived at the Fox Stern office late that afternoon. As she started going through the contents, Elena found not only documents, but a thumb drive. Nothing among the papers was work product, but neither were they in any way significant to Owens's case. Then Elena popped the drive into her computer. It contained a video file that showed the street in front of the restaurant taken from the security camera at the convenience store across the street. The date displayed on the video was the same date as the diner murders.

As the video reached the end, Elena grabbed the phone and called Greg. "You need to come in here. You're not going to believe what I just received from the AG's office." As soon as Greg walked into her office, Elena said, "I'm going to show you the last three minutes of the video file on this thumb drive. The important part is right at the end."

Greg sat silently as he watched. Just as the time displayed on the video reached 5:37 a.m., a car appeared, accelerating quickly as it crossed in front of the restaurant from west to east, toward I-75.

"So what?" he asked. "That's not Owens's car. It's a black sports car."

"It's not just any black sports car," Elena said. "It's an older model Camaro matching the description of the vehicle used in the robbery and murder at the convenience store three weeks earlier."

Greg was thunderstruck. He stared at Elena in utter disbelief. "How could Delaney possibly have missed that?"

"I wondered the same thing. So I looked at the video file included in the materials Delaney sent to us. That video stops about forty-five seconds before the black Camaro appears on the screen."

"How can that be?" Greg asked, clearly agitated by what Elena had just said. "Are you saying that the copy of the video file Chastain produced to Delaney before trial was missing the scene at the end with the black Camaro?"

"I don't know how else to explain it. I find it hard to imagine that the final forty-five seconds was omitted inadvertently when making the copy since the copying process is automated. Someone would have had to set the copying equipment to thirty-six minutes exactly, rather than thirty-six minutes and forty-five seconds."

That evening, Greg couldn't sleep. He kept thinking about the seriousness of what they had uncovered. Chastain was widely regarded as one of the toughest but also one of the best and most ethical prosecutors in the state. Yet, like Elena, Greg didn't believe the final 45 seconds of the video were omitted inadvertently. He looked at his clock. Twelve thirty, and he still couldn't sleep. He got out of bed, quietly closing the bedroom door behind him to avoid disturbing Elena.

On the one hand, he thought to himself, it seemed highly unlikely that a subordinate in Chastain's office would commit such a serious act without Chastain's implicit, if not explicit, approval. On the other hand, it was equally unlikely, if not impossible, to believe that Chastain, with his golden reputation, would allow or tolerate such conduct, especially in a capital case.

After an hour or so of pondering what to do, Greg felt himself growing weary and headed back to bed. Although he usually was the first to get up in the morning, Elena woke him at seven thirty. Quickly showering and dressing, he went into the kitchen for breakfast, where Elena was finishing her coffee.

"Did you decide to sleep in this morning?" she asked whimsically.

"No, I just had trouble getting to sleep last night. I couldn't stop thinking about that video and its implications, not only for Joseph's case, but for Georgia's use of the death penalty."

Elena looked Greg in the eyes, her face growing concerned, and asked, "What do you mean?"

"Here's the thing. If a high profile, widely respected DA such as Chastain would do such a thing, I can hardly imagine the tactics police and prosecutors engage in elsewhere around the state to improve the chances of success in capital cases. How many more people sit on death row because of evidence that was withheld or altered by the prosecution? How many innocent people have been executed?"

Elena could see fear take hold of Greg. She'd seen this look before, but thought he'd been making progress with the psychologist.

"Greg, look at me," Elena commanded. "Where are you? What are you thinking about?" He closed his eyes and kept them shut for a while. When he opened them, he seemed more like himself.

"I don't understand," Greg said. "For some reason, I started thinking about Ford again. I'm not sure what triggered it this time."

"Do you think you should talk about this with Beth?"

"Yes, I will. I'm seeing her again on Thursday."

CHAPTER FORTY-SEVEN

In his office later that morning, Greg was determined to keep his focus on Owens. He opened the trial transcript on his computer and began searching for every question Delaney asked regarding the video.

Repeatedly, Delaney asked the police witnesses whether any video of the street in front of the diner around the time of the murders showed a white Ford Focus, such as the one owned by Owens. The answer, which was truthful, was that no such car appeared on any video.

Delaney either did not receive a copy of the full video that included the black Camaro, or if he did, he not only failed to keep a copy in his files, but he also failed to make the connection between the black Camaro and the murder at the convenience store. That seemed highly unlikely, but there was only one way to find out.

"Mike, Greg Williams here," he said as soon as Delaney answered. "I need to show you something when you have a few minutes. Any chance you could stop by my office today or tomorrow?"

"Sure," Delaney said. "I just got out of a meeting close to your office, so I can come by now if you like."

·   ·   ·   ·   ·

"Your firm must've dropped a bundle building out and furnishing these offices," Delaney said as soon as Greg arrived in the lobby to escort him to a conference room. "I'm not sure I'd get any work done if I had an office like this one."

"Not that I take it for granted," Greg said, "but I'd rather the firm spent a little less on decorating its office space and a little more on things that matter."

"Like what?" Delaney asked.

"Well, not that we don't make generous contributions, but at times like this, increasing our annual donation to legal aid organizations would be a good place to start," he replied.

"That'd be wonderful," Delaney replied, "but for now, I'm just glad they allowed you and Elena to take on this case."

Elena was waiting in the conference room with the original video cued up on her laptop. As the two men took their seats, Delaney asked, "So what can I do for you?"

"Mike, do you recall if Chastain provided you copies of all the video recordings the police obtained from the night of the murders?" Greg asked.

"Yes, I had at least three such recordings," Delaney said. "One was taken from the convenience store camera across the street. The two others were from street cameras between the restaurant and Owens's home. None showed a white car such as Owens owned, which I thought was a big hole in their case."

"You're correct about that," Greg continued. "But there's more. Elena, play the video file you showed me this morning."

"This is the video taken by the camera from the store across the street from the diner," Elena said. "If you don't mind watching from the beginning, we need to know if you recognize this video as one that was provided to you by the DA before the trial."

After about five minutes, Delaney said the video looked familiar. "I feel certain this is something the DA gave us a few weeks before the trial started," Delaney said.

"Okay," Greg said, "keep watching and tell us if you see anything you don't believe you've seen before."

When the video reached 5:37 a.m., and the black Camaro raced across the screen toward I-75, Delaney seemed perplexed. "Wait," he said. "Can you rewind that and replay the last minute again at a slower speed?"

When Elena did so, Delaney started shaking his head. "That dark car passing in front of the restaurant minutes after the shooting . . . I don't believe I've ever seen that before," he said. "I know I would've asked some questions about it if I'd seen any car pass by around that time. Obviously, it could've provided a lead on another suspect."

"Do you recognize the make and model of the car?" Greg asked.

Delaney looked at the video in slow motion one more time. "No, can't say that I do, but I'm not much of a car buff. Is there something particularly noteworthy about it?"

"What if I tell you it's an older model black Camaro?" Elena said. "Would that mean anything to you?"

"That son of a bitch!" Delaney screamed. "Chastain kept that from me because he knew what I would've done with it. It would've brought the case against Owens to a screeching halt. I want him disbarred for this."

"I agree," Greg said. "This video file came from a file labeled as work product, which the habeas judge ordered Chastain to turn over to us, but which was not produced to you before the Owens trial."

"Work product, my ass," Delaney yelled, thoroughly incensed. "There's no way—*no way*—this video file is work product. This was a 100 percent intentional *Brady* violation," referring to the US Supreme Court case that requires prosecutors to disclose to the defense any material in their possession that may prove a defendant's innocence.

As Delaney calmed down and processed what he'd just learned, the look on his face went from anger to dismay. "I can't believe it," Delaney said. "Chastain has his faults. But I've never known the man to alter or withhold exculpatory evidence in any case, let alone a capital murder case. I'm in shock."

"We checked the video that was in the files you sent over to us and found a file that ended right at 5:36:15 a.m., less than one minute before the Camaro appeared on the screen. So we suspected Chastain didn't provide you with a complete copy," Elena said. "But we needed to show it to you to see if our suspicion was correct."

"What are you going to do with it?" Delaney asked.

"We're going to ask for a meeting with the lawyers in the attorney general's office who are defending the habeas case," Elena replied. "Even if they've looked at the video, I doubt they'd understand the significance of the black Camaro because none of them were involved in the investigation of the convenience store shooting. But we'll explain it to them and let you know what happens."

CHAPTER FORTY-EIGHT

Moments after Delaney left, Greg suggested to Elena that she ask for a meeting with LaToya as soon as possible. "Keep it vague because I want to watch their faces when we show them the video," he said. "Let 'em know we've got something that's extremely important for them to see."

Elena placed the call immediately. "Hi, LaToya, it's Elena Samuels. How are you doing today?"

"Fine, if you don't count the two briefs on my desk I need to finish reviewing today and a trial I have starting on Monday," Palmer said. "What can I do for you?"

"I think we need to get together so I can show you something," Elena replied. "I know your schedule is crammed, but can you squeeze fifteen minutes out of your day today or tomorrow?"

Palmer sighed. "How urgent is this?" she asked.

"Very," Elena replied. "I wouldn't ask otherwise. I have something you need to see, and not just for the benefit of my client."

"Well, I'm intrigued, but two of these briefs need to be filed by five o'clock today," Palmer said. "Can you come by at five thirty?"

•   •   •   •   •

When Greg and Elena walked into the Georgia Department of Law reception room, Palmer was standing at the desk talking to Elizabeth Austin. Although they'd never met, Elena recognized Austin from seeing her interviewed on the news several times about significant cases the AG's office was handling.

"Elena, this is Elizabeth Austin," Palmer said. "From the tone of your voice and the urgency of your request for a meeting, I've asked her to join us. I hope that's okay with you."

"Of course," Elena replied. "It's a pleasure to meet you. This is Greg Williams, the lead partner on the case. We appreciate you taking the time to hear what we have to say and, more importantly, to see what we have to show you."

"My pleasure," Austin said. "LaToya tells me you're a straight shooter. So am I. Let's go in my office." They sat at a conference table in a room that, Elena noticed, adjoined the attorney general's office. Austin offered coffee or soft drinks, but they declined.

"I promised to keep this short, so if you don't mind, let me explain why I asked for this meeting," Elena said. "I have two videos that I want to play for you. The first one is on a thumb drive that was produced by District Attorney Chastain to Michael Delaney, Owens's trial counsel, a few weeks before the trial."

Elena walked around the conference table and turned her computer around so Austin and Palmer could see the screen. "This is almost twenty minutes, and I'm glad to show you the entire recording if you'd like, but the significant part is at the end. So, to save time, I'll show you only the last few minutes, but I'll leave a copy of the thumb drive with you so you can view the entire recording at your convenience if you'd like."

Elena played the last three minutes of the video produced by Chastain to Delaney before the Owens trial. When it ended, the time displayed on the screen showed 5:36:15 a.m. on the morning of the murders. When it was over, Austin looked puzzled.

"What am I supposed to take from that?" she asked.

"The answer to your question is in the second video," Elena said. "You noticed, I trust, that this first video ended at 5:36 and fifteen seconds, which, based on the evidence at trial, would have been anywhere from six to ten minutes after the shootings." Austin and Palmer both nodded.

"That video is the one produced to Owens's trial attorney, Michael Delaney, by the district attorney before the trial," Elena said. "A few days ago, as LaToya knows, she sent us a box of items that Chastain had improperly withheld from Delaney based on his claim it was his office's work product, which is confidential. Among the items provided to us was a second, *almost* identical, video file. Again, I'm going to play the last few minutes of the second video file. I believe you'll understand why we're here once you see it."

Austin and Palmer watched as, in the last few seconds, the black Camaro raced across the screen, passing in front of the Harrington Diner. Both raised their eyebrows and had questioning looks on their faces. "I take it you're suggesting that the district attorney cut off the video he provided to Mr. Delaney just before that black car appeared in the video," Austin said.

"Exactly," Elena said.

"Okay. Is there some reason that black car is significant to your client's case?" Austin asked. "Because, honestly, I'm still not clear what your point is here."

"Ms. Austin," Elena said, "this video was taken from a camera outside of a convenience store located across the street from the diner. That convenience store had been robbed, and the attendant shot and killed, about three weeks before the murders of Mr. Tillotson and Mr. Gonzales."

"Go on," Austin said.

"The assailant remains unidentified and at large. But here's a photograph the police took from the very same video camera on the night of the convenience store robbery and murder. As you'll see, the car exiting the convenience store parking lot and turning left toward the interstate appears to be identical to the one seen at 5:37 a.m. on the video I just showed you."

Austin studied the photograph. "Run that last minute again, please," she asked.

After viewing the video again, Austin asked, "Ms. Samuels, are you absolutely certain that the video produced by Mr. Chastain's office to Mr. Delaney ended before the black car crossed in front of the diner?"

"Here's an affidavit from Mr. Delaney," Elena said, "attesting that the first video I showed you, which I've marked as Video File No. 1, was the only version he received from the district attorney's office. He also states, under oath, that until yesterday afternoon, when we showed him the video we've marked as Video File No. 2 containing the footage of the black car crossing in front of the restaurant at 5:37 a.m., he'd never been provided with or seen that footage."

Austin turned to Palmer. "To your knowledge, have there been any arrests in connection with the convenience store robbery and murder?"

"I don't recall hearing about any arrests in that case," Palmer said, "but I'll check on it first thing in the morning."

Austin thanked Elena and Greg for bringing the information to her attention and promised to investigate the situation expeditiously. "What are you asking the State to do based on this video?" she asked.

"We believe the State should move to vacate the conviction of Mr. Owens and dismiss all charges against him," Elena said. "If the DA had provided the complete video to Mike Delaney, he certainly would've argued that the driver of the black Camaro was the murderer in both the convenience store killing and the diner killings. So you know, Mr. Owens drove a 2006 white Ford Focus that didn't appear on this or any other video taken by cameras in the vicinity of the crime scene that night."

"We'll investigate this thoroughly," Austin said. "But I can't make any promises about what action, if any, the State will take until our investigation is complete. And that may take some time."

"Time is one thing our client doesn't have a lot of," Elena said. "So we'd ask that you expedite your investigation not just for his sake, but because if what we're saying here is right, a murderer who has struck twice and killed three people is on the loose, and could strike again at any time."

Then Greg, who had been sitting quietly, jumped in. "Respectfully," he said, "we also believe your office should investigate the circumstances under which the last forty-five seconds of this video was deleted, and an altered file produced to the defense in the Owens case. At the very least, it was unethical and should lead to disciplinary action being taken against anyone involved in such conduct. At worst, it may well have been a criminal act, but I leave that to your office to determine."

Austin stood up and shook hands with Elena and Greg. "We'll be in touch," she said.

Once they were outside, Greg looked at Elena and said, "Nicely done. I think you hit just the right tone and got their attention. It's got to scare them. It scares the hell outta me."

"We'll see," she said. "Getting their attention is one thing. Getting them to do something about it may be an entirely different matter."

CHAPTER FORTY-NINE

After completing an internal review of the case, Austin and Palmer met with Attorney General Josephine Marshall. The first Black woman to serve as attorney general in Georgia, Marshall had been elected on a platform of strongly supporting law enforcement so long as law enforcement played by the rules in its interactions with all citizens, including those who are Black, Hispanic, Asian, LGBTQ+, or other minorities.

"That certainly hasn't always been the case in Georgia," Marshall said during her campaign for office. "But it will be if I'm elected attorney general." Her background as a former police chief in a moderately sized city in south Georgia before going to law school and becoming a prosecutor gave her the creds to take such a position without being viewed as anti-law enforcement.

Austin emailed Marshall alerting her "to a serious issue that's arisen in a high-profile habeas case we're defending. Please let me know when you have time on your schedule for us to meet. It's urgent."

"Tomorrow 8:00 a.m.," Marshall responded almost instantly.

Austin and Palmer walked into the reception area of the attorney general's office at 7:50 a.m. the next morning. The reception area alone was as large as Austin's office and considerably better furnished. "Wow," LaToya whispered to Austin. It was her first time there.

"Maybe I should apply to be her assistant. I'd have a much larger, wooden desk, credenza, and a more comfortable desk chair."

"You wouldn't want the job," Austin whispered back. "She runs through assistants about every six months on average. The last one only hung around for three weeks."

"You may go in," the assistant said a few minutes later.

As Austin opened the large, wooden door with the Seal of the State of Georgia on it, Marshall was already out from behind her desk and walking toward the door to greet them. The office had burled-wood paneling and plush, blue carpeting. Marshall's large, ornately carved wooden desk sat in front of a matching credenza and bookshelves filled with law books.

"Wonderful to see you, Elizabeth," Marshall said. "It's been too long. And who's this?"

"General, allow me to introduce you to LaToya Palmer, one of our star assistant AGs. She's taking the lead on the Owens habeas case," Austin said.

"It's a pleasure to meet you, LaToya. How long have you been working here?"

"Eighteen months," LaToya replied. "I came over from the Atlanta City Attorney's office."

"Wonderful. Elizabeth is excellent to work with and a wonderful source of advice for young lawyers." Marshall paused a moment before adding with a smile, "And older lawyers as well." Then, turning to Austin, she asked, "What's up?"

"We have a problem with a murder prosecution that was tried up in Noonan County around eighteen months ago. It was the case involving the murder of two men in a restaurant known as the Harrington Diner. They were shot to death—one of them execution-style to the head—in the early morning hours as they were getting ready to open for the day."

"Noonan County, you say. That's Paul Chastain's jurisdiction. What's the problem?" Marshall asked. Austin turned to Palmer, who gave Marshall an overview of the murder and the trial before discussing the recent developments in the habeas case.

"The habeas lawyers, Greg Williams and Elena Samuels, are very sharp. They were on the verge of obtaining an order that would have compelled Chastain to identify, and justify having withheld from Owens's trial lawyer, anything he claimed was attorney work product. I offered, in advance of the court entering such an order, to review the documents myself and evaluate whether each was properly withheld. When I did, none of the documents qualified as work product.

"Most of it was irrelevant," Palmer continued, "but there was a thumb drive containing video of the front of the Harrington Diner on the morning of the shootings. In the last forty-five seconds, the video showed a black Camaro passing in front of the restaurant just minutes after the murders took place. That Camaro matched a car caught on video leaving the site of another unsolved robbery and murder—at a convenience store located *directly across the street* from the Harrington Diner—that took place just three weeks earlier."

"Wait," Marshall said. "Are you telling me that Paul Chastain withheld a thumb drive that would've pointed defense counsel toward someone other than Owens as the likely suspect in the diner murders?"

"It's worse than that," Austin said. "Chastain produced a similar, but not identical, version of the video file to Owens's defense counsel. That version had the final forty-five seconds of the video cut off."

"Oh, my God!" Marshall exclaimed. "How can that possibly be?"

"I can't imagine. There's just no question that, had the complete video been turned over to Delaney, he would've moved to have the case dismissed, which almost certainly would've been granted by Janice Hinton," Palmer replied. "And even if the case wasn't dismissed by the judge, the video almost certainly would've resulted in an acquittal."

"So, where are we now?" Marshall asked.

"Owens's lawyers are demanding that we move to vacate the conviction and release their client in the interest of justice."

"And what's your recommendation?"

"We think that if we refuse to vacate the conviction, Owens is all but certain to have his conviction overturned. Not only will Chastain look bad, but you'll also look bad for failing to act when presented with clear evidence of extremely serious—and I think, intentional—prosecutorial misconduct. But I don't think we should release Owens until we make our own independent investigation of the case and decide whether there's enough credible evidence to warrant a retrial."

Recalling her days as a police chief and later as a prosecutor, Marshall didn't take long to respond. "I agree," Marshall said, her face showing the pain of what she had to say next. "As you review the video and conduct your investigation, I want you to assess as best you can whether there's any chance this was an inadvertent error. If not, I also want you to assess, as best you can, whether there's credible evidence that Chastain, or anyone in his office, knowingly altered or caused someone else to alter the video on that thumb drive. I want to know who is responsible for this travesty of justice. You report that portion of your findings to me, and me alone, orally. Do you understand?"

"Yes, ma'am," Austin responded. "Understood."

"And make this your top priority," Marshall said. "There's a man sitting on death row who may not belong there."

Two days later, without making an appointment, Austin, Palmer, and an investigator from the AG's office showed up in the Noonan County District Attorney's Office. "I am Deputy Attorney General Elizabeth Austin and we're here to see the district attorney," Austin told the receptionist.

"Is he expecting you?" the receptionist asked.

"No," Austin replied.

"I'll have to check on whether he's available," the receptionist said. After disappearing for a couple of minutes, the receptionist returned and said, "Mr. Chastain is in a meeting and says it will be about thirty minutes. He asked me to have you each take a seat—"

"You tell Mr. Chastain to get out here right this minute!" Austin commanded.

The startled receptionist stood up and walked back toward Chastain's office. Moments later, an aggravated Chastain came flying out of his conference room and into the reception area.

"Who do you think you are, Ms. Austin?" he demanded. "You don't get to barge in here and interrupt my schedule without an appointment."

"Mr. Chastain, this is a subpoena *duces tecum* from Judge Parsons, who is presiding over the Joseph Owens habeas case, ordering you to turn over immediately all records, video discs, thumb drives, and other recordings of the video you recently produced to Mr. Owens's attorneys in that case. I also have here an emergency notice of deposition, approved by Judge Parsons, for the employee who was in charge of duplication of videos in the time leading up to the Owens trial."

Chastain, never known to be at a loss for words, was speechless. After a few moments, he said, "We'll need a few hours to review the subpoena and gather the materials listed in it. I can have it for you before the end of the day if that's satisfactory."

"When can I take the deposition of your employee? I don't expect it to take more than an hour or so, depending on what he or she has to say."

"I'll need to check on his availability. But may I ask what this is all about?"

"No, sir, you may not," Austin said coldly.

"Am I, or anyone in my office, the target of a criminal investigation being conducted by the Attorney General's Office?"

"At least for the moment, this is a civil investigation," Austin responded. "But that could change, depending on the evidence we uncover." Chastain stared at Austin for a few moments before turning and walking back to his office without saying another word.

The documents were turned over shortly before 6:00 p.m. and the deposition was scheduled for the following afternoon. The testimony confirmed that the video produced to Delaney shortly before Owens's trial lacked the last forty-five seconds, which showed the black Camaro passing in front of the diner. "Didn't happen while I was in the office, I can tell you that for sure," said Jesse Rutherford, Director of the DA's Division of Records.

"Who else in the office knows how to run the duplicating equipment on which this thumb drive was made?" Austin asked.

"My deputy director, Belinda Jones, and I are the only people allowed to use that equipment. Since I kinda had an idea of what you'd be asking about here today, I've already asked Belinda, and she said she knew nothing about anyone making a copy of the video on that thumb drive."

"How difficult would it be to make a copy that left out the last forty-five seconds?"

"The equipment is really pretty simple to use. There's a slot to insert the original thumb drive and another for the blank. When you push the button to make a copy, you either have to punch a button that says copy the whole thing, or otherwise you can enter a specific range of time if you don't want the whole thing copied, like copy from minute 2:30 to minute 4:30, or whatever you want."

"Could Mr. Chastain have made the copy himself?" Austin asked.

Rutherford appeared to be stunned by the question and stared at Austin, as if in disbelief that she would suggest such a thing. "I'm sorry, Ms. Austin, but I just don't believe Mr. Chastain would ever do such a thing. He's the most honorable man. . ."

"I'm not asking what you believe, Mr. Rutherford. My question is only whether it's possible that Mr. Chastain could have made the copy himself."

"Possible, I suppose, but highly unlikely."

"Who besides you and your deputy have access to the duplicating equipment?"

"Mr. Chastain, Mr. Maxwell, and all the department heads have keycards that would allow access to that room."

"And are electronic records kept of the cards used to access the room?"

"I reckon so, but I've never had occasion to ask."

"How about if we take a quick break for you to check on that. And, assuming such electronic records exist, bring me a printout here and now of everyone who accessed the room in which the copying device is kept during the three days prior to the date this office produced the thumb drive to Owens's lawyer."

When Rutherford returned twenty minutes later, he handed Austin a computer printout. "If I'm reading this correctly, Mr. Rutherford, it shows that three people other than yourself, including Mr. Chastain, entered the records room on the day before the thumb drive was produced to Mr. Owens's attorney, correct?"

"Yes, ma'am, that's what it shows."

"Two of the people apparently were in the room for only two or three minutes, but Mr. Chastain was in there for eleven minutes, correct?"

"Yes, ma'am."

"How long would it take to make a duplicate of the thumb drive?"

"Well, if you know what you're doing, just a few minutes."

"Less than eleven minutes?"

"Yes, ma'am."

Austin reported the results of the investigation to Marshall, who shook her head in dismay. "The video definitely was altered," Austin said, "even if we don't yet have proof of who altered it. But there's no question that it couldn't have happened without Chastain's implicit, if not explicit, approval and/or participation. Unfortunately, since we could not establish with certainty the date on which the copy of the thumb drive in question was made, the electronic access records maintained by the DA's office, while suggestive, are inconclusive."

Three weeks later, Elena received a call from Austin.

"Attorney General Marshall has directed me to move to vacate Mr. Owens's conviction based on the failure of the district attorney to turn over the complete video taken by the camera across the street from the diner," Austin told her. "However, the charges against Mr. Owens will remain in place, and he'll remain in prison, until the investigation is complete, and she decides whether to press any further charges."

In a press release, the attorney general stated that failing to produce the complete video "was, by any standard, unduly prejudicial to Mr. Owens's defense. The portion of the video that was withheld from his lawyers showed a black Camaro crossing in front of the Harrington Diner minutes after the shootings, and just three weeks after an apparently identical car, also with a single male occupant, was seen fleeing the scene of a murder at a convenience store across the street from the diner. The convenience store murder remains unsolved. Mr. Owens's defense counsel unquestionably was entitled to the complete video before the trial."

The decision wasn't just extraordinary. It was unprecedented in Georgia history.

Chapter Fifty

By the time they arrived at the office the next morning, Greg and Elena each had a pile of congratulatory messages waiting for them. There was a nonstop flow of lawyers coming by to shake their hands, including Fisher, Petroff, and Miller. Even Jack Stephenson, who was typically up to his eyeballs in federal tax cases, took the time to send a quick email saying, "Well done! Good PR for the firm."

"Congrats! When's the celebration?" Katherine Bergman asked.

"Thanks, Katherine," Greg said, "but Owens is still facing a retrial, so we've got more work to do to nail this down. No celebration until he's fully exonerated and released from prison."

"That makes good sense," Katherine replied, "but you and Elena deserve a lot of credit for getting it this far. I hope you can put it to bed before too long."

Around ten thirty, as he was getting off a call with a thrilled Rebecca Masters, there was a knock at his door. Greg turned to see Clay Morrisey standing there with a big smile on his face.

"I just wanted to offer my sincere congratulations," Clay said as he reached out to shake Greg's hand, "and to let you know that, despite those harsh words between us, I'm truly proud of what you've accomplished."

Greg remained seated at his desk, his facial expression revealing the anger he was feeling at Clay's two-faced offer of well-wishes. "Proud enough to restore the $50,000 you took out of my compensation for last year?" Greg fired back.

Clay's face turned sour. "Damn it, Greg, you know I can't go back and change last year's numbers. That money was paid to the partners out of last year's profits."

"I accept personal checks," Greg said sharply.

Clay glared icily at him.

"And so does Elena. I hope you're ashamed enough of what you did to me, but the $20,000 you took from her comp was utterly disgraceful."

"Go to hell, Greg," Clay said. "I warned you."

"You warned me? Is that what you call it?" Greg asked, as his face turned red and his voice rose so other attorneys and staff could hear him clearly in the hallway and adjoining offices. "I'd describe it as an unethical attempt to coerce me into ending the case quickly, even if it wasn't in our client's best interest. You would've had me sell out Owens by negotiating a plea deal that would've kept him in prison for decades for a crime he didn't commit."

Clay started to respond, but Greg wasn't finished. "Which, by the way," he continued, "you knew I would never do. *Never!*"

"Are you finished?" Clay asked contemptuously.

"What's really disgraceful, though," Greg continued as he came up out of his chair and was face-to-face with Clay, "was that you weren't satisfied with punishing me by cutting my distribution. No, you decided to whack Elena's compensation as well, even though she's had no control over what happened."

"Screw you, Greg," Clay shouted, his temper now burning out of control. "Oh, sorry, that's Elena's job." Greg froze, shocked beyond imagination by the hideous, sexist words his long-time friend and partner had just said to him. But before he could respond, Clay continued. "Y'know, I've never heard a word of complaint from Elena about her compensation. Not one word. But here you are complaining about it for her. Perhaps she's just a timid little girl who's afraid to speak for herself, so she lets her big, strong, boyfriend speak for her? Is that it?"

"No, I can speak for myself just fine," said Elena, who had stepped into the doorway of Greg's office in time to hear the sexist taunt. Clay's head swiveled around quickly to see Elena glaring at him. Instantly, a look of horror came across his face.

"So you know," Elena said in a calm tone that didn't reveal the anger and revulsion she was feeling at hearing Clay's words, "my complaint for your demeaning and sexist comments will be in the hands of the firm's general counsel and the members of the management committee before the end of the day. You have no business being a partner in this firm, let alone managing partner."

"Elena, I apologize. I sincerely and profusely apologize," Clay said as his face reddened. "Greg and I were having a terrible disagreement. I was angry and thoughtlessly struck back at him with the first words that came to mind. I never meant that as a disparagement of you."

"The hell you didn't," she said, her voice rising with each word. "Those words couldn't have come out of your mouth so quickly unless you already had such misogynistic thoughts about me in your mind. Now I understand why so few women progress to the top echelon of partners around here. We're nothing but window dressing to you. Figments of your vile, sexist imagination. I guess it's just women clients such as Carrie Melton, who pay the firm millions of dollars in fees, that you respect. Or do you?"

"Despite what you think, I'm truly sorry," Clay said, and stepped toward the door to leave Greg's office. Elena stared Clay down before stepping aside to let him pass.

But before he could get out the door, Greg spoke up. "Just so there are no more, quote, misunderstandings, I want to make sure you understand that the Owens case is not over."

"What the hell are you talking about?" Clay snapped. "I thought the State dismissed the case."

"They are vacating the conviction, but keeping Owens in prison on murder charges while they continue to investigate the murders. That ends the habeas case, but we're not going to walk away from Owens until he's fully exonerated."

"How much longer will that take?"

"I've no idea. But since you're so very proud of us, I'm confident we'll continue to have your full support for however long it takes, right?"

Clay stormed out of Greg's office without another word.

CHAPTER FIFTY-ONE

"Elena, we need to keep the heat on the AG's office," Greg said as they started the drive south to the prison to deliver the news of the State's decision to Owens. "I don't want Joseph to linger in jail for another day while they fool around trying to identify the murderer. He deserves to get his life back."

The now-familiar drive took them past mile after mile of undeveloped, wooded acreage filled with oak and pine trees amid overgrown brush, interrupted occasionally by billboards advertising gasoline stations and fast-food restaurants available at the next exit.

"How do you think he's going to react to the news?" Elena asked.

"It's going to be confusing for him. He won't understand why he's not being released immediately. And who can blame him? I don't understand it myself. They wouldn't have sufficient evidence to arrest him now, so how can they justify keeping him in prison?"

"They can't," Elena said. "But I guess they'll at least move him off death row, don't you think?

"I think so," Greg replied. "He's no longer under a death sentence, so there's no justification for keeping him on the row."

As they pulled into the parking lot in front of the prison, Elena asked, "Are you feeling okay about going back into the prison?"

"I'm good," Greg said with an air of confidence Elena hadn't seen in him during any prior visit to the prison. "Dr. Morrow thinks I've turned the corner. She says I'm doing a much better job of controlling my emotional reaction to the stimuli that brought on my panicked response."

"How do you feel about it?"

"Yeah, I definitely feel like I've made good progress. I'll keep seeing her for a while—probably a little less frequently—and if everything continues to go well, the visits will taper off over the next two or three months."

As they passed through security and walked to the conference room to wait for Joseph, Elena sensed that Greg had regained his confidence. His face no longer showed any trace of the anguish and fear that had overcome him during earlier visits.

Once Joseph came into the conference room, Greg said, "We have some very good news for you, but also a little bad news that we think is only temporary."

"Okay. So what's the good news?"

"The good news is that the State has agreed to vacate your conviction."

"What does that mean exactly?" Joseph asked.

"It means that, once the State files the necessary papers in court and the judge approves, you'll once again be an innocent man."

Joseph jumped to his feet, but Greg quickly said, "Wait, wait. Let me tell you the rest of it." As it became clear to Owens that he wouldn't be a free man anytime soon, his mood became somber.

"I wanna get *outta* here," he cried out. "I didn't kill nobody. I shouldn't be in here." Greg had to remind Joseph that he'd be getting off death row and that, while the State reserved the right to try him again, it wouldn't make that decision until after it concluded its investigation into the significance of the mysterious black Camaro.

"How long will that take?" Owens asked.

"We can't answer that for you," Elena replied. "But we're going to keep the pressure on. You have a right to a speedy trial under the

Constitution, but exactly what that means under these circumstances is hard to say. I know you're eager to go home to Jasmine, but as hard as this is, you need to be patient. "

"How patient would *you* be?" Owens asked.

"Not very," Elena conceded. "But the longer the State takes to decide, the more difficult it'll be to proceed against you. And if they do bring you to trial again, Michael Delaney will use the video of the black Camaro to create doubt in the mind of the jurors about whether the actual murderer has managed to evade justice. "

"No!" Owens replied sharply, shocking both of them. "I don't want Delaney to represent me at a new trial. He screwed up the first time. I want you two to be my lawyers."

"Joseph," Elena said, "Greg and I aren't criminal defense lawyers. Neither of us has ever represented a defendant in any criminal case. Not even in traffic court. You need an experienced criminal defense lawyer to represent you."

"Have you ever done one of these habeas cases before?" Owens asked.

When Elena shook her head, Owens said, "So you learned what you needed to know for this case, and you can do it again for a criminal trial. Besides, you say Delaney's experienced, but he didn't find out about this video. *You* did. I trust you, not him."

"This wasn't his fault," Elena said. "The district attorney altered the video, so Delaney never saw the black Camaro passing in front of the restaurant minutes after the murders." She immediately felt bad for not telling Owens it was Delaney's fault as well for not challenging Chastain's assertion of the work product privilege.

Before she could correct herself, however, Greg was explaining to Owens that the courts have special rules about which lawyers can represent defendants in death penalty cases. "Those rules require that the lead attorney have substantial experience in murder cases before representing a defendant in a capital case. We don't qualify. In fact, we don't have *any* criminal defense experience. So even if we were willing to represent you, the court wouldn't allow it."

Owens looked down and thought quietly for a few moments. "Okay, but you could help Delaney, right? And you could be there for the trial."

"If there ever *is* a second trial," Elena said. "We think there's a pretty good chance the State won't put you on trial again. Or, if you want to be a real optimist, it's possible the State will track down the driver of this black Camaro and decide he's the person who shot Tillotson and Gonzales. If they do that, they'll have to drop the charges against you."

"Yeah, right," Owens said. "You'll forgive me if I don't start celebrating just yet."

Greg looked a bit sheepish, turned to Elena, and saw a look on her face he had seen during other cases they'd handled together. She wanted to do it.

"I'll tell you what. We'll talk to our firm and to Delaney. If the firm and Delaney are agreeable, we'll work with him to try to persuade the attorney general to drop the charges against you and, if she refuses, we'll assist him in preparing for a new trial. That's all I'm prepared to say for now."

"You guys are the best," Owens said as a grin spread across his face.

PART THREE

CHAPTER FIFTY-TWO

On a desolate stretch of Interstate 10, about fifty miles west of Tallahassee, Trooper J. L. Ross of the Florida Highway Patrol was sitting on the median, concealed from westbound vehicles by an overpass, with his radar monitoring the speed of traffic. Suddenly, a flashing light alerted him to a car doing eighty-four miles per hour— nineteen miles per hour over the speed limit. Ross quickly flipped on his blue lights and took off in pursuit.

It took him a few minutes to catch up, but just before Exit 142, which provides access to the panhandle towns of Marianna and Blountstown, Ross notified FHP dispatch that the car had pulled over. He ran a check on the license tag, which was from Georgia. The check came back clean. Ross exited his cruiser and approached the car, a black 2014 Camaro, on the driver's side. It appeared to be occupied only by the driver. As he neared the vehicle, Ross could see that the driver had lowered his window and his hands were visible on top of the steering wheel.

"Driver's license, please," Ross said. The driver quickly handed over his license, which identified him as Craig Martin Young, a twenty-eight-year-old resident of Farnsworth, Georgia, a rural community thirty miles northwest of Atlanta. The name and address matched the vehicle registration information that was returned on the license tag check.

"Was I going too fast, Officer?" Young asked.

"It's trooper, not officer," Ross responded. "And yes, I clocked you at eighty-four miles per hour. The limit here is sixty-five. Have you been drinking alcohol this evening, Mr. Young?"

"No, sir," Young replied. "I'm driving to Mobile to visit some friends, and I'm running late, so I pulled off the interstate in Tallahassee to grab a burger and a shake to go, and was trying to make up some time. I've got the bag right here if you want to see it."

Ross said nothing, but took the license back to his patrol car. After a check of the Florida and national crime databases came back clean, he returned to the car and handed Young his driver's license along with a citation for speeding. "The citation shows you where and when you're to appear in court. If you don't want to contest the ticket, you can sign at the bottom and mail it to the court clerk with a check for $358. But if you don't either appear in court on the date shown or send in the ticket with a check before the scheduled court date, the court will issue a warrant for your arrest. Do you understand?"

"Yes, sir. I'm sorry, Trooper," he said.

"You don't have to apologize to me," Ross replied. "I'm not angry with you. Just slow down and drive safely."

"Yes, sir, thank you."

A couple of miles down the road, with the trooper no longer behind him, Young reached below his seat, pulled out a .45 caliber handgun, and returned it to the glove compartment.

CHAPTER FIFTY-THREE

"Hey, Captain," Shorter called out from his desk, "I've got somebody on the phone named Austin who says she works in the Attorney General's Office and wants to speak to you." Smith was on the phone catching up on old times with a buddy at the Atlanta Police Department.

"You know somebody named Austin in the AG's office?" he asked his friend.

"Elizabeth Austin?" his friend responded.

"I only know I have someone on the other line holding for me named Austin who claims to be in the AG's office."

"Take the call," his friend said. "If it's Elizabeth Austin, she's the Chief Deputy AG, number two in that office." Smith hung up with his buddy and picked up the other line. "This is Captain Smith. How can I help you?"

Austin introduced herself and told Smith she was reviewing the Harrington Diner double murder case and needed to meet with him to discuss an issue that had arisen. "How about 10:00 a.m. tomorrow at my office?"

"In Atlanta? Ms. Austin, my schedule's full up. Can we possibly do this by phone?"

"Captain, as you may be aware, our office has agreed to vacate the conviction of Joseph Owens. We're now—"

"You did *what*?" Smith screamed into the phone so loud that everyone else in the office stopped what they were doing and stared through the glass window at him. "That was a righteous investigation. I led the investigation personally. Why on earth would you even *think* about letting Owens go free?"

"Slow down, Captain. We haven't decided to release Owens. He's still in prison and will remain there until we conclude our inquiry. As I was saying, we're trying to decide whether to retry him. It would help Attorney General Marshall and me very much to review with you certain evidence that's critical to our decision. Now, if you have a scheduling problem, I'd be glad to speak to your chief to free you up for the meeting."

Smith got the message loud and clear. "What time did you say you want me there?"

"Ten in the morning."

"Got it."

CHAPTER FIFTY-FOUR

At exactly 10:00 a.m. the next day, Smith walked into the reception area of the Georgia Department of Law and told the receptionist he was there for a meeting with Elizabeth Austin.

"Yes, Captain, she's expecting you," the receptionist said. "Please have a seat, and I'll let her know you're here." Five minutes later, Austin walked into the reception area and introduced herself to Smith. "Thank you so much for making the trip here on such short notice."

"No problem," he replied, even as he grumbled to himself about her rather unsubtle offer to call his chief to free him up for the meeting.

Austin led Smith through a different door from the one through which she had entered the reception area. Following Austin into an ante room and then an inner office, Smith recognized Attorney General Marshall, who stood up from behind her desk and strode across the large office toward him. The participation of the attorney general not only was a surprise, it put Smith on edge.

"Pleasure to meet you, Captain," Marshall said as they shook hands. "Thank you for making time in your busy schedule to visit with us this morning."

"Always glad to assist the State Law Department in any way I can."

"You've met Chief Deputy Attorney General Austin, and we're also joined by Deputy Attorney General LaToya Palmer, who'll explain why we asked you here today."

Palmer started the discussion by telling Smith she was the attorney handling the day-to-day work in the habeas lawsuit filed by the new lawyers for Owens. "This isn't Michael Delaney we're dealing with anymore," she said. "These lawyers are from Fox Stern, one of the top law firms in the state, and the firm has assigned a team of their best attorneys to get Owens freed.

"One of the first steps the Fox Stern lawyers took was to demand production of all documents relating to the Owens prosecution in the district attorney's possession, including documents that the DA withheld from Mr. Delaney on the basis they qualified as attorney work product.

"I'm not going to bore you with an explanation of attorney work product, but the important thing is that I reviewed everything the DA withheld to be sure they properly classified it as work product. Regrettably, none of those documents were work product, so we had to turn them over to Fox Stern."

"Okay," Smith said impatiently. "So what?"

"Captain, you're leading the investigation into the robbery and murder that took place at the convenience store across the street from the diner about three weeks before the Harrington Diner murders, correct?"

"Yes. Unfortunately, we've not been able to identify the suspect in that case. We're still searching for him, but we've pretty much run into a dead end. Why do you ask?"

Austin jumped in at that point. "Did the police consider the possibility that the same person who robbed the convenience store and shot the attendant there also committed the diner murders?"

"Of course we considered it, being that the crime scenes were just across the road from each other and the shootings were so close in time.

But we saw nothing to make us think it was the same perpetrator. All the evidence we gathered in the diner shootings pointed to Owens, who had motive, since he'd been fired a few days before the shootings, and was known to have an explosive temper. He also had opportunity since he knew when Tillotson and Gonzales arrived each morning and when other employees would show up at the restaurant. And since his wife worked the night shift that night, nobody would've known if he'd left the house for a couple of hours."

Austin nodded at Palmer, who picked up a thumb drive and placed it into a video player. "Captain, did you see the video that was taken on the night of the diner shootings by the surveillance camera at the convenience store?" Palmer asked.

"Yes, I'm certain I looked at that."

"I'm going to show you the last two minutes of that recording. Take a look and let me know if this is the videotape you saw during your investigation."

"I think that's the same video I saw. But to tell you the truth, I really can't say for sure. It's been too long since I last looked at it. Was this taken from our file?"

"No, this came from the district attorney's work product file. Let me ask you to look again at the last minute of the video and focus on the car that passes in front of the diner in the eastbound lane." As the video file reached the last minute, Smith appeared to be startled. "Wait, I know I haven't seen that last scene before. You say it was in Mr. Chastain's files?"

"Yes, it was in a box in the DA's storage room. When we reviewed the thumb drive, we realized the work product doctrine did not protect the video from disclosure, so we turned it over to Owens's habeas lawyers, who showed it to Delaney. That's when you-know-what hit the fan. Delaney realized the DA had duped him, because the video file they'd given him didn't contain the last forty-five seconds in which the black Camaro appeared."

"Are you suggesting that the black car appearing at the end of the video is the same one the assailant used to flee from the convenience store killing three weeks earlier?" he asked.

"We don't know for sure," Marshall said. "But certainly it was something that should have been investigated and considered before charging Owens."

"I agree," Smith said.

"So there are two separate issues we're dealing with here. First, without question, Owens's trial lawyer was entitled to receive this complete video and to argue to the jury that the black Camaro provided a reasonable doubt about whether Owens was guilty."

"No question," Smith said.

"The second issue, of course, is whether you saw this complete video and properly followed up on the presence of a black Camaro at the diner at the time of the murders."

"General Marshall," Smith said, "I want to assure you that I've not seen the last minute of this video before this moment. Had I seen it, we would've spared no effort to identify the driver of the Camaro before taking any action against Owens."

"C'mon, Captain, your detectives were the ones who would've obtained this video from the convenience store as part of their investigation. Do you seriously expect me to believe they didn't show it to you immediately?"

"I can't explain how this happened sitting here now, but I've not seen the video of the Camaro passing in front of the diner until today," Smith replied. "Let me assure you I'll look into this immediately and determine who was responsible for obtaining and reviewing the video, and why it wasn't brought to my attention."

"If you'd seen this video, Captain, you would've thought twice before charging Owens, wouldn't you agree?"

"That was the DA's decision, not mine."

"Did you tell Mr. Chastain you disagreed with his decision?"

"Not to be disrespectful, General, but do you know Mr. Chastain very well?"

"Only by reputation," she said.

"Well, I can tell you that once he makes a charging decision, he's not interested in hearing anyone else's opinion, including mine. And there certainly was more than enough evidence to charge Owens at the time."

"Only if you disregarded this video."

"Or hadn't seen it."

Marshall looked at him dubiously. Then she took the thumb drive out of the player and handed it to him. "It's not too late to investigate further, Captain. This is an extra thumb drive for you. Study it and let us know ASAP whether it causes you to think differently about the case. We have twenty-eight days to respond to a motion filed in the trial court filed by Michael Delaney to reopen the case and to dismiss all charges against his client for prosecutorial misconduct and based on actual innocence."

After he left, Marshall told Austin and Palmer she thought Smith was lying. "His story's just not credible," she said. "I've been in his shoes when I was a police captain and later as a police chief. There's just no way the captain in charge of the investigation wouldn't have reviewed every minute of all the crime scene video obtained during the investigation. And even assuming for a moment that he didn't immediately recognize it as a Camaro, which is unimaginable coming just three weeks after the convenience store murder, at a bare minimum he would've ordered his subordinates to have the car's make and model identified."

Austin nodded her agreement.

"He had to know," Marshall said. "Something's just not right here."

Back in his car, Smith reflected on the meeting. It left him with a bad feeling, one he had never experienced during his career in law enforcement. He knew his integrity and reputation were at issue, and he needed to try to get ahead of it fast. On his way back to Harrington, he called Detective Gloria Riggs.

"Gloria, get everyone who worked on the Owens case together and have them in the conference room for a meeting at one o'clock," he said. "There's been a new development."

"Okay, Captain," Riggs said. "But it's Stone's day off."

"I don't care," Smith said. "Locate him and tell him to get his ass into the station. We've got a problem."

CHAPTER FIFTY-FIVE

"Greg, you're unusually quiet this evening," Elena said as they sat in the living room enjoying a second glass of cabernet sauvignon from a bottle Greg had opened for dinner. "Is everything okay?"

"Everything's fine," he said. "I just have a few things on my mind."

"For instance?"

"I'm thinking about the confrontation with Clay last week. Obviously, we're going to do everything we need to do for Joseph. But I think we've reached the point of no return at Fox Stern."

"What do you mean?"

"I mean our support within the firm has evaporated. Whoosh! Gone. Clay wouldn't behave the way he did unless he was feeling the heat from some of the big hitters in the firm who want an ever-increasing share of the profits. It's disappointing and disheartening, after all these years, but times have changed in the law business, and not for the better as far as I'm concerned."

"I'll tell you what it means to me," Elena said. "It means this firm has lost its way. All Clay wants is to drive up net profits in order to merge with a national firm based in New York, LA, or Chicago, that has even higher net profits. I've sensed that for some time. And I'm not the only one around here who thinks so."

"It makes sense," he replied. "Clay's always wanted the firm to be the most profitable in Atlanta. Now that he's there, he wants to take it a step farther and move onto the national stage."

"We need to find another place to work," Elena said. "Someplace where we can make a good living, but where the partnership's commitment to equal justice for all is real, not just a bunch of happy talk to make law students feel good about coming to work there."

"I agree. Completely. Between us, I'm confident we've got enough clients we can take with us to attract interest from other firms. But first things first. We've got a commitment to Owens that we have to meet regardless of whether we're getting paid for it, and it's not realistic to move firms in the middle of the case. So let's buckle down, do what we need to do for our client, and return to this discussion once he's free."

Elena nodded.

"By the way, did you actually file a complaint against Clay for what he said about you?"

"I surely did. And I'm serious about it."

"What are you asking the management committee to do?"

"I asked that Clay be required to attend gender equity training and to apologize to both of us in front of the entire partnership. I also asked that his compensation be cut $25,000 and the money be contributed to the Georgia Women Lawyers Foundation to support gender equity training programs."

"Well done! I'm not overly optimistic, but I hope the management committee will have the backbone to do something meaningful."

"We'll see," Elena said. "One of the management committee members reached out to ask some questions two days ago. I expect I'll be hearing from them very soon."

CHAPTER FIFTY-SIX

"First," Smith barked as soon as he closed the door to the conference room, "what we discuss in here stays in here. Nobody is to say a word outside of this room about what we're going to talk about now. Not today, not tomorrow, not ever. Not with the chief, not with your spouses, not with your dogs. Do each of you understand what I'm saying?"

They all nodded their heads.

"Riggs, do you understand?"

"Yes," she said.

"Harris?"

"Yes, got it, Captain," he said.

"Stone?"

"No problem, Captain. I understand."

Each of the detectives listened quietly as Smith told them what transpired at the meeting in the AG's office and how he responded to the questions relating to the black Camaro. "What's unbelievable," he said, "is that the original thumb drive remained in the DA's records. Somebody's going to lose their job over that."

"Where do we go from here, Captain?" Riggs asked.

"I'm going to have a drink with Chastain this evening after work to tell him we're reopening the investigation into the diner murders.

Frankly, I don't think it'll get us anywhere, but we've got no choice. One of you send out an APB with a description of the Camaro and photos taken from the video at the convenience store shooting and at the diner shootings. Let me know immediately if we get any responses.

"In the meantime, I want the three of you to review your files in both cases. Go back over your interview notes and see if there are any stones left unturned. Review all the evidence to see if we've missed something that would lead us in a new direction. We'll get together to discuss it again first thing tomorrow. Understood?"

All three detectives nodded.

Driving to the meeting with Chastain, Smith went over and over in his mind how he'd come to be in this fix. He'd had doubts when Chastain insisted on bringing the charges, but Chastain wasn't hearing any of it. Then, as the DA built his case against Owens, Smith actually came to believe it was Owens who killed Tillotson and Gonzales. All the pieces seemed to fit, especially once the New Jersey organized crime connection and the .45 missing from the pawnshop came to light. Now, however, the doubts had resurfaced. The presence of the black Camaro was even more troubling in the absence of any video showing Owens's white Ford Focus anywhere near the crime scene on the morning of the diner murders. Smith had pushed that issue out of his mind as he pursued Owens. Now, however, he couldn't ignore it any longer.

They met at the Blue Mountain Pub, a favorite watering hole in Stone Valley, just a fifteen-minute drive from Harrington, and sat at a booth in the back corner. When the waiter came over, they ordered a couple of beers. Smith handed the waiter a $20 bill and asked him to keep the booth next to them empty.

"Why the hell'd you keep that thumb drive?" Smith asked.

"I didn't know we kept it," Chastain said. "I told Carson it was a duplicate of what we had in the file and could be discarded, but I guess he either forgot or misunderstood. We got a break when Delaney didn't push to review the original before the trial after I classified it as work product. But these new lawyers are damn hound dogs. They don't let up once they get the scent. There's nothing I can do about it now but plead harmless error."

Smith looked at him in disbelief. "Harmless error? The AG is going to kick Owens free unless we come up with something better than that. They've got twenty-seven days left to respond to a dismissal motion filed by Owens's lawyer, and they're looking to us to explain why we didn't attempt to identify the Camaro driver before charging Owens."

"Easy for them to say. They weren't facing reelection with two unsolved murder cases and three victims hanging over their heads. The television stations and newspapers were eating us alive. I had to do something."

"Well, what are you going to do now? I don't think Marshall is going to let this go without finding out who is to blame for Owens's wrongful conviction. And when she figures it out, heads are going to roll."

"Just relax," Chastain said. "We can ride this out."

"*You* can ride it out," Smith shot back. "You've been reelected and announced you'll be retiring at the end of this term. But I'm twelve years shy of being eligible for full retirement. If Marshall gets the notion that I didn't pursue every piece of evidence regardless of where it might lead, my career is over and I'm totally screwed."

"My lips are sealed," Chastain assured him. "Besides, we still don't know if the Camaro driver who shot the convenience store clerk also was the person who shot the diner victims. It might have been just a coincidence that an identical black Camaro happened to be in the wrong place at the wrong time. There's just no way to know."

"Oh, please! This isn't a scene out of *My Cousin Vinny*," Smith said, his voice dripping with sarcasm. "This is real life. I told you we needed to run down that Camaro and you went ahead with charging Owens, anyway."

"I had no choice. The community might have eventually forgotten about the old guy killed in the convenience store. He was a widower and didn't have any survivors. But the widows and young children of the victims at the diner were another matter entirely. That was not going away until the killer was captured and convicted."

"I'm going to pursue any new leads that turn up on the convenience store murder," he told Chastain, "including renewing our search for the black Camaro. But I won't make any public statements about reopening the investigation."

"Okay. I appreciate that."

"Unless we manage to find the Camaro and its driver. If we do, all bets are off."

CHAPTER FIFTY-SEVEN

Smith was sipping his coffee and enjoying a chocolate glazed donut Carole had brought in that morning, pondering next steps in the convenience store investigation, when his phone rang. "Smith," he said as he picked up the phone.

"Captain Smith, this is Trooper J. L. Ross of the Florida Highway Patrol. I just saw your APB, and I may have stopped your suspect in a black Camaro two nights ago for speeding along I-10 in North Florida."

"Hold on, Trooper, while I get my sergeant in here to hear what you have to say." Smith put down his donut and yelled out for Riggs to get into his office immediately. "Okay, Trooper Ross, I have Sergeant Riggs with me. Please tell us about the Camaro you stopped two days ago."

Ross told them about the stop and his exchange with the driver. "He had a Georgia driver's license that identified him as Craig Martin Young, a white male, twenty-eight years of age, and a resident of Farnsworth, Georgia. I can email you a copy of the speeding citation I issued to him. It'll give you all of his personal information and his license tag number. The only thing is the car is a 2014 model, not a 2012 or '13 as stated in your APB. But I checked and Chevy made just a few, relatively minor, changes to the 2014 Camaro, so it easily could have been mistaken for the earlier model."

"Okay," Smith said, "we might've been off on that. Can you give us a description of the driver?"

"I didn't ask him to exit his vehicle, but I'd guess he was about six feet tall, husky build, fair skin, and brown hair cut short."

"Did you notice whether he had a mole on his chin?"

"Sorry, Captain, I didn't. But I certainly might have missed something like that so late at night."

Riggs asked about Young's demeanor.

"Courteous and compliant. Apologized for speeding," Ross said. "I asked him if he'd been drinking and he denied doing so. His driving was fast, but not erratic. He spoke clearly and responded to my questions, so I didn't have any reason to question him further or to conduct a sobriety test."

"Trooper, you've made my day. Please email the citation as soon as you can so we can get out an updated APB. We owe you a big one."

"Oh, and by the way, I don't know whether he was telling the truth, but Young told me he was heading from Atlanta to Mobile to visit a friend," Ross said.

As soon as he received the citation, Smith gave it to Riggs, who issued the updated APB within thirty minutes. It showed the suspect may have been stopped two days earlier driving a black 2014 Camaro on I-10 near Marianna, Florida, and was believed to be headed west toward Mobile, Alabama. "The suspect," it went on, "is wanted for questioning in connection with an investigation into a robbery and murder at a convenience store in Harrington, Noonan County, Georgia. He should be considered armed and extremely dangerous. Approach with caution."

When Riggs left his office, Smith called Chastain.

"Paul, we just received what may be a significant lead on the Camaro," Smith said. He waited a moment for a reply, but Chastain said nothing, so he continued. "A black Camaro with Georgia tags was stopped by a Florida Highway Patrol trooper heading west on I-10 two nights ago. We have a copy of the operator's driver's license and the license tag number, so we're issuing an updated APB."

"Okay," Chastain replied. "But that doesn't make him our suspect in either of the shootings."

"Paul, the driver's a resident of Farnsworth," Smith said. "From the photo on his driver's license and the description the trooper gave me, he matches up pretty well with the guy we saw on the video running out of the convenience store."

"Okay," Chastain replied, somewhat brusquely. "But that's only one murder. Keep me updated."

Riggs assigned Harris to lead the investigation into Young. "I want to know everything there is to know about him. Get down to Farnsworth ASAP. Keep me updated and let me know *immediately* if you find anything, no matter how remote or seemingly insignificant, that connects him to either of the crime scenes."

Chapter Fifty-Eight

The next morning, after giving a courtesy call to the Farnsworth police, Harris and Stone headed there to dig up any background information they could find about Young. The address on his driver's license turned out to be an old, dilapidated house on a dirt road. There was no answer when Harris knocked at the door and no cars in the driveway.

There were four other houses on the street, so Harris and Stone each took two of them. Nobody was home at the first house Stone approached. But as he walked up the driveway to the second house, an elderly man in overalls and using a cane came outside onto the porch.

"What's your business?" the man asked.

Stone showed him his badge and said he was looking for information about the guy who lived down the street, gesturing toward Young's house.

"Don't know his name. Not very neighborly-like. As fer as I can tell, he keeps to hisself. Don't seem to have many visitors. At least, I ain't never seen no other cars in the driveway. He in some kinda trouble?"

"I just want to talk to him," Stone replied. He asked how long it had been since the man had seen Young.

"Three, maybe four, days, as best I kin recollect." After a pause, he added, "I'm thinkin' it was three days ago."

"Can I leave my card with you and ask you to call if you see him about?"

"Okay, just s'long as you don't tell him how you found out he was there. I don't want him comin' over here and shootin' up my place."

"Why do you think he would shoot up your place?"

"Cause that's what he's doin' most of the time. Hardly an afternoon goes by that he's not firin' off a gun or a rifle of some kind or 'nother, taking target practice out in his backyard. One time I saw him firin' at some birds that were flyin' over his yard. I went over there and asked him why he was shootin' at the birds, and he just said somethin' like, 'well, them birds invaded my airspace.' I'm a-tellin' ya, there's a screw or two loose in that fella's brain. I reported it to the police, and they sent someone 'round, but it didn't do no good at all."

"How long ago was that?"

"Oh, I 'spect it was a good two or three months ago."

Back in their car, Stone told Harris about the elderly man's comments. "Sounds like Mr. Young is just a little off. This guy says he called the police on him a few months back for firing his gun at birds who were flying over his backyard. Let's see if we can find the report on that and talk to whoever came out here."

"We also need to get a search warrant for Young's house," Harris said. "If he's cleared out, we may not find much of anything. But it's worth a look."

Stone tracked down the Farnsworth police officer who responded to the initial call from the neighbor. Officer Peggie Gibbons told Stone the man who came to the door that evening was a white male, about six feet tall, around 180 to 190 pounds. "He was polite, responsive to my questions, but clueless—or pretending to be clueless—about there being any problem taking target practice in his backyard. I told him firing weapons is illegal in a residential neighborhood except to defend himself against attack, which didn't include birds flying over his backyard," she said with a bit of a chuckle. "He said he hadn't realized that. Really. I don't think he was being coy."

Stone shook his head in disbelief. "Anything else?" he asked.

"I asked permission to enter and walk through the house to make sure everything was okay, and he immediately stepped aside. I walked into each room and then stepped into the backyard, but saw nothing out of the ordinary. So I cautioned him again and left."

The next day, with the warrant in hand, Harris, Stone, and a forensic team arrived at Young's house. After forcing open the door, Harris worked with the group that searched inside the house, which appeared to have been vacated. Stone worked with a team that combed through the backyard with the help of a metal detector.

About an hour after they arrived, Stone came walking into the house, went up to Harris, and said, "Guess what we found out back?" He held up two sealed evidence bags containing an assortment of thirty-six empty shell casings. "How much you wanna bet that at least a few of these were fired from a .45 caliber gun?" Stone sent the shells to the Georgia Bureau of Investigation crime lab, which took just one week to send back its report. "Twenty-six shells were from an AK-47 and fourteen shells were from a .45 handgun," it said.

Then came the stunner.

"A comparison of the .45 caliber shells found in the backyard of the Young property in Farnsworth to the shells recovered by Harrington Police from the crime scene at the Harrington Diner show virtually identical markings on both sets of shells," the GBI report stated. "Consequently, it is highly probable the weapon fired in the backyard of the Farnsworth residence of Mr. Young was the same weapon used in the murders at the Harrington Diner."

Smith issued an urgent update to the APB within an hour saying, "Young is wanted in connection with a second murder investigation involving two additional victims shot to death during a robbery at the Harrington Diner. Extreme caution should be used in approaching the suspect, who also is suspected of committing an unsolved robbery and murder at a convenience store located across the street from the diner."

CHAPTER FIFTY-NINE

Greg and Elena were enjoying a quiet Friday night at home, snuggled on the couch, and watching the movie version of *To Kill a Mockingbird*, Elena's all-time favorite book, when Greg's cellphone rang shortly after nine thirty.

"Whoever it is will leave a message," Elena quickly said, knowing it was a futile effort to keep Greg from answering his phone and destroying the romantic moment.

"Hello," Greg said.

"Mr. Williams, this is Captain Smith of the Harrington Police Department."

"Hello, Captain," said Greg, more than a bit surprised by the call. "What can I do for you?"

"It's the other way around. I just thought you'd like to know we've gotten a lead on the black Camaro. With a little luck, we may have this guy in custody before too long."

"Where is he?"

"I can't share that information since this is an ongoing investigation. I've probably already crossed the line, but I wanted to give you a heads-up because evidence we've uncovered in the course of our investigation ties this guy to the Harrington Diner murders, as well as to the convenience store murder."

Greg was stunned. He remained silent for a few seconds, contemplating what Smith had just revealed to him. Elena was staring at him with a look of concern mixed with bewilderment on her face. "Captain, I'm sure you understand, but regardless of whether you catch this guy, we'll need you to share on the record, at the appropriate time, the new information your investigation has developed."

"I do understand. But that's beyond my pay grade. Any disclosure will have to come through the Attorney General's Office, so it may take a few days. If you don't mind, please wait for them to contact you, and don't let on that I've tipped you off. I wouldn't want to get called on the carpet for speaking with you before letting them know about this development."

"Of course. I'm very, *very* grateful. And not to look a gift horse in the mouth, but do you mind if I ask why you decided to call me this evening?"

"Well," he said, drawing the word out for a second or two while he thought about his answer, "let's just say I felt like I owed you one."

"For what?" a startled Greg asked.

After a few more seconds of silence, Smith said, "The donuts. Those were damn good donuts you brought to the station a few months ago." Before Greg could say a word, he heard the line disconnect. Then he put his telephone down, looked at Elena, and just grinned.

Elena, desperate to know what the call was about and baffled by Greg's big smile, jumped up and said, "What was that all about?"

"You're not going to believe me if I tell you."

"Believe *what*? Who was that?"

"We can start thinking about where we want to go," he said.

"Go? Go when? Go where? We can't think about a vacation until the Owens case is over."

"It's over."

"What?" Elena gasped.

"That was Captain Smith," he said. "He wanted to tell me confidentially, even before he tells the AG's Office, that they have new evidence that links the person who killed the convenience store clerk to the murders at the diner."

Elena's jaw dropped open. "Oh, my God! Oh, my God! What is it? Tell me what it is."

"He didn't tell me what the new evidence is," Greg said. "He said he would tell the AG's Office, and we'd hear from them in a few days."

"Do they have the suspect in custody?"

"Apparently not yet, but he seemed confident they'd have him before too long. I guess it's just a matter of time now."

"Did he say why he was tipping you off in advance?"

"Yes. Donuts."

"What?" Elena exclaimed.

"He said he owed me one, and when I asked why, he went silent for a few seconds and then he said it's because of the donuts I brought to the police station when I went to see him."

Elena stared at him with raised eyebrows and a dubious look on her face.

"That's what he said. I guess they worked," he said as they snuggled back up on the couch and resumed watching as Atticus Finch valiantly tried to save his client from the gallows.

CHAPTER SIXTY

Young wasn't sure where he was heading in the long run. But following his encounter with the Florida Highway Patrol trooper on I-10, he decided it would be best to get off the interstate. After deciding to spend the night in a motel in Pensacola rather than going on to Mobile, Young drove north on Highway 29. When he reached Andalusia, Alabama, he decided to head west on Highway 84.

Young had a cousin who lived in Louisiana, just south of Shreveport, where he could hide out for a while. Winding through Alabama and into Mississippi, he spent the night in a motel near Natchez. The next morning, Young continued west on Highway 84, which took him through central Louisiana. As he approached Interstate 49, Young noticed a car trailing about fifty yards behind him that he'd first noticed soon after he'd passed Winnfield. It made him uncomfortable, so he sped up, and felt relieved when the other car disappeared from his rear-view mirror.

Not long after, as he neared the intersection with Highway 171, where he would turn north toward his cousin's home in Mansfield, Young came around a curve and saw a Louisiana State Police patrol car about twenty yards ahead, blocking both lanes, with its lights flashing. As Young hit the brakes, two police officers, who stood behind the open car doors with guns drawn, yelled at him to get out of his car slowly with his hands showing.

For a split-second, Young thought about trying to flee by making a U-turn. But a quick look in his rearview mirror revealed the unmarked car that had been following him, now blocking the road heading east, with blue lights flashing through its windshield and on its front grill. Two more officers stood behind their opened car doors, also with guns trained on him.

He rolled down his window and yelled out that he was surrendering, then held his empty hands out through the window. Young slowly reached down with his right hand and opened the door. As he got out, keeping his hands raised, two officers approached him, while the others kept their guns trained on him.

"This must be some kind of mistake," Young said to the officer who told him to turn around, place his hands on the top of his car, and spread his legs. "I'm just heading up to Mansfield to visit my cousin."

The officer remained silent as he pulled Young's arms behind him, put him in handcuffs, and told him he was under arrest.

"What am I being arrested for?"

"Murder and armed robbery," the officer replied coldly, offering no more details. Young said nothing. Once he was in the patrol car, he asked where he was being taken.

"The Shreveport jail," the officer said, "at least until they can send you back to Georgia."

A few hours later, a Shreveport jail officer came to his cell and put Young back in handcuffs. Then he took Young to a small conference room partitioned by bulletproof glass. A woman sat on the other side of the glass.

"You have fifteen minutes," the officer said.

"Who are you?" Young asked the woman after she picked up the telephone receiver on her side of the partition.

"My name's Jennie Sanders and I'm your court-appointed lawyer. For now, anyway. Once you're returned to Georgia, there'll be a public defender there assigned to represent you, unless you're able to pay for a lawyer."

"What am I charged with?"

"Three counts of murder and two counts of armed robbery. What I need to know is whether you're willing to waive extradition proceedings, which is the formal process by which one state asks another state to turn over a prisoner to face charges in the requesting state. If you waive extradition, they will transfer you to Georgia within a few days. If you don't, we can delay things and make Georgia jump through a bunch of legal hoops, but ultimately, extradition is a virtual certainty."

Young thought for a few minutes. "I'm in no hurry to go back to Georgia. Maybe we can negotiate something. But for now, I want to fight it."

"Okay. I'll prepare the papers to challenge extradition. But if you want to negotiate with the DA in Georgia, I suggest you do so quickly. If so, I'm going to have to get a Georgia lawyer involved. Is that okay with you?"

"Sure," he replied.

"Can you afford to hire a lawyer?"

"No, sorry."

"That's okay. I'll check with the public defender's office that serves the Harrington area." The Georgia public defender assigned to represent Young was Roger Castillo. Sanders told Castillo that Young wanted to negotiate a deal to waive extradition in return for Chastain taking the death penalty off the table.

"That just isn't going to fly," Castillo said. "The DA knows Young will lose his fight to avoid extradition, so agreeing to come back voluntarily won't be enough of an incentive to get him to the negotiating table. But I'll talk to him and see what I can do."

A few hours later, Castillo called Sanders to say that, as expected, Chastain rejected the offer out of hand. "But the DA said something really interesting. He said that if Young will plead guilty to the two murders at the diner and to another robbery and murder that took place three weeks earlier at a convenience store across the road from the diner, there might be something to talk about in terms of avoiding the death penalty. That's not an offer, of course, but talk to Young and let me know if he's interested in discussing it."

Sanders asked Castillo if he had any idea why the DA might agree to such a deal.

"I'm only guessing here," Castillo said, "but he's taken intense heat for seeking and getting the death penalty against an innocent man. And rightly so, especially since he did it during a bitterly contested reelection campaign. I also think he's concerned that, with all the publicity the Owens exoneration has received, it'll be difficult for him to persuade another jury to sentence a different defendant to death for the same crimes. Bottom line is he wants to save face and get all of this behind him."

CHAPTER SIXTY-ONE

Sanders went to the Shreveport jail first thing in the morning. When she explained to Young how the DA reacted to the proposal, he surprised her. "I thought that's what he'd say. I wanna talk to the Georgia lawyer. Can you work that out?"

It took a little doing, including a call from Chastain to his counterpart in Shreveport, who called the warden of the Shreveport jail. The next day, a three-way call between Castillo, Sanders, and Young took place. Young wanted Castillo's opinion on the likelihood of a jury giving him the death penalty if he pled not guilty, but was convicted of the three murders.

"There's going to be some resistance in the county for sure because of the wrongful conviction of Owens," Castillo said. "But here's the problem. If I was Chastain, I'd tell the jury that because you kept quiet while Owens, an innocent man, was put on trial, convicted, and sentenced to death for your crimes, you should be put in the position that Owens was in after his conviction. That argument, frankly, is likely to have some appeal to jurors."

"So, what's your advice?"

"I wouldn't take that chance. Especially because of another development I learned about this morning."

"Oh?" Young said. "What recent development?"

"The Louisiana authorities recovered a .45 caliber handgun from your car after your arrest. I assume that's not a surprise to you."

Young didn't respond. After a few seconds of silence, Castillo continued. "Chastain told me the Harrington Police Department found two empty shell casings at the Harrington Diner on the morning of the murders, which established that the perpetrator shot the victims with a .45 caliber weapon. They also obtained a search warrant for your home in Farnsworth, and the search turned up shell casings fired from a .45 caliber pistol in your backyard. The GBI compared those shell casings to the ones found at the diner, and they were a match.

"So," Castillo said, "if the weapon found in your car when you were arrested is the same weapon you fired in your backyard, the GBI's ballistic test results will establish it was the weapon used in the Harrington Diner murders and, I suspect, the convenience store murder across the street."

"Make the deal," Young said with a touch of urgency. "I'll waive extradition and plead as long as the death penalty is off the table."

"You understand that'll mean life in prison without the opportunity for parole, right?"

"Make the deal."

Three days later, Castillo called Young back. "I think we have a deal," he said.

"You think? What the fuck does that mean?"

"The DA has one question he wants you to answer before he signs off. He wants to know why you tied Tillotson to a chair and shot him in the head. He says he hasn't been able to get that scene out of his head—or make any sense of it—since the morning of the shootings."

The query from the DA mystified Young. "What fuckin' difference does it make?" he yelled into the phone. "Dead is dead."

"You'll need to answer his question if you want this deal. I think what he really wants to know is whether you knew Tillotson and had some kind of grudge against him, or what?"

"No, I didn't know him. When I first went in through the back door, which he'd left unlocked, his back was to me. I crept up behind him, put my gun to the back of his head, and told him not to turn around if he wanted to live. He started talking 'bout a better way of life and changing my ways to save my soul. He was getting all religious on me and said he would pray for me. I kept telling him I didn't want him or nobody else to pray for me, and to shut the fuck up. But he just kept on talking, kept on preaching at me.

"Then I told him to open the safe. I stayed behind him as we walked over, keeping the gun to the back of his head. Once he opened it, I moved him to the side and reached in to get the money. But when I turned back to him, the stupid bastard had turned 'round and was looking at me, smiling and still preaching about how much Jesus loves me. God, that *pissed me off*," Young said, his voice rising in anger with each word he spoke. "So I dragged him over to the chair and tied him to it so he couldn't follow me or get to a phone to call the cops. And *still* he wouldn't shut up. It's his own damn fault he's dead."

There was a silence on the other end of the line for a few seconds.

"Mr. Young, look, I'm sorry, but I think the DA's gonna ask why you didn't just shoot Tillotson as he was standing by the safe instead of taking him into the dining room, tying him up, and putting the gun to his head as he watched?"

"I just told 'ya," Young screamed. "I didn't *plan* to kill the guy. I didn't *want* to kill the guy, but he was making me crazy. He gave me no fuckin' choice. Just like that old guy in the convenience store. He wouldn't shut up, neither."

CHAPTER SIXTY-TWO

"I'm not expecting any visitors today. Who is it?" Owens asked Sgt. Charlie Bailey, the supervisor who took him to the visitation area.

"They don't tell me that when they call up here," Bailey said.

Since he no longer was on death row and had somehow managed to avoid trouble since his move into the general population, Joseph wasn't required to be shackled for the walk to see his visitors. As they passed by the glass windows into the visitation room, he could see Greg and Elena sitting inside, and instinctively became fearful that there was bad news coming. As he entered, though, Joseph could see they were smiling. He gave each of them a hug.

"What's up?" he asked.

"We have some news," Elena said.

"Good news?"

"I received a call this morning from Elizabeth Austin. She's the deputy attorney general who's supervising your case. She told me that police in Louisiana have arrested a man based on a warrant issued in Noonan County for the convenience store murder three weeks before the murders at the diner."

Joseph's brow furrowed and his eyes squinted as he processed the news. "So, what's that got to do with me?"

"The guy's now confessed not only to the convenience store murder, but to the murders of Steve Tillotson and Eduardo Gonzales," Elena said, choking up with a mixture of joy and relief as she spoke. Joseph closed his eyes and, after a few seconds, tears began to flow as he reached out to hug Elena and then Greg.

"I'm going home?"

"You're going home," Elena said. "Austin says they will release you as soon as the paperwork is complete, likely within a day or two. They'll notify us as soon as they know, and we'll be here with Jasmine to pick you up."

"Jasmine knows?" he asked, suddenly getting choked up.

"She knows," Greg said. "We stopped by to see her on our way down here. Everyone within two blocks of your home knows because she started screaming for joy and couldn't stop for five minutes."

"You guys," he said, pausing as he looked at each of them, "you guys have saved my life."

Greg thought about that simple, but immensely powerful, and deeply meaningful statement. It was a transcendent moment for him. He always enjoyed winning, but this one—this victory—was different. This case, unlike his usual cases, was not about money. It was about nothing less than life and death. In that instant, he felt as though, somehow, he'd not just helped save an innocent life, but also helped redeem a system of justice gone astray.

The evening news on Channel 3 led off with Young's arrest and confession to committing the murders at the diner and at the convenience store. Chastain praised Captain Smith for the great work of his detectives in cracking both cases.

"The spent shell casings found in Young's backyard had markings that matched the shells found at the Harrington Diner on the day of the double murder there," Smith told the media. "We're confident that Young committed the robbery and murders that took place there, as well as the robbery and murder three weeks earlier at the convenience store across the street from the diner."

Then the newscaster added, "We at Channel 3 are proud to say that the lawyers who represented Joseph Owens in this case, Elena Samuels and Greg Williams, are also our station's attorneys. We congratulate them on their extraordinary commitment to justice by exonerating Mr. Owens and freeing an innocent man from prison."

CHAPTER SIXTY-THREE

At Fox Stern, there was a celebration in honor of the victory. While Greg and Elena accepted the congratulations of most of their colleagues graciously, Greg shocked a group of partners he was speaking with by conspicuously turning his back as he saw Clay approaching.

Clay got the message and veered off toward Elena. He'd tried to mend fences with her by apologizing publicly at a partners' meeting after receiving an admonition from the management committee for the derogatory comment he'd made in Greg's office a few weeks earlier. But the ice had not melted.

"Congratulations, Elena," Clay said. "We're very proud of what you and Greg have accomplished."

She was having none of it.

"I could tell you were so proud of me all along," Elena responded as she stared unflinchingly into Clay's eyes, "by the decrease in my paycheck at the end of last year, and the demeaning comments about me that you made to Greg. Honestly, you've got a lot of nerve coming to this celebration."

A few people who were in earshot of the conversation gasped at Elena's bluntness. But Clay, trying to turn the other cheek, told Elena she had a very bright future at Fox Stern.

"I do think I have a bright future in front of me," she told him, "but it isn't going to be here."

Stung by Greg's conspicuous snub and Elena's sharp rebuke delivered in front of several partners and associates, Clay left the celebration and headed back to his office, fuming about being turned into a villain rather than getting any credit for approving their request to take on the Owens case. After all, he thought to himself, it was just part of his job as managing partner to keep a close eye on the cost of the case.

CHAPTER SIXTY-FOUR

"Here he comes," Elena said excitedly as the gray metal door to the prison office swung open. Joseph walked out into the sunshine, wearing khakis and a blue shirt Jasmine had brought for him. He came to a stop as soon as he saw Jasmine smiling on the other side of the gate that was sliding slowly open. After hesitating for a moment, he turned to look toward the door as though waiting for someone to tell him he had permission to leave, but it was closed. He turned back toward his wife and stepped through the open gate. Jasmine broke down in tears as they embraced.

After a few moments, Elena stepped close and told them Greg had brought his car around and was waiting to take them home. At first, Elena thought they hadn't heard her as they lingered in an embrace that was six years in the making. Then Joseph took Jasmine by the hand. "Let's get away from this place," he said. "Let's go home."

Once they were in the car, Greg drove slowly through the parking lot and along the prison road that led to Georgia Highway 36, where he turned right toward Interstate 75. Minutes later, he turned onto the access road heading north for the drive to the home in southwest Atlanta where Jasmine had moved to be closer to the prison. She'd become uncomfortable living in Harrington, where the looks she got from everyone made her feel uneasy. Greg looked in the rearview mirror and saw Jasmine wiping away tears as Joseph held her close.

At their home, friends and neighbors had gathered for a welcome home celebration. When he got out of the car, the first person to grab Joseph was his brother, Hector. "Welcome home, bro. I knew in my heart this day would come. I knew it. Praise the Lord!"

One after another, his friends embraced Joseph and welcomed him home, offered toasts to his freedom, and laughed with Jasmine as she celebrated the homecoming. Greg and Elena stayed for thirty minutes before telling Joseph they had to get back to the office.

"You're a free man," Greg said. "Enjoy it, soak it in, and take your time getting readjusted. Listen, it may be a bit harder than you expect. For six years, the guards told you what you could do and when you could do it. Readjusting to freedom after such a long time in prison can be a challenge, but Elena and I are here to help in any way you need. And when you're ready, we can talk about your right to sue the district attorney for what he did to you. But there's no rush."

"I don't know what to say," Joseph said as he teared up. "Without you two, I'd still be in that hellhole of a prison. I owe you guys my life."

"You owe us nothing," Greg said. "But I do have one very important request. Jasmine told me that, before you were arrested, she and Hector were trying to find a counselor for you. I think it's even more important now for you see a counselor to help you readjust to life outside of prison and to cope with the emotional issues you were dealing with before your arrest. Please promise me that you'll see a counselor."

Jasmine, who was listening to the conversation, said Hector already was making some inquiries. "If Hector has any problem finding someone or if you just want some more recommendations, Elena and I know some people who can help. Please don't hesitate to call. This is really, really important."

Their friends and family kept the celebration going for a couple of hours before they started heading out. Finally, after all the guests had left, it was just Joseph, Jasmine, and Hector sitting in the living room.

"It must have been hell in that place," Hector said. "How'd you deal with all of it?"

"I don't wanna talk about that, Hector," Joseph said in a sharp tone. "Not now. I've spent the last six years just trying to survive in that place, eating the crap that passes for food, following orders from the guards that made no fucking sense, and dealing with some of the sickest perverts in the world. I need to get it out of my mind. Understand?"

"I'm sorry, man. I didn't realize . . ." he said, his voice choking with emotion at having caused his brother such pain. "I just thought talking about it would help."

"Look, Hector, I'm sorry. I shouldn't have talked to you that way," Joseph said. "Maybe someday we can talk about it. But not now. I need some time."

"No problem. If you're ready, whenever you're ready, I'll be here. In the meantime, though, I'm gonna get to work on finding you a counselor who can help you deal with all this."

Joseph stood up and reached out to embrace his older brother. "I'm not upset with you, man," he said. "You got that?"

"Yeah, I got it," Hector replied.

After a few minutes of silence, Jasmine said, "Hector, have I mentioned that it's been six years since Joseph and I have been alone together?"

"Oh, sorry, Jaz," he said with a sheepish smile on his face as he headed for the door. "I'll be in touch. But not too soon."

Jasmine walked over to Joseph, took his hands, and gently pulled him up out of his chair. She embraced and kissed him, softly at first, then with more urgency. When she broke the embrace, she took Joseph by the hand and led him toward their bedroom.

"Wait," he said, stopping suddenly.

"What's the matter?"

"It's been a long time," he said as a look of embarrassment came across his face. "I just don't know if I can . . . y'know . . ."

Jasmine smiled and pulled him close. "You let Mama worry about that," she said as she led him through the bedroom door.

CHAPTER SIXTY-FIVE

"Here you go, bro," Hector said. "These here are two psychs that, from what I've been told by some friends who've done some time, know what they're doing. Give 'em a call." When Joseph called the first, she said she didn't have an opening on her schedule for six weeks. The second could see him in two weeks, but his fee was $175 per visit.

"We can't afford that," he told Jasmine. "I'm not sure what to do." With her encouragement, Joseph picked up the phone and called Elena.

"I'm really sorry to bother you," Joseph said. "But the counselors Hector came up with aren't going to work out."

"Joseph, I'm really glad you called. I was going to call soon to check on how you were doing," Elena said.

"Okay. I'm doing okay. Y'know, taking it day by day."

"Give me a couple of days and I'll get back to you. I think we can help you out with this." When the phone rang late that afternoon, it surprised Joseph to hear Elena's voice on the other end. "You have a piece of paper and something to write with?"

"Don't tell me you've come up with somebody already?"

"Yep. His name is Dr. Stephen Gray. One of my partners knows him and thought he might be willing to help you. So I called him and it turns out he's counseled some other people who've served time in prison. He's willing to see you this week."

"Man, that sounds great. But lemme ask you something. Do you know how much he's gonna charge?"

"Joseph, I explained your circumstances to Dr. Gray. He'd read some newspaper articles about you being exonerated and released from prison. When I told him we had represented you without charging a fee, he volunteered to help you at no charge." There were a few moments of silence on the phone. "Joseph, did you hear what I said?"

"Yeah, I heard," Joseph said, choking back the emotional reaction that had overcome him. "You guys busted your butts all this time, working day and night, to prove I wasn't no murderer, and you didn't charge me a penny. Nothing. Now you find this guy who's willing to help me and he's not gonna charge me nothing. What I wanna know is, what've I done to deserve people like you and Greg and this shrink to help me like this?"

"Joseph, you're a good person who's been to hell and back in the last six years, through no fault of your own. It means a lot to Greg and to me to help you. Your thanks are all the payment we need. Now, take down Dr. Gray's phone number and call him. And stay in touch to let me know how you're doing."

The first appointment was that Friday. Dr. Gray's office was in an old, eight-story brick building just north of downtown Atlanta. His office was furnished simply, with a brown leather sofa and matching chair and a cherry table and chair that served as Dr. Gray's desk. Jasmine drove Joseph to the appointment, but stayed in the waiting room while he met with the psychiatrist.

"It's good to meet you," Dr. Gray said as he shook Joseph's hand.

"Thanks for seeing me so quickly," Joseph replied.

"How've you been feeling since they released you?"

"It varies from day to day, and sometimes from one minute to the next. It's hard to stop thinking about being in prison and the idea that I'd die in that place for a crime I didn't commit. I'm angry a lot of the time, but happy to out of there and thankful for the people who've helped me. Mostly, though, I'm exhausted from all this stuff."

"Let me assure you that your feelings are entirely normal. One hundred percent normal. Being in that place was traumatic. It would be for anyone, and the trauma is even worse when the person imprisoned is actually innocent."

"So, can you help me?"

"I can help you help yourself," Dr. Gray replied. "This isn't like when you have a cold or the flu. There's no pill I can give you to make the pain go away in five days. It's a process where I guide you to cure yourself by talking about what you've been through and to release those feelings that have built up over—what?—six years of being locked away from your wife, your family, and your friends."

Dr. Gray saw Joseph once a week for the first two months and every other week for the next four months. Satisfied that Joseph was making excellent progress and readjusting to life outside of prison, he reduced the visits to once a month for three more months. After the last meeting, Gray told Joseph that he didn't think they needed to schedule another meeting, but he'd be available anytime Joseph thought he needed to talk. "You're doing really well. But I'm here if you need me."

"Doc, I don't know how to thank you," he said.

"Your smile is all I need. Take care of yourself and call if you need me."

Although Joseph didn't know it, as he began making progress in his treatment, Dr. Gray had called Elena to ask whether they could help Joseph find a job. "It would be very helpful to his recovery from the emotional trauma," he told her. Soon thereafter, Greg arranged for Joseph to get a temporary job loading cargo for a trucking company that was a client of the firm. After four weeks, the supervisor was so pleased with Joseph's work and attitude that they offered him a job as a permanent employee. His salary was more than he'd ever been paid, and the job also included health insurance and other benefits.

"Joseph, Elena and I are so proud of you, man," Greg said when he called to congratulate him on getting hired permanently. "You're back on your feet in record time."

"I'd be nothing without you guys," Joseph managed to say as he was choking up. "I'd be a number, not a man, and I'd be lost in that iron jungle."

The words of gratitude meant everything to Greg and made him appreciate even more what he and Elena had been through at the firm. It also made him realize how right he'd been to stand up to Clay. However, their work for Owens was not quite over.

"Now that you've settled back in and got your feet on the ground with a good job, we need to talk about your right to sue the district attorney for violating your civil rights," Greg said.

"Can I do that?"

"Yes, although it's a complicated process, and I want you to know at the outset that these cases are very difficult to win. But I think you've got a good case against Chastain. Can Elena and I come by one day this week to talk to you and Jasmine about it?"

"I'm a working man now," Joseph said with a laugh. "But I get off at three each day. How about Wednesday around four?"

"See you then," Greg said.

The lawsuit was filed two months later and immediately attracted the attention of the media all over the state. "Released Prisoner Sues Noonan DA" read the front-page headline in the Harrington Post:

Former Harrington resident Joseph Owens has filed a civil rights suit against Noonan County District Attorney Paul Chastain, alleging that, at his direction, an employee in his office intentionally altered and withheld video evidence, leading to Owens being falsely convicted for the two murders at the Harrington Diner, and sentenced to death, in violation of his constitutional rights.

Owens's conviction was vacated after the State conceded that Chastain's office had altered a critical piece of evidence. He is seeking six million dollars in damages for the district attorney's misconduct, one million for each of the six years he spent in prison.

"The State cannot give my client back those six years," said one of Owens's attorneys, Greg Williams, a partner at the Fox Stern law firm. "But we're hopeful it will do the right thing and agree to a fair amount of

compensation for the horrendous and inexcusable conduct of the District Attorney.

Chastain hung up the telephone when reached by a reporter who asked for a comment on Owens's lawsuit.

CHAPTER SIXTY-SIX

Chastain hadn't spent one moment thinking about the injustice he'd done to Owens or to the families of the victims, to the jurors, the judge, or the taxpayers who had footed the bill for the trial and for Owens's confinement. "It was," he told Austin when she called to inform him of the attorney general's decision to release Owens, "an unfortunate oversight, resulting from an inadvertent error made by a clerk while copying the video file on the thumb drive."

Since the only person who knew otherwise—Captain Smith—could hardly reveal the truth about what transpired without admitting his own complicity, Chastain believed he was immune from the potential legal, ethical, and political consequences of wrongly prosecuting and convicting Owens. But after hearing about Chastain's "unfortunate oversight" remark, followed by his announcement that he would retire at the end of his current term, Smith knew it was now or never. He picked up the telephone and called Austin.

"I'd like to come see you and, if possible, General Marshall," he said. "I need to get something off of my chest."

Three days later, back in the same conference room where he'd met with them months earlier, Smith told them, "I need to come clean about what happened with that video file."

"Are you looking for anything from us in return for providing us with this information?" Marshall asked.

"Absolutely not," Smith replied. "Not that my saying so will make the slightest difference, but you do whatever you think you need to do with the information I'm going to share with you. If you think I acted inappropriately, I'm prepared to take whatever consequences come my way. Frankly, it's better than living with this on my conscience.

"So," he went on, "when I saw the video with the black Camaro and brought it to Chastain's attention, he told me to leave it with him. I said, 'Paul, we need to pursue this. It can't be coincidental that a black Camaro was outside of the diner minutes after the shooting.'"

"What did Mr. Chastain say to that?" Austin asked.

"He gave me ten days to identify and arrest the driver of the Camaro. It was an impossible task, especially since we didn't have a license tag or anything else to go on. When I came up empty, and despite my protests that I needed more time, Chastain went forward with presenting the case to the grand jury and seeking an indictment of Owens."

"Why do you think he did that?" Marshall asked.

"Because he'd heard from reliable sources that a well-qualified and well-financed opponent planned to challenge him in the upcoming election. It may not be apparent to everyone, but if you're around Paul very much, you know his ego is all tied up in never having lost an election. Hard to believe, but despite all the tough talk and bravado, deep down, the guy's as insecure as anyone I know."

"I'm grateful, Captain," Marshall said. "Coming forward like this is no less than what's required of you, but not everyone in your shoes would have done so. Thank you."

CHAPTER SIXTY-SEVEN

Two weeks after watching as Judge Hinton took the guilty plea from Craig Young and sentenced him to three life sentences without parole, to be served consecutively, Chastain was pleased to receive an invitation from Attorney General Marshall to meet with her. He'd seen Marshall speak at several law enforcement conferences, but never had the opportunity for a private discussion.

"I'm going to be out of the office tomorrow morning," Chastain said to Maxwell. "Can you cover the arraignment in the Yates case?"

"Sure," Maxwell said. "Where're you going to be?"

"I received an invitation from the attorney general to meet with her," he said proudly. "I've got a few things on my mind to speak with her about, such as getting her support for more funding from the General Assembly at the next session."

"You think that's why she invited you down there?" Maxwell asked.

"It's just an invitation to meet with her," Chastain said. "The letter doesn't say there's an agenda."

"Okay," Maxwell replied.

"I've seen that look from you before," the DA said. "You think she has an agenda?"

"Might have to do with the Owens case," Maxwell said. "Leastwise, it seems a bit strange to get an invitation out of the blue right after the case was closed with the new conviction." Chastain thought for a few moments while he pondered Maxwell's comment.

"Well, I'd think if that was the case, she'd have said as much. But if that's what she wants to talk about, I can deal with it. It's not the first wrongful conviction in Georgia. The State may have to pay the guy some money, but there's insurance for that."

When he arrived for the appointment at 11:00 a.m., Chastain was ushered into the AG's office immediately. He was a little surprised, and a bit alarmed, to find he was not alone in the office with Marshall. He had anticipated having a private tête-à-tête with the state's chief lawyer. But the presence of another person—especially *this* other person—suggested Marshall wanted a witness to anything that was said.

"Paul, I appreciate you coming to Atlanta to meet with me," Marshall said. "Let me introduce you to Chief Deputy Attorney General Elizabeth Austin."

"We've met previously," Chastain said with a sneer, "in my office." Austin didn't reply, but kept a slight smile on her face.

"General, it was kind of you to invite me here," he said, trying to take control of the meeting. "I've been looking forward to having an opportunity to meet you and discuss how prosecutors in the field could benefit from stronger relationships with your office."

"That's an important topic," Marshall acknowledged. "But that's not the purpose of this meeting."

"Oh? What *is* the purpose?"

"You," Marshall said with a bit of an edge in her voice. "You're the topic. I'm going to ask Elizabeth to explain." Chastain, startled by the tone of Marshall's voice, looked bewildered as he turned his gaze toward Austin.

"Mr. Chastain, I was the lead attorney for the State in responding to the motion filed by the attorneys for Joseph Owens to have his conviction overturned, after the video containing the black Camaro surfaced in the habeas proceeding. As I'm sure you'll agree, that was not the State's finest moment."

"Mistakes are made from time to time," Chastain said. "I'm glad the full video came to light because it eventually led us to the person who committed not only the diner murders, but the murder of the gas station attendant across the street from the Harrington Diner. And as I'm sure you know, the perpetrator has now pled guilty and been sentenced to three consecutive life terms."

"Yes, that's certainly good news for everyone," Austin replied. "But now we're dealing with a civil lawsuit filed by Owens's lawyers. They're asking for $6 million in damages for your violation of their client's constitutional rights."

Chastain sat silently, keeping his gaze on Austin.

"So the questions we asked you here to discuss are how and why the video you produced to the public defender during the trial was altered by deleting the scene showing the black Camaro passing in front of the diner within minutes of the murders of Tillotson and Gonzales?"

Chastain looked stunned and started to protest, but Marshall quickly cut him off.

"That's not all, Paul," the AG said. "Another important question we need to discuss is on what basis you tried to do the same thing in the habeas case—again under the preposterous guise of work product? You know as well as I do that there's no way on earth you could classify that video as work product."

"Well, I don't know about that," Chastain started to say, but Marshall was having none of it.

"Paul, don't go there. Your position is indefensible. Worse yet, of all people, you should understand that your conduct not only was unethical, but it also may well have been criminal. Am I making myself clear enough?"

"I don't appreciate the tone of your comments, General. I'm an elected district attorney and I answer only to my constituents. If you want to pursue this discussion, you can send your questions to me in writing, and I'll respond accordingly." Chastain immediately stood and started toward the door.

"*Sit down*, Paul," Marshall commanded sternly. "We're *not* done here."

Chastain stopped and turned around, but didn't move back to the chair he'd been occupying. He stood silently, waiting for Marshall to continue.

"Your conduct of the Owens investigation and trial is not merely unethical, it is disgraceful and indefensible. The fact that the critical, final forty-five seconds of the video, was deleted from the video file your office produced to Owens's defense lawyer *could not possibly* have happened by accident. Somebody in your office had to program the duplicating equipment to do that. And it's my strong belief, sir, that it was done either by you or at your direction, because I just cannot imagine for the life of me that anyone in any DA's office would do such a thing other than with the DA's express or implicit direction."

Chastain remained silent as his face turned ashen.

"Even if you didn't give the order, I've not the slightest doubt that, at a bare minimum, you knew the video file on the thumb drive produced to Owens's trial attorney wasn't complete, and you chose to look the other way. It is, sir, a disgraceful, dishonorable, and dishonest way to end a fine career."

"General," Chastain said, starting to protest, but Marshall again cut him off.

"Paul, if I were your attorney, which I most certainly am not, I'd strongly advise you to remain silent. We're talking here about the alteration of evidence by the State in connection with a capital murder case. Beyond the criminal implications," she paused for a moment and saw Chastain's eyes open wide, "there's the matter of the waste of taxpayer money on the Owens trial, the cost of the subsequent investigation by my office, and the considerable sum it's going to take to settle the lawsuit filed against the State on Owens's behalf by his attorneys. I have to say I'm not sure if that case will settle before Owens's attorney takes your deposition, but for your sake, I certainly hope so. If not, I'd *strongly* suggest you hire a lawyer to represent you at the deposition. Do you understand?"

"What do you want from me?" a beaten down Chastain asked.

"Your resignation," Marshall answered immediately. "If you resign your office within seventy-two hours, you can make whatever statement you want about your reasons for leaving. You're tired, you want to spend more time with your family, you want to travel, or whatever makes you comfortable."

"And if I choose not to resign?" Chastain asked.

"Thanks for coming to see me, Paul. I wish you well."

Two days later, residents of Noonan County were stunned to learn that District Attorney Chastain had left office before the expiration of his term. "I've accomplished everything I wanted to accomplish over my almost twenty-two years in office," he said in a press release that was issued only after he had cleared out his office and had a private talk with key members of his staff to inform them of his decision. "It's time to turn the office over to my Chief Deputy, Roger Maxwell, who will be the acting district attorney until my successor is elected. The people of Noonan County are in good hands with Roger at the helm."

As he attempted to exit the building without being noticed through a back stairwell, it surprised Chastain to see a Channel 3 television news reporter and camera crew waiting for him there. The reporter asked whether the outcome of the Owens case and the pending civil lawsuit had anything to do with his decision to resign.

"Absolutely not," Chastain said indignantly.

"So why now?" the reporter asked. "Aren't you embarrassed by seeking and obtaining the death penalty against an innocent man? Does that weigh on your conscience?"

Chastain stared at the reporter for an uncomfortable moment, then turned and walked away.

CHAPTER SIXTY-EIGHT

"The offices aren't nearly as swanky, and the views here aren't nearly as good, as they are on the fiftieth floor of Fox Stern's offices," Greg said with a smile when Katherine Bergman stopped by for a visit a week after he and Elena announced their departure from the firm. "But the atmosphere here is a lot better. Not as much hot air, if you know what I mean."

They had signed a lease for a small suite of offices on the sixth floor of a building in midtown Atlanta. It had enough room for them plus an assistant, a paralegal, a conference room, and two extra attorney's offices. The move had come about quickly following final dismissal of the charges against Owens.

Greg sent his resignation letter to Morrissey one week after the firm's celebration of their victory. He also copied each of the other members of the firm's management committee.

Dear Clay,

I'm sure it will come as no surprise to you that I am resigning from Fox Stern effective immediately. Notwithstanding our many years of working together for the good of our clients and for the firm, we now have very different views of what it means to have a successful law practice.

Your unrelenting focus on increasing firm profits at the expense of partners who honor the firm's long tradition of providing free legal services to the poor is deeply disturbing. Worse yet, the withdrawal of your support for our representation of Joseph Owens during the midst of the case, and your retaliation against Elena Samuels and me by severely cutting our compensation when we refused to "find a way," as you put it, to bring the case to an end prematurely, was not merely unconscionable, it was unprofessional and unethical.

Attached hereto are letters from eight clients authorizing me to take their files with me. Immediately upon informing them of my departure from Fox Stern, each asked me to continue to represent them at my new firm. You are welcome to verify this with the clients if you so choose. I anticipate more clients following suit shortly.

Greg

Minutes later, Morrissey and the management committee received a resignation letter from Elena. Although disappointed, they had been expecting Elena's announcement that she'd be taking some clients with her, two of which had each paid Fox Stern over $350k in fees in the last twelve months for litigation work Elena had handled. But the third client Elena was taking, a hot tech company embroiled in a dispute growing out of its recently completed initial stock offering, which threatened to erupt into a federal securities lawsuit at any moment, brought Clay up short.

"How'd Elena manage to get that client to move firms with her?" an upset Clay demanded from George Cummings, the corporate securities partner responsible for managing the firm's relationship with the client. "I thought you had a strong relationship there."

"I do, Clay, but the real question is how the hell did you let Elena get away?" Cummings replied. "She's incredibly personable and talented. At your suggestion, I introduced her to the general counsel of the company, who immediately asked to have Elena assigned to the company's litigation files."

"Did you try to persuade him to leave the files with us?"

"Him, who?" Cummings asked.

"The general counsel?"

"Good grief, Clay, what century are you living in? The GC is Paulette Wilkes-Jones, the former Southeast office enforcement chief for the Securities Exchange Commission who, like Elena, graduated from Yale Law School. So, no, I don't think it'd be wise to try to persuade Paulette that the lawyer I introduced her to a just a few months ago, and who's already achieved excellent results for the company, suddenly isn't the best person to handle the company's litigation just because she's left the firm."

The uproar over the departures of Greg and Elena had not settled down when Morrissey and the management committee received an unexpected resignation letter from Katherine Bergman. In the letter, Bergman said she "was offended to learn of the firm's actions in financially punishing Greg Williams and Elena Samuels for their exemplary service on behalf of Joseph Owens. Fox Stern is no longer the kind of firm at which I care to practice law, so I will join Greg and Elena at their new firm."

Four members of the management committee demanded an immediate meeting to discuss the defections. Since the firm's bylaws required Morrissey, as chair of the committee, to call a meeting at the request of a majority of the members, he had no choice. The meeting was scheduled for 5:00 p.m. that same day.

"What the hell've you done, Clay?" demanded Jeff Fisher. "You've driven away three of our top litigation partners who, between them, not only generated more than five million in fees last year, but were among the only ones trusted by some of my most important clients to handle their cases."

"I did exactly what this committee asked me to do," Clay responded angrily. "The firm's growth over the last five years has brought us to the verge of being included on the list of the hundred most profitable law firms in the nation. The Owens case threatened our ability to achieve that goal, so I merely encouraged Greg to find a sensible, but, of course, ethical way to bring the case to a close."

"Sounds like you did more than encourage," said Susan Petroff. "And, besides, since Owens was actually innocent, what kind of compromise was even possible short of the DA conceding error and releasing Owens? Did you want him to plead to a crime he didn't commit and serve twenty years or more in prison?"

"I suggested no such thing," Clay said dismissively. "I trusted Greg to reach a satisfactory compromise short of taking the case to trial."

"That's *bullshit*, Clay. It didn't exactly take a rocket scientist to understand there was *no possibility* of reaching a compromise," Petroff yelled. Clay started to turn red in the face and rise out of his chair, but he regained control and sat back down without responding to the taunt. "So," Petroff continued, "the bottom line is that, without consulting us, you penalized Greg and Elena by cutting their distributions last year for working on a *pro bono* case that not only did we authorize, but in which all of us took great pride. I find that utterly disgraceful, if not unethical."

"I take offense at that," Clay said indignantly, this time unable to restrain himself. "There's nothing unethical about reducing a partner's share of the profits when his collections decline. We do that all the time."

"No, we *don't*!" Petroff pounded her fists on the conference room table. "We don't agree to take on a case that we know up front will cost the firm millions of dollars in free legal services, allow two of our partners to devote hundreds or thousands of hours of time to save our client from being wrongfully executed for a crime he didn't commit, and then thank them for their important work by shifting a disproportionate share of that financial burden onto them. Shame on you. And shame on us for not catching it and stopping you."

"Let's try to lower the temperature in here," said Gene Miller. "What's done is done. The important thing now is that we act immediately to stop this from causing more disruptions and more departures from the firm." Turning to face him, Gene said, "Clay, I hate to say this, but I think the only way to get past this without inflicting more damage is for you to step down as managing partner."

"I disagree," said Jack Stephenson. "This seems like a rather drastic action to take against the person who guided us through a deep recession followed by the largest period of growth the firm has ever enjoyed."

The debate went on for almost two hours, after which an exhausted and chastened Morrisey called for the meeting to end. He promised to consider all the opinions expressed in the meeting carefully and to inform the committee within a day or two whether he would step down as the managing partner.

Two days later, after notifying each of the committee members personally, Morrissey emailed all attorneys in the firm. It said, "I will step down as chair of the firm's managing partner after eight years because it's time to turn the management of the firm over to the next generation of leaders."

CHAPTER SIXTY-NINE

The fuzzy explanation for Morrissey's decision to step down fooled nobody at Fox Stern, where the grapevine among attorneys and staff had been burning up with news about each of the partner resignations, as well as the emergency management committee meeting, minutes after each had occurred. Speculation was rife about who would serve as the firm's new managing partner.

Two weeks later, and notwithstanding Clay's decision, the firm's situation grew significantly worse. For decades, Fox Stern's largest client was Southern Family Financial, Inc., a private investment firm for one of the nation's wealthiest families. Clay, who oversaw the client's corporate acquisitions practice, had taken over as the principal contact for SFF when founding partner Bill Fox retired.

Because Greg and Elena had successfully handled two large securities fraud cases for SFF, Clay quickly decided to invite Hugh Wilson, the CEO of the company, to lunch at the firm so he could meet some other litigation partners. When Wilson asked what happened to Greg and Elena, Clay told him, "They've had a bug for a while to start their own firm and, despite my best efforts to talk them out of it, they decided to go ahead with their plan. We're going to miss them."

The next evening, Clay's cell phone buzzed, and he saw there was an incoming call from Wilson. "Tell me something," Wilson started out without so much as a greeting. "Did you think that after two hugely successful federal trials with Greg and Elena representing us, I wouldn't call to wish them well at their new firm?"

Clay, startled as much by the tone of Wilson's voice as by his words, said, "Hugh, what do you mean? I told you they left to start their own firm, and they did."

"Did you inadvertently leave out the fact they effectively were forced out by having their income slashed for handling that death penalty case you approved?" Wilson asked.

"They told you that?" Clay asked incredulously.

"I asked them why they left the firm," Wilson said, "and, unlike you, they answered honestly."

"Greg and I had a difference of opinion about that, but—"

Wilson cut him off, not wanting to hear another word. "Transfer all our litigation files to Greg and Elena first thing in the morning," Wilson demanded. "I admire their courage and their willingness to put principle above profits, unlike you. I'll let you know where to transfer the corporate and real estate work soon."

"Hugh, Southern Family has been a client of Fox Stern for more than twenty years," Clay said. "I think we deserve to be treated better than this."

"That's funny, Clay," Hugh said. "Greg and Elena used pretty much those exact words to describe how they felt about the way you treated them." Then Clay heard the call disconnect.

News of the loss of one of Fox Stern's oldest and most important clients spread through the firm quickly and rattled many of the partners. Concerned that the defections of more partners and clients could lead to a collapse of the firm, the new managing partner, Karen C. Gonzales, emailed the entire firm first thing the next morning. "Clay Morrisey has resigned from the firm, effective immediately, for personal reasons," it read. "We wish him well."

CHAPTER SEVENTY

Even as Fox Stern was celebrating the victory, Janice Hinton was questioning whether she wanted to continue as a judge. "I don't know if I can keep doing this," Hinton told her husband, also a lawyer, after the release of Owens. "If Owens had been executed before this new information came to light, how could I have lived with myself?"

"You can't blame yourself for Chastain's misconduct," Hinton's husband said, trying to comfort her.

"No, of course not. But the evidence against Owens was not overwhelming. I contemplated granting the defense motion to dismiss the capital murder count after the State rested its case, but I decided to put my trust in the jury to get it right."

"What's wrong with that?" her husband asked.

"It was a cop-out on my part. Part of my job is to be the gatekeeper. If I believe the evidence is insufficient to convict, it's my responsibility to stop the case from even getting to the jury. I didn't have the courage to trust my instincts and do my duty. Now, it hurts to think about what could've happened — what would've happened — if those lawyers hadn't volunteered at the last minute to represent Owens and uncovered the district attorney's treachery."

"Y'know, what's apparent to me is that you take this job very seriously, as you should. And just as many people experience when they become judges before you, there's a learning curve."

"A learning curve is a bad thing when a person's life is at stake," Hinton replied.

"You're right. And in fairness, you were a bit unlucky to get a case like this assigned to you for your first murder trial. But like any good judge, you've learned from your mistakes and you've got a conscience. I'd hate to see you give up on yourself now."

•   •   •   •   •

Across town, without a companion to help her work through the pain, Elaine Jessup suffered alone in her two-bedroom wood cabin on the outskirts of Harrington. Convinced it was her testimony that led to Owens's conviction and death sentence, Jessup had to cope with having been so terribly and unimaginably mistaken about what Gonzales had meant — if he had meant anything at all — by the sound he uttered just before he died. A deeply religious woman, she'd prayed for the Lord's forgiveness. But she knew her prayers weren't enough. So Jessup decided to do the only thing she could think of to ease her conscience. She wrote and rewrote the letter, time and again, apologizing for the unforgiveable mistake she'd made when she testified at his trial.

"I don't ask for your forgiveness because I can't even forgive myself," she scribbled in an unsteady hand, "but I couldn't live with myself without telling you how truly and deeply sorry I am for the awful mistake I made, and for the pain you and your family have endured."

Jessup had written her letter to ease her conscience and mailed it without the slightest expectation of receiving a reply. The very thought didn't even cross her mind.

But seven days later, when she opened her mailbox, she saw an envelope with her name and address scrawled on it. Her knees buckled slightly, and she felt dizzy as her heart started pounding. There was no return address, but it didn't need one. Jessup knew instantly who it was from. Her eyes watered as fear gripped her. Her nerves were rattled so badly that she remained frozen in place for what seemed like hours, gripping the mailbox for support, unable to move or to retrieve the envelope.

Finally, Jessup snatched it from the box and walked slowly back inside her cabin. She steadied herself as she sat down and placed the envelope on the hand-knotted lace tablecloth atop her antique walnut dining table. Not in any hurry to see what was inside, she hesitated, staring at the envelope for a few more minutes, taking several deep breaths as she pondered the message inside. Finally, she carefully opened the envelope and removed a folded piece of plain, white paper. Written on it, in the same scrawl as was on the envelope, she read, "You spoke what you believed to be true on behalf of the friend you had lost. Go in peace."

Jessup clutched the letter to her chest as she cried the tears of relief that came with being graciously and undeservedly unburdened of a terrible guilt. It was a gift from a man who owed her nothing. And it meant everything.

Acknowledgements

I started working on this book confident that I knew how to write. I've been writing most of my adult life, starting as a college journalist, then as a daily newspaper reporter, and later writing legal briefs. What could be so hard about writing a novel? When none of the many agents I queried showed the slightest interest, I finally recognized that I didn't have a clue. Brian Tomasovich was the first to take on the task of teaching me how to think about writing a novel. He has a gift for teaching and the patience to help a struggling, would-be novelist, learn the essentials. Pamela Taylor, an author and editor with whom I connected through my publisher, *Black Rose Writing*, provided invaluable guidance in a wonderfully collaborative way. I'm also grateful to Chad Rhoad, an editor I met through the Atlanta Writers Club, for his feedback.

I cannot begin to thank adequately family members, friends and colleagues who read and, in some cases, re-read, drafts of my novel. My brother, Jerry Rothman, was a thoughtful reader and critic. Jennifer Shelfer, Lynne Shelfer, Kevin Getzendanner, Toby Steinberg, Nancy Scott Degan, Lisa Ihns, Robin Maher, and Bob Carlson each provided valuable comments, criticism, and encouragement, at various stages of the writing process. If I have omitted others who read and commented along the way, it is through sheer inadvertence, and not for a lack of gratitude.

About the Author

Bob Rothman was a newspaper journalist for six years before attending law school. After graduation, he became a trial lawyer at an Atlanta law firm, where he practiced for more than 38 years. Although he primarily handled business disputes and media defense work, Bob also spent ten years representing a death row inmate in post-conviction proceedings. He is a member, and has served as chair, of the American Bar Association Section of Litigation. He also served as chair of the ABA Death Penalty Representation Project. Bob and his wife, Dee, live in Atlanta. *A Terrible Guilt* is his first novel.

Note from Bob Rothman

Word-of-mouth is crucial for any author to succeed. If you enjoyed *A Terrible Guilt*, please leave a review online—anywhere you are able. Even if it's just a sentence or two. It would make all the difference and would be very much appreciated.

Thanks!
Bob Rothman

We hope you enjoyed reading this title from:

www.blackrosewriting.com

Subscribe to our mailing list – *The Rosevine* – and receive **FREE** books, daily deals, and stay current with news about upcoming releases and our hottest authors.
Scan the QR code below to sign up.

Already a subscriber? Please accept a sincere thank you for being a fan of Black Rose Writing authors.

View other Black Rose Writing titles at
www.blackrosewriting.com/books and use promo code
PRINT to receive a **20% discount** when purchasing.